REMO BRACED FOR THE ATTACK

His hands shot up instinctively to ward off the killing blows.

But in the instant before his hand reached Remo's throat, the Master of Sinanju's expression suddenly changed. The blank stare flashed to a look of deep annoyance. For that sliver in time he looked himself again.

Remo hesitated. And in that moment of uncertainty, Chiun's darting hand shot through his pupil's defenses.

Remo had but a split second to come to terms with his imminent death. But instead of a killing blow, a scolding hand smacked Remo hard on the back of his head. Afterward, Chiun's hand retreated inside the sleeves of his kimono.

"Let that be a lesson to all who would dismiss the abilities of the elderly," the old man sniffed haughtily.

Remo rubbed the back of his head. "That hurt," he groused.

"The best lessons come from pain."

Other titles in this series:

Created by Murphy & Sapir

THE Destroyer™

MARKET FORCE

A GOLD EAGLE BOOK FROM
W🌐RLDWIDE.®

TORONTO • NEW YORK • LONDON
AMSTERDAM • PARIS • SYDNEY • HAMBURG
STOCKHOLM • ATHENS • TOKYO • MILAN
MADRID • WARSAW • BUDAPEST • AUCKLAND

First edition April 2002

ISBN 0-373-63242-8

Special thanks and acknowledgment to
James Mullaney for his contribution to this work.

MARKET FORCE

Printed in U.S.A.

To Dick and Sue Mullaney & Al and Betty Carter.

And to Benjamin R. Kostman,
thanks to Joel S. Kostman, and vice versa.

And to the Glorious House of Sinanju,
e-mail: housinan@aol.com

PROLOGUE

The blood was everywhere. On the floor, on the bed. It had even splattered into the hallway outside the hospital room. God, it looked as if someone had stomped on a blood-filled balloon.

Given the condition of the two bodies discovered so far, the fact that the blood had shot out as far as the hall didn't surprise Detective Ronald Davic. Not with the inhuman force that had been employed against the poor dead doctor.

"Damn, what a mess," Detective Davic muttered as he circled around the far side of the corpse.

This was definitely one for the books.

The body was hanging from the wall. Actually *hanging,* like a cow on a slaughterhouse hook. That was a twist Detective Davic had never seen before. And it wasn't as if he was new to this sort of thing. Before coming to town, he'd spent fifteen years working homicide in New York City.

Fused. The back of the dead doctor's head had been fused with the wall. There was no other way to describe it.

The body hung in defiance of gravity. The dangling toes brushed the floor. The skull had hit so hard it had split at the back, creating suction that was proving difficult to pop. The police were through examining the body. At the moment, the coroner's boys were trying to pry the head loose. They were hoping the body would drop once the head popped free.

It was all too much. When he'd first stepped into the hospital room, Davic was forced to walk on tiptoes to avoid the grisly puddles of sticky blood. The floor, the far wall, the nightstand, the bed. God, it was everywhere.

Like nothing he'd ever seen before.

"Jesus, what could have done this?" Davic muttered as the men from the coroner's office worked around the doctor's suction-stuck skull.

"Some of these crazies have strength like you wouldn't believe. Like superstrength or something. This is one for the books, though. At least it's new to me."

Detective Fred Wayne was trying to put on a nonchalant front. Davic ignored his partner.

The kid didn't really need to point out that this was beyond his police experience. Even if Davic didn't already know it to be true, he could have figured it out by the way Wayne blew his lunch out in the hallway the moment he'd gotten his first glimpse inside the room.

Wayne was trying to mask his earlier loss of control with phony bluster. It wasn't working. He still looked green around the gills. The younger detective was looking everywhere but at the body as he talked.

"Uniform is searching the grounds," Wayne said.

"Jackson and Javez are keeping an eye on them. Making sure they don't make too big a mess."

"The guy who runs the place back yet?"

"Not yet," Detective Wayne replied. "He phoned his secretary yesterday to say he was on his way. Some kind of business trip. But that was long before all this. She said she has no way to reach him. Guy doesn't even know what he's coming back to."

"What about the assistant? He was supposed to be at work, right? He turn up yet?"

Wayne shook his head. "We're still searching inside. He could have left the building for something, maybe didn't tell anyone. Or he could be another victim. I guess we won't know until he turns up."

"*If*," Davic muttered to himself.

A sucking crack came from the rear wall.

The coroner's men had managed to unstick the body from the wall. They tried to catch it, but it lurched forward, falling facedown in a heap on the floor. The blossomed head cavity yawned up at the cold fluorescent ceiling lights.

Detective Wayne immediately grabbed his mouth and ran out the door. The sound of dry-heaving came from the hall.

Detective Ronald Davic decided the kid might have a good idea. He needed some fresh air.

Leaving the men in the room to load the doctor's body onto a stretcher, Davic stepped into the hallway.

Another coroner's crew was at the end of the hall rolling a gurney with the second body—this on a nurse—through the fire doors.

"Hold up," Davic called.

A man in white held the door for him, and Davic slipped into another short hallway.

They rolled the gurney past a few windows that looked out over water. A left from this hall and they were in the main basement corridor. At the end were fire doors. Once through them, they carted the stretcher up the stairwell to the first-floor landing.

Davic scooted ahead. He held the door for the men as they rolled the stretcher out into daylight.

A silent ambulance was parked at the side of the building, its back door open.

The men loaded the sheet-draped body of the unlucky nurse inside. As they strapped it in, Detective Davic tapped a cigarette from the pack in his pocket.

He had misplaced his lighter days ago and hadn't yet picked up a new one. Davic was afraid for a minute that he had lost the book of matches he'd scrounged from the back of a kitchen cupboard. He found them in his raincoat pocket.

As the men were closing the door on the dead nurse, Detective Davic lit up. He pulled in a deep, thoughtful lungful of smoke as he watched them move to the front of the ambulance.

The ambulance drove slowly from the side parking lot. Davic walked along behind it. He stepped into full daylight when he rounded the front of the building.

There were three other ambulances there, as well as two fire trucks, five police cruisers and a handful of unmarked cars.

Davic wondered why it was that men in official cars always seemed to park where they'd cause maximum inconvenience for everyone else. Probably just because they could.

The ambulance had a hard time threading its way through the traffic jam of parked cars. The driver bumped the right tires through the snow of the front yard to get around the landscaped rotary. It was clear sailing after that.

Lights off, the ambulance with the dead nurse drove down the great gravel driveway and passed through the wrought-iron gates. Siren silent, it drove slowly away.

Back up the driveway, Detective Davic dropped his cigarette. The wind whipped his thinning hair. He ground out the butt under his toe. Cursing the habit and the job that had forced it on him, he turned back.

The building loomed high above him. On one of the windows, someone had taped a cardboard angel, ringed with holly. A pathetic attempt to welcome in the season.

Alone in the main driveway, the police detective shook his head. "Merry Christmas," Ronald Davic grumbled.

His words were blown away in a swirl of winter wind.

With a deep frown on his doughy face, the Rye, New York, police detective trudged slowly up the broad front steps of Folcroft Sanitarium.

1

When the plane touched down at John F. Kennedy International Airport in New York, the tired passenger at the very back of the coach section released a silent sigh of relief.

With weary eyes the bland man in the gray suit watched the tarmac speed by. When the glass-encased terminal building rolled up to meet the plane, he exhaled once more.

Dr. Harold W. Smith was grateful to be home.

When the plane had fully stopped and the passengers were given permission to deplane, Smith stayed in his seat. Not wanting to fight the crowd or draw attention to himself, he let others grab for their bags and cram the aisles. Only when the crowd had thinned did Smith get wearily to his feet.

Smith had been pressing a battered briefcase between his ankles for most of the flight from South America. Picking it up, he set it onto his seat. Reaching up, he unfastened the overhead compartment. He pulled out a small black suitcase.

Age had worn the frayed plastic corners of the once sturdy nylon bag. The zipper on the small side pocket no longer worked. It was stuck permanently shut, a few strands of black nylon thread jammed firmly in the metal teeth.

For years now Smith had kept the same carry-on at work just in case he was called away on emergencies. Of course, the types of emergencies that would likely pull Harold Smith from his desk were the kind for which packing was most times impossible or pointless. Impossible because he never knew what sort of climate he might land in, pointless because he might never return. How could one pack for every conceivable climate on the planet and why would one need a spare pair of underwear if one was dead?

In the bag were three pairs of socks and underwear, a spare white shirt, a shaving kit and a toothbrush.

The toothbrush was a promotional item Smith had gotten from his dentist. For decades now after each of his yearly dental appointments, Harold Smith had made certain to collect the free toothbrush and small tube of toothpaste Dr. Rohter, his dentist, supplied his patients. One time back in the 1970s Smith had forgotten to collect the free items and had driven all the way back to the dentist's office to get them. He wasn't embarrassed in the least to do so. After all, the dentist got them for nothing from his suppliers. As a patient in good standing, Harold Smith was as entitled to his free toothpaste and toothbrush as any other patient.

In the bathroom cupboard of Smith's tidy little home at the edge of the Westchester Golf Club was a shoebox filled with free toothbrushes and tiny tubes of toothpaste. The contents of some of the toothpaste tubes had liquefied from sitting unused for so long.

Smith placed his carry-on next to his briefcase as he pushed shut the door to the overhead compartment.

The bag was a nuisance that he hadn't really needed to bring with him on this trip.

A pragmatic soul, Smith had at one point considered bringing the bag home for good. It was only taking up space in his office closet. But in the end he had decided that it would be more suspicious to board an international flight with only his battered leather briefcase. And one thing Harold W. Smith did not crave was attention.

Smith picked up his two pieces of luggage.

Before the crowd had thinned completely, Smith fell in with it. He left the plane without the flight attendant at the door even making eye contact. Few people ever took notice of Harold W. Smith. He was just a nondescript gray man with a worn overnight bag and briefcase.

Smith walked briskly through the terminal and out into the cold winter day without a single person glancing his way.

The sky above New York was a sallow gunmetal gray. The color of the day seemed reflected in the gaunt man with the worn bags who hurried up the broad sidewalk.

Everything about Smith seemed tinged in grays, from his three-piece gray suit to the pallor of his skin. The only splash of color that stained his otherwise absolute grayness was the green-striped Dartmouth tie coiled around his neck like a knotted snake.

His sheer ordinariness was the perfect camouflage.

No one would have guessed that this shivering gray man hurrying through the parking lot of John F. Kennedy International Airport was more than just the sum of his gray parts.

Harold Smith was much more.

Smith was director of CURE, a secret agency whose existence was known only to the highest level of the executive branch of the United States government. CURE's mandate was to work outside the Constitution in order to protect it. As head of CURE, Harold W. Smith controlled forces far greater than any other man on the face of the planet. The fact that he looked even more boring than the average dull, gray businessman hurrying to his car on a shivering winter day was Smith's greatest shield. His ordinariness turned away prying eyes, preventing discovery of America's greatest, most terrible secret.

At the far end of the airport parking lot was Smith's trusty station wagon. Like its owner, the old car was showing signs of wear but, like its owner, it stubbornly kept on going. The station wagon had seen Smith through myriad crises, political and social upheaval, seven presidents and just over thirty New York winters.

Unlocking a rusted door, Smith put his suitcase on the back seat near his neatly folded overcoat and scarf. He'd known he wouldn't need the garments in South America, so he'd left them in his car. He was grateful to shrug on the heavy coat and draw the scarf around his thin neck.

He placed his briefcase on the passenger seat beside him as he slid in behind the wheel.

The parking slip was in the sun visor where he'd left it five days earlier.

When he'd left on his trip, Smith knew there existed a very real chance he might never return. Since the car wasn't even worth its weight in scrap metal, he figured he'd just abandon it at the airport. Someone would eventually notice the rusted car and have it towed somewhere for disposal.

But Smith was alive, his car was waiting for him on his return and—even on a cold December day like this—the engine turned over on the first try.

Smith allowed himself a rare smile. Just because a thing was old did not automatically mean it was no longer useful.

He backed carefully from the space and drove to the booth. After paying his parking fee, he headed for the exit.

The traffic from the airport was no worse than normal. Smith scarcely noticed. So bone tired was he, he allowed himself to drive on automatic pilot. Before he knew it, he was driving through the center of his own town.

There was no need to go directly home. Before assuming the reins of CURE, Smith had worked for the CIA. His wife was accustomed to mysterious absences. Still, he had one thing to check on before going to work.

He drove through the congested center of town. A new street built in the 1980s led to the rear entrance of a big apartment complex. A dozen four-story buildings squatted on what had once been farmland.

Smith parked his car in front of Building B. Briefcase in hand, he headed for the door.

A row of doorbells was lined neatly on a panel. Smith ran an arthritic finger down the list of names next to the door. He stopped at the one labeled Mark Howard.

Smith pressed the bell.

Howard was Smith's assistant. The younger man was supposed to have been filling in for his employer at work these past few days. But Smith had phoned the office a few times while he was away, and Howard had failed to answer.

At first Smith thought something might be wrong. But he had used his briefcase laptop to check the phone lines and the CURE mainframes for tampering. The agency was secure.

Smith was going to phone his secretary, but decided against it. He didn't want to involve her if it turned out to be a CURE problem. She had no idea what her employer actually did for a living. Besides, Smith suspected he knew what the problem was.

Mark Howard had not been feeling well these past few weeks. He seemed to be suffering from some form of mental exhaustion that was affecting his work. Smith had even given Howard some time off, but when the crisis in South America came he was forced to call his assistant back to work.

Smith wound up staying in South America longer than he had expected, to make certain the danger that took him there was completely eliminated. If Mark's condition had worsened in the five days Smith was away, the young man might have gone home to rest.

At least that's what Smith had assumed. But if Mark was home, he should have answered his door.

Smith rang the bell again. When there was still no answer, the CURE director frowned. A tingle of concern fluttered deep in his belly.

He picked a name at random on another floor and pressed the glowing yellow doorbell.

"Yeah, what is it?" a gruff male voice asked after an agonizingly long moment.

"Exterminator," Smith replied. His lemony voice was crisp and precise. "Maintenance called about a cockroach problem in—" he read the name and apartment number from the tag "—the Robertsons' apartment next to yours. I'm here to spray."

"Why didn't maintenance let you in?"

"I was given the passkey to the apartment, but the custodian failed to give me the key to the front door," Smith said into the speaker. "He was called away on an emergency in another building. It doesn't matter to me if you don't let me in. However, the insects are in a breeding cycle right now. If I have to leave now, this entire building could be infested by the time I get back."

The unseen man exhaled angrily. "Those people are animals," he grunted.

There was a buzz and the security lock opened. Smith slipped inside. He took the stairs to the second floor and hurried to Howard's apartment.

The door was locked. However, unlike the security door downstairs, this one was just a standard dead bolt. Smith took out his wallet and removed a small set of burglary tools. With a few deft wiggles he picked the lock.

The apartment was dark. The curtains were drawn on the dreary morning. Smith shut the door behind him, feeling on the wall for the light switch.

''Mark?'' Smith called.

No answer. Smith wasn't carrying a weapon. Stepping cautiously, he did a quick search of the apartment.

He found no one. However, there were droplets of water in the shower stall. In the kitchen, a banana peel in a bag under the sink had not yet fully blackened. A cereal bowl in the sink had a small amount of milk in the bottom that had not yet soured. Clearly, his assistant had showered and eaten breakfast in his apartment that morning.

Mark Howard was a hardworking and conscientious young man. His condition had to have worsened after Smith had left, necessitating the need to take a few days off. But he was obviously feeling better, for he had to have returned to work.

Smith shut the lights off and let himself out.

The older man didn't feel any guilt for breaking into Howard's apartment. Such things came with the job.

Outside, Smith climbed back behind the wheel of his car and headed off to work.

He found no traffic on the isolated road that ran

beside Long Island Sound. A wall rose beside the car. Beyond it loomed the familiar ivy-covered building that had been Smith's true home for the past forty years.

As he turned into the drive of Folcroft Sanitarium, Smith noted that the bronze plaque on the main gate had begun to lose its luster. He was making a mental note to send someone from the custodial staff out to polish it when he spied the police cars parked in front of the building.

What little natural color Smith possessed drained from his ashen face. His thudding heart rose into his constricting throat.

With an outward calm that belied his inner panic, he pulled his station wagon onto the shoulder of the main drive. He retrieved his cell phone from his brief-case.

He dialed with shaking hands. It was his secretary, not Mark Howard, who answered the ringing phone.

"Dr. Smith's office."

"Mrs. Mikulka," Smith said, trying to keep his voice even, "is there something wrong at Folcroft?"

"Oh, Dr. Smith. Thank goodness you finally called." Mrs. Mikulka sounded desperate. "I didn't know how to reach you. It's one of the patients. He went—I don't know what. *Homicidal.* He killed three people. The police are here."

Smith felt some of the tension drain from his shoulders. It was a Folcroft matter. Nothing to do with CURE.

"I know they are," he said.

"Oh," Mrs. Mikulka said. "Where are you?"

"In front of the building. Where is Mr. Howard?"

"He's missing," Mrs. Mikulka said, her voice tight with apprehension. "He wasn't feeling well these past few days, so he stayed home sick. He came back just this morning, before all this happened. Now he's missing and the police are saying— Oh, Dr. Smith, I hope he's all right."

Mrs. Mikulka was clearly distraught. Smith was surprised at himself for the level of concern he felt for his young protégé. But there were matters more important than Mark Howard or Harold Smith.

"Which patient was it?" Smith pressed.

"One of the ones from the special wing," Mrs. Mikulka said. "They're saying he must have gone berserk. He killed a doctor and two nurses before he disap—"

Smith didn't give her the chance to finish. He clicked his phone shut and dropped it into his brief-case.

He knew exactly which patient it was.

With wooden movements he put his car in gear and continued up the driveway. Skirting the emergency vehicles, he steered around to the side of the building. He parked his car in his reserved space in the employee lot.

He left his suitcase in the back seat. Taking his briefcase in hand, he ducked inside the side door of Folcroft's executive wing. With calm, deliberate steps he climbed to the second floor.

When Smith stepped into her office from the hallway, Mrs. Mikulka's broad face brightened with relief. There was a man waiting in his secretary's office.

"Dr. Smith," Mrs. Mikulka said. "Oh, thank goodness. This is a detective with the Rye police. I'm sorry," she said to the man, "I forgot your name."

"Detective Ronald Davic," the policeman replied, offering Smith his hand. "I'm glad you're back, Dr. Smith."

Even as he shook the detective's hand, Smith was gesturing to his office. "I understand there has been some difficulty," Smith said. "Please step inside."

Leaving his flustered secretary alone in the outer room, he ushered the detective through to the inner office.

Smith noted as he rounded his desk that nothing looked out of place. With police snooping around Folcroft, he had been concerned that they might have found their way in here. He would have to do a search of the room once he was alone.

"I spoke to my secretary on the phone a few minutes ago," Smith began as he settled into his chair. "I have the rough details. What is the current situation?"

"You've got three on your staff dead—a doctor and two nurses—one man missing and the killer still at large."

"Do you believe he is still on the grounds?"

"We're searching. We've turned up nothing yet."

"When did this happen?"

"About three hours ago. Just after seven this morning. Dr. Smith, you realize it's your assistant director, Mr. Howard, who's the missing staff member?"

"Yes," Smith said.

"Did he have any kind of special relationship with the patient? Friend, relative, anything like that?"

Smith's brow formed a dark V. "No. Mr. Howard has only been on staff here for a year. The patient has been in a medicated coma for the past decade. Why?"

Davic fished in his pocket, producing a folded piece of paper. When he opened it up, Smith saw it was a standard Folcroft medical chart. They were normally left on a clipboard in a patient's room so that sanitarium staff could log test results and keep track of medications. With a finger yellowed from years of smoking, the detective tapped one of the top lines on the paper.

"Your patient's sedatives were canceled five days ago," Davic said as he set the paper before Smith. "I talked to one of your staff doctors. Your assistant isn't medical staff, so he shouldn't be messing around with which patients get what drugs. But he's the one who signed off on the change. Now, since you say he doesn't even know this guy, can you guess why he'd do something like that?"

Smith blinked behind his rimless glasses. The detective was right. According to the logs, Mark Howard had changed the prescribed medications for the patient in Folcroft's special wing. And in so doing had set free one of the greatest threats CURE's personnel had ever faced.

Smith was stunned to silence. He felt as if he

should do something. As he reexamined the paper, he shifted in his chair. For the first time he noticed that the chair no longer squeaked. It *always* squeaked. Smith had been meaning for years to have it oiled but had never gotten around to it.

Somehow, in a moment when a missing squeak should have been the last thing on his mind, the silence of his chair roared like thunder in his ringing ears.

"I...am at a loss," Smith finally managed to say.

"Really." It was a statement, not a question. "Well, with luck we'll find him alive and ask him."

The detective held out his hand for the paper. Smith surrendered it reluctantly. His mind reeled as he considered how Mark Howard might deal with being questioned by the police and what it could mean to Smith's covert organization.

"Wait a moment," Smith said abruptly. "What was the name of the doctor? The one killed?"

Davic supplied him the name from a small notebook in his jacket pocket.

"Oh, my," Smith said quietly.

"What? Is something wrong with the doctor?"

Smith looked up with worried eyes. "A few months back he asked me about the sedatives that were being administered to that particular patient. He had wanted to cut the dosage back then. He was adamant, but I overruled him. I am afraid he might have used my absence to convince Mr. Howard to sign off on a change in the patient's treatment."

Of course it was nonsense. A hasty cover concocted on the spur of the moment.

One day months ago the doctor in question had indeed questioned Smith about the meds for the patient in the special wing, but he had not pressed the issue since then. The man had always done exemplary work at Folcroft. But the doctor was now dead, and Smith was willing to sacrifice the man's spotless reputation for the sake of Mark Howard. Not that he would hesitate to take harsh action against his young assistant if Howard had betrayed CURE. But that was a matter to be handled internally—away from prying eyes.

The detective seemed to accept Smith's story.

"About this patient of yours," Davic said as he folded the chart and returned it to his pocket. "Just what's his story exactly? What he did to those people downstairs—" Davic shook his head "—I've never seen anything like it."

"He is a unique case," Smith explained. "He is a John Doe remanded to our custody by the federal prison system. There was some hope that we might be able to treat him. We couldn't. His brain is completely unable to regulate the release of certain chemicals in his body. As a result, he is able to display what would be seen as incredible physical feats. But this only lasts for short spurts. He was kept medicated for his own good. Like a subject who ingests PCP, he is oblivious to the damage he is causing himself. He will continue to push and push until he tears his body apart."

Lies piled on lies. Smith was amazed at how easily they came. Not that he could very well tell the truth. He was grateful that he'd had the foresight to concoct a cover for the patient in question years ago. A check of federal prison records would corroborate his story.

"It's not *his* body I'm worried about, Dr. Smith," Detective Davic said.

"I share your concern," Smith said. "Our John Doe is a special case. I advise against any physical confrontation with him. Bullets might not be enough to stop him. I'm sure you're aware of cases where police have had difficulty subduing men who were shot multiple times. I'm afraid this could happen here. Do you have tranquilizer guns?"

Davic thought the old man was joking. But there was nothing but deadly earnestness on that gray face.

"No," the detective admitted.

"Get some. Try the local animal control. In the meantime you may use ours. There are two air dart handguns locked in a security locker in the basement. I will retrieve them for you. Also, I'm uncomfortable with many police in the building. I understand your need to search, and clearly you must be thorough given the circumstances, but the needs of this institution's other patients cannot be ignored. When you are finished looking, please remove your men at the earliest opportunity. Their presence will only alarm patients and visitors. Ultimately, I believe a search of the building is pointless. Offered his freedom after all this time, our Mr. Doe would not dawdle. It's my belief that he has already fled the grounds. And I would appreciate it if you removed the police cars and other vehicles from the drive at once. I could barely fit past them."

Detective Davic wasn't used to being given orders from a civilian. The way this Dr. Smith barked them out, it sounded as if he were used to being in command during times of crisis.

"I'll see what I can do," Davic offered cautiously.

As the detective spoke, one of the phones on Smith's desk jangled to life. There were two phones, one black and one blue. They were both old rotary sets. None of the lights were lit on the black one.

Smith didn't look at the ringing blue phone.

"Thank you, Detective," the Folcroft director said. He made not a move toward the telephone.

"Aren't you going to answer that, sir?"

"Yes," Smith said. The strained smile he plastered across his face made him look like a grimacing corpse. "Of course I am." Heart pounding, he picked up the blue phone's receiver. "Dr. Smith here," he said stiffly.

"Took you long enough," the voice on the other end of the line growled. "What, were you out frisking the nurses for swiping copier paper again?"

"Oh, hello," Smith said, scarcely hearing the caller's words. "Yes, that is fine. But I'm busy right now, Aunt Mildred. I'll have to call you back."

"Smitty, maybe you should drop the Aunt Mildred thing. At your age, any aunt you'd have would have to be a hundred million years old. Listen, we're done in Europe, but Chiun's acting screwier than usual. I need some busywork just to get a break from him. Gimme another assignment.''

"That's wonderful news, Aunt Mildred," Smith replied. "Thank you for calling. But I really must go now. Give my regards to Uncle Martin."

He hung up the phone.

"I apologize for that," Smith said to Detective Davic. He held his unnatural smile. "You were saying?"

The instant Davic opened his mouth to speak, the blue phone began ringing once more.

Smith grabbed the receiver. "Hello?"

"Are you on drugs?" demanded the caller angrily.

Without saying a word, Smith pressed the phone to his gray vest. He felt the outline of the poison pill that he kept in his pocket press against his narrow chest.

"Forgive me," Smith said tightly, "but this is an important business call that I need to take. Will you excuse me for a moment?"

"Yes, sir," Davic said. The detective left the office, pulling the door tightly shut.

"I can't talk at the moment," Smith said into the phone. "There's a crisis here."

"Crisis shmisis," the voice on the phone dismissed. "Are you gonna give me another assignment, or do I have to scrape one up on my own? And believe me you wouldn't like that. I'm in an 'international incident' kind of mood."

Smith hesitated. This was one of only two men on Earth who might be able to help right now. On the other hand, with the police here, he might just invite more questions.

Smith booted up his computer. He found an active file at the very top of CURE's target list. Spitting out a few rapid commands, he hung up the phone.

Quickly shutting off his computer, he headed back out to find the detective. When he entered his secretary's office, he found Davic talking excitedly on a cell phone.

"I'll meet you out front," he was saying. He clicked off the phone, stuffing it in his pocket. "We found another body," Davic said to Smith. "Out in the woods near the north wall. They think it might be your assistant."

Mrs. Mikulka gasped. Pressing one hand to her open mouth, she fell back into her chair. She looked up at Smith with frightened, tear-filled eyes.

Standing next to her desk, the Folcroft director put an arthritic hand on her shoulder. He gave a comforting squeeze. It was a greater show of emotional support than he'd given her when her husband had passed away of a sudden heart attack eighteen years before.

"I am going with you," Smith insisted to Davic.

It was clear by his tone that there would be no arguing.

Detective Davic made a quick decision. "Let's get those tranquilizer guns," he said, spinning for the door.

As the two men hurried from the office, Smith already had his key chain in hand. And etched in the lines of his patrician face were equal parts determination and dread.

2

His name was Remo and he wasn't quite sure of the correct spelling of the word *traitor*.

Remo had bought the newspaper at the airport in Miami, taking it with him when he boarded his plane. He had dropped into the seat and opened up to the entertainment section. Forced to bum a pencil from a flight attendant because he'd forgotten to buy one of his own, he had settled down with the crossword puzzle on his knee and a very determined look on his face, and he got stuck on his very first word.

Traitor should be an easy word to spell. But from taxiing to takeoff, he just couldn't seem to get it right. Was it *e-r* or was it *o-r?* He wrote it a bunch of times in the margin around the otherwise blank crossword puzzle. He wrote it so many times that both versions were starting to look just as right to him.

The plane was flying over the Gulf of Mexico and Remo still hadn't gotten it. He decided that it was high time he got some help.

"Hi," Remo said enthusiastically to the passenger in the seat next to him. "Could you tell me the proper spelling of *traitor?*"

Diet Pepsi launched out both of the man's nostrils.

"What?" he gasped, nearly dropping his soda can.

"Traitor," Remo repeated. "I can't seem to get it right." He held the newspaper out for inspection.

Remo's seatmate saw the word in question. It was written in between every available column space and all around the margins of the paper. Over and over. In script, printed out. In capitals and in lowercase letters.

As he read that carefully written word, Alex Wycopf's world collapsed. His mind whirled. His nostrils burned from Pepsi. The knees of his white cotton pants where he'd spit his mouthful of soda were stained brown.

"You know how you get stuck on a word and you just can't seem to get it?" Remo asked. He smiled a disarmingly innocent smile.

"I...what? Oh. Yes."

Alex Wycopf didn't know how he'd even managed to say that much. His blood sang a concert in his ears. For some reason his eyes were watering, even though he was too afraid even to cry. And through Wycopf's near-panic attack, the man sitting next to him continued to stare that vacant stare and smile that little knowing smile and hold out that scrap of paper with that incriminating word emblazoned a hundred times over for all the world to see.

"So do you?" Remo asked.

"Do I what?" asked Alex Wycopf, his face turning as white as a crisp sheet of first-grade notebook paper.

"Do you know how to spell *traitor?*" Remo asked.

"Oh." Wycopf blinked. "Um, no. No, I don't."

Remo's face grew disappointed. "No? Oh."

He returned to his crossword puzzle.

A passing flight attendant noticed that Alex had had some kind of trouble with his drink. He offered the shaken man a napkin to dry his pants before going off in search of a towel.

"I don't like traitors," Remo announced abruptly once the flight attendant was gone. "Whether or not they're with an *e* or an *o*. I happen to love America. Don't you love America?"

"I, um, sure," Alex Wycopf said. He was dabbing at the knees of his pants. His slick wet palms soaked the flimsy paper napkin.

"I don't mean as an angle or a dodge or a way of making a quick buck selling her out," Remo said. "I mean really love America. In the patriotic sense. That's the way I am." He tapped his pencil on his newspaper. "It's funny that I still do. I've seen so much over the years, you'd think my attitude would have changed. But I've been doing a little soul-searching these past few months and when I think about it—really think about it—I do still love America. Funny."

The flight attendant was back with a wet towel. Remo shifted in his seat, and the man cleaned the sticky soda off the back of the seat in front of Wycopf. He took a few swipes across the floor before retreating to the galley.

Alex Wycopf didn't know what to do. He just sat there looking dumbly ahead. He was staring at a rivet on the back of the seat in front of him. Suddenly that rivet was the most interesting thing on the face of the planet. Nothing else mattered—not the plane, not this trip, not his seatmate who somehow knew the truth even though no one should have.

"Crossword puzzles are hard," Remo observed, shattering Wycopf's brief moment of terrified solitude. "I remember the nuns used to make us do them sometimes back in grade-school English class. They did it at the very end of the year, just before summer vacation. It was supposed to be fun. Most of the year wasn't fun, and I guess crossword puzzles were their way of letting us let our hair down. Some of the kids seemed to like it. The ones like me in the back of the class would rather have been pounding erasers out in the recess yard than doing crossword puzzles. Hey, there's another one. *Eraser.* Does that have an *o* or an *e*?"

By now Wycopf had regained composure enough to speak. "That's an *e*," the traitor said.

"So you're certain eraser has an *e* but you're not sure how to spell *traitor*?" Remo said. "That's funny. You'd think you of all people would be able to spell *traitor*."

Alex Wycopf couldn't believe it. He had held out some hope that this was all a bizarre fluke. That he hadn't really been found out. He wanted to leap out of his seat. He wanted to run for the exit, kick it open and take his chances jumping out over the Gulf of Mexico.

But his seatmate was no longer paying attention.

Remo was engrossed once more in his crossword puzzle.

Maybe Alex was getting worked up over nothing. Maybe this was an innocent mistake after all. Maybe the guy sitting next to him was just someone doing a crossword puzzle who happened to be stuck on the word *traitor*. Maybe he didn't know anything at all about the treasonous acts Alex Wycopf had performed in the past and was about to perform again. Maybe his world wasn't about to come crashing down.

All at once, his seatmate looked up from his newspaper.

"I know," Remo said firmly.

And as he looked into those deep-set brown eyes, Alex Wycopf knew with cold certainty that he was staring into the very eyes of his own death.

"'Mother on *The Brady Bunch*,'" Remo said, reading another clue from the puzzle. "Do they mean her real name, or her name on the show? And what about those of us who've never seen an episode? Who writes this stuff?"

He scribbled something on the page, thought better of it, then erased it.

Alex Wycopf gripped the arms of his seat. His knuckles ached from clutching so hard. The whine of the propellers was so loud he thought he'd go deaf.

"Gee whiz, you sure sweat a lot, don't you?" Remo said.

Beside him, Alex Wycopf's face had gone from white to red. He was panting now, his heart thudding madly in his chest. It was as if he were suffocating. There was plenty of air. He was pulling it into his lungs, but it wasn't doing any good. Hyperventilating, Wycopf was on the verge of passing out when Remo tsked unhappily.

"Now, now," Remo warned. "This isn't the time for anxiety attacks. I need you around a little longer."

Remo stuck his hand behind Wycopf's back, manipulating a cluster of nerves at the base of the man's spine. Alex felt the breath return to him. He filled his lungs with air. The deafening propeller noise receded to its normal hum.

Alex Wycopf was himself again. Alive, breathing and terrified out of his mind. He moaned pathetically.

"How do you know?" Wycopf whispered sickly.

"Hmm?" Remo asked, looking up from his puzzle. "You mean how do I know you've betrayed not only your country but the entire Western world? That's a long story."

This was the God's honest truth. It *was* a long story. It had started a couple of decades before when an innocent beat cop named Remo Williams was sentenced to die in the electric chair for a murder he didn't commit. The chair hadn't worked, and Remo awoke in Folcroft Sanitarium with a new face and a new life. He was to be the enforcement arm for CURE, America's extralegal last line of defense.

At Folcroft, Remo was remanded to the custody of the Master of Sinanju, a Korean martial artist whose wizened form was the perfect camouflage for the most dangerous man on the face of the planet. The skills he imparted to his young student changed Remo Williams, heart, mind and soul.

With Sinanju a man could perform seemingly impossible feats of strength, speed and skill. For those blessed to view life through the prism of Sinanju, it was as if the normal world were slowed down and slightly warped.

Remo had learned and learned well, eventually attaining full Masterhood himself. At the moment his official title was Transitional Reigning Master. It was only a matter of time—a short time if his teacher could be believed—when Remo would become the Reigning Master of Sinanju. The one man in a generation permitted to accept that proud mantle.

Surprisingly, Chiun—Remo's mentor and the current Reigning Master of Sinanju—was okay with surrendering his title to his pupil. Remo was okay with it. Everyone who mattered was okay with it, and all was right with the world.

Until two days ago.

For the past few months Chiun had been writing and mailing some sort of mysterious letters. Every time Remo had asked what they were all about, he was told by his teacher to mind his own business. Remo knew in his gut it was going to be bad news for him. Everything was always bad news for him. And Chiun certainly hadn't been skulking around these past months planning a surprise party.

Of course Remo was right.

Two days ago he had seen one of Chiun's shiny

silver envelopes on the table of an assassin in Switzerland.

There was no mistaking it. This killer-for-hire who Remo had never met before had for some reason received a note in the mail from the Master of Sinanju.

Chiun confiscated the letter and killed the killer before Remo had a chance to find out what was going on.

On their way out of the country, Chiun mailed five more envelopes, said they were the last, told Remo not to ask again or else and then lapsed into some kind of weird melancholic funk. It was almost as if he had decided his work on Earth was done. Now that he had an heir apparent in Remo, there were no more challenges for the old man to face.

On one level Remo felt guilty. After all, in a way it was his fault that Chiun was feeling his productive days were over. Of course it was silly to think such a thing. Remo couldn't very well stagnate, locked in a state of perpetual apprenticeship for the sake of his teacher's ego.

Whatever Chiun was feeling right now would pass.

After he and Chiun landed back in the States, Remo phoned his employer for another assignment. It didn't have to be big, just something to get him out of Chiun's hair for a little while. Maybe alone the Master of Sinanju would be able to sort through whatever baggage he needed to.

Remo's boss had been strangely terse on the phone. Almost as if he were afraid to talk, even on a secure line. Something about some piddling little crisis. He had given Remo the Wycopf assignment and hung up quickly.

And so Chiun returned to Folcroft Sanitarium by taxi while Remo boarded a plane for Mexico.

Although he felt selfish admitting it even to himself, Remo was grateful for this side trip. It gave him a chance to recharge his batteries and escape the funereal air that had descended on his teacher of late.

Beside Remo, Alex Wycopf had fallen into frightened silence. He remained mute for the rest of the trip to Mexico. When the plane was ready to descend over Cancún, he had to be told three times to buckle his seat belt. He heard the stewardess talk, but the words didn't seem to register.

Alex Wycopf prayed for a bumpy landing. If they crashed, maybe he could escape in the confusion.

It was a picture-perfect landing on a sunny Cancun day.

When the plane stopped and the door was sprung, Remo tapped Alex Wycopf on the knee.

"Time to depart."

"Don't you mean deplane?" Wycopf asked hopefully.

This time it wasn't a crossword question, and this time Remo wasn't smiling. He folded his newspaper under his arm and ushered a weak-kneed Alex Wycopf up the aisle.

Off the plane and through the terminal, Remo hailed a cab outside.

"You're giving directions," Remo said to Wycopf. He pushed the traitor into the back seat.

As the cab pulled away from the curb, Remo let the newspaper fly out the window. The crossword puzzle that didn't contain any clues about six letter words for "one who commits treason" landed facedown in the dirty Mexican gutter.

GENERAL ZHII ZAW of the People's Liberation Army sat in a big, comfortable chair in the living room of the elegantly furnished Mexican hotel suite.

A pall of choking cigarette smoke filled the room.

The sun blazed hot and white over Cancún. Had the balcony doors been open, a delicate breeze off the ocean would have refreshed the stale air of the room. But the sliding glass doors were closed, the drapes tightly drawn. The air conditioner worked overtime to remove the smoke and human odors from the sprawling suite of rooms.

General Zhii Zaw was not alone. A dozen other men were in the suite with him.

Most were Chinese security forces, although there were one or two scientists thrown in the mix. They had arrived singly or, at most, in groups of two over the past three days. They had come to Mexico via South America and they had assembled in these rooms. To wait.

The scientists were there to make certain they were getting what they paid for. The security personnel were there to see to it that the data got back to China safely.

The general's mission was absolutely critical. He

had been told by no less than the director of state security that China's entire future was at stake.

Thanks to a program of stunningly successful espionage, for a few years America's secrets had been wide open to the People's Republic of China. Spies in Washington and in the American nuclear program had been more than willing to betray their country, their loved ones and the security of the entire free world for thirty pieces of silver.

But that was all over now. These past few years it had become next to impossible to procure new technology. And China *needed* American technology.

China couldn't produce anything of value on its own. Everything it possessed had to be procured elsewhere. Without its ability to steal and reverse engineer, China was little more than a clumsy, overpopulated Third World power. The premier knew it, the leaders in the National People's Congress knew it and General Zhii Zaw knew it.

The general stabbed out his cigarette in a candy dish that sat on the end table next to his chair.

"What time is it?" he demanded.

"Eight forty-two," an aide replied. Like the other Chinese agents, he wore a plain blue suit. "The plane landed twenty-five minutes ago. I called the airport to confirm."

"He should be here soon. Radio to our man in the lobby. I want to know the instant the American arrives."

"There is a problem with communications, General," the aide said nervously. "I tried to call downstairs a moment ago and there was no response. His radio must be broken.''

The general's waxy face normally sagged like melting bags of flesh at his big jowls. The jowls sank even deeper as he frowned.

"Must I do everything?" he demanded. "Send a man down with a replacement."

"Yes, General."

The man in the lobby wasn't really necessary. Even without his early warning, General Zaw wasn't worried that anyone other than the American traitor, Alex Wycopf, would get through. In the hallway just outside the hotel room door stood General Zaw's personal bodyguard, Luo Pong.

Luo Pong was only five feet tall and nearly as wide, all muscle. In the name of state security, Luo Pong had been known to dismember uncooperative prisoners with his bare hands and, on occasion, eat the remains. Anyone in his or her right mind steered clear of that squat, terrifying man with hands like catcher's mitts and a taste for human flesh.

The general's aide had scraped up a replacement walkie-talkie for the lookout in the lobby. He was reaching for the doorknob when the hotel-room door suddenly sprang open.

Startled, the aide jumped back as something big and round rolled into the room.

The rolling round something had eyes.

When Luo Pong's severed head came to a stop at the toes of his shoes, General Zhii Zaw was already leaping to his feet. At the same instant, Alex Wycopf came stumbling into the room, propelled forward by a thick-wristed hand.

"What's a four-letter word for 'what you're all about to be'?" Remo announced to the gathered Chinese agents.

The agent near the door pulled a gun on Remo. Remo planted the man's own barrel so deep in his face loose brain matter dribbled out the back of his head like gray oatmeal.

"That's right," Remo said to the security officer with the revolver in his face and the gun-barrel blossom out the back of his head. "The correct answer is 'dead.'"

The reaction of the others in the suite had been slow until now. But when their comrade with a gun instead of a nose fell to the floor, nine hands flew to holsters.

Before a single weapon could aim for the man at the door, Remo was whirling into the crowd of Chinese agents.

"How about a four-letter word for 'how Chinese spies who steal American secrets will wind up from now on'?" Remo asked.

A pair of guns drew a bead on him. Remo ducked as the men squeezed their triggers. The two Chinese agents inadvertently blew each other's face off.

"That's right," Remo said. "Same answer. Dead."

He was up in the air. His heel caught the top of a Chinese agent's head and with a twist he sent the man's chin cracking down through his own sternum.

Even as brittle bones compressed, Remo was

launching himself from the collapsing man. Two toes took out the throats of a pair of Chinese soldiers while simultaneous flashing hands reduced the beating hearts of another pair of soldiers to gurgling paste.

The final two security agents didn't even have time to process the sudden, brutal deaths of their comrades before Remo was on them. They saw black. Then they saw red. Then they saw nothing at all.

Remo turned from the last dead security agents.

All that remained was General Zaw and the pair of scientists. The latter had been brought along to confirm as genuine the schematics and other data Alex Wycopf had stolen from his job as undersecretary in the U.S. Department of Energy. For good measure Remo mashed the heads of the two Chinese scientists through a wall. Their skulls cracked the porcelain tub in the adjacent bathroom in two.

In a matter of seconds, General Zhii Zaw of the People's Liberation Army saw his entire entourage of highly trained agents reduced to a pile of bloodied, twitching limbs.

The American who moved faster than the general's eye could follow turned his level gaze on General Zaw.

"You General Seesaw?" Remo asked.

The general pulled himself up tall. No American— no matter how fast—could make him surrender his pride.

"I am General Zhii Zaw," the general said, sneering. His jowls waggled with proud defiance.

"I kind of figured. Why is it all you big Chinese

commie mucky-mucks look like you've taken the slow boat from Madame Tussaud's Wax Museum?''

''Your insults are nothing to me,'' the general insisted. ''Do what you came to do, and let it be done.''

The old man puffed out his chest, awaiting the end.

Remo shook his head. ''It's not gonna be that easy,'' he said. ''I've got a little mission for you.''

The general laughed. ''You are mad if you think I will do anything for you, imperialist running dog.''

At that, Remo smiled. It was a cold, evil smile.

''Here is the message you will deliver. Tell those thieving rice herders in Beijing the next time they screw with America—'' He thought carefully, trying to remember the exact phrase he'd been told to use. '''The Yangtze flows red with their blood.' Yeah, that's it. And tell them this isn't a threat. Tell them it's a promise. To them from me, personally.''

General Zaw scowled derisively. ''I will do no such thing,'' he mocked. ''Who are you that you make such demands?''

And for Remo Williams, the words came, easier now than they had in the past. They were filled with pride of history and humility of responsibility.

''I am the soon-to-be Reigning Master of the House of Sinanju, duck droppings,'' Remo said. ''And you live this day only because Sinanju requires a messenger.''

The general's jaw dropped lower than his jowls. Eyes of brown grew very wide, stretching the big pouches that sagged beneath them.

"Sinanju," the general hissed. "You are legend." His voice trembled with the beginnings of fear.

Remo fixed him with an icy stare.

Alex Wycopf was shivering in fright on the floor where Remo had first tossed him. China's top nuclear spy in the United States cringed as Remo dragged him up off the floor. Remo stood Wycopf before the People's Republic general.

"Here's a little visual aid," Remo said. "Paint this picture for those pajama-wearing Mr. Magoos you work for."

Remo placed his hand on Alex Wycopf's face, fingertips fanned out and pressed lightly to flesh.

Wycopf inhaled fearfully.

Remo's hand remained still for a moment, so that the general could get a good clear mental image.

With a sudden spin of his fingers, Remo proceeded to scramble Alex Wycopf's face.

Bones broke swiftly and cleanly, allowing Remo to shift them with delicate nudges. Thumb and fingertips kneaded flesh, shifting soft muscle beneath.

When Remo was through seconds later, General Zaw gasped in horror.

The general had no idea how the American had done it, but the traitor's nose was now on his chin, bracketed by a pair of misplaced ears. An eye was on the forehead, while the other eye butted up against the mouth, which was now where the nose had been. Remo had rearranged the features without even breaking skin. Wycopf looked like a living Picasso painting.

Alex Wycopf's misplaced lips puckered. Only one of his eyes still possessed the ability to blink. It did so, to freakish effect.

"Picture the entire Commie leadership in Beijing singing 'Nearer My Mao To Thee' from their knee-caps," Remo said.

He finished Alex Wycopf with a slap to the forehead so hard it made the traitor's entire brain splat like a wrinkled gray snowball against the balcony windows.

As the shell of Alex Wycopf dropped to the floor, General Zhii Zaw joined him.

"Master of Sinanju, forgive me!" the general cried. As he crawled on his knees, his hands encircled Remo's ankles. His dry tongue tried to lick the toes of Remo's loafers.

Remo kicked him away.

"*A* Master," Remo said. "Not *the* Master. Not yet. Consider yourselves warned. Next time, no Mr. Nice Guy."

His last word delivered, Remo slipped out of the hotel room and was gone.

Still on his knees, General Zaw looked around at the room smeared with blood and brains.

It had all happened in the wink of an eye. As the realization sank in, his terrified stomach clenched.

General Zhii Zaw puked his breakfast onto the sensible blue carpet. Afterward he bowed his head deep into the puddle of his own stomach contents. In supplication to the awesome power of the glorious Masters of Sinanju.

WHEN REMO STEPPED off the elevator downstairs, he found a bunch of very pale vacationing American college kids crowded around the lobby television set. They were watching a show about a group of people who had been stranded in a remote location and were forced to use their wits to survive.

On the screen were printed the flashing words "You will not change the channel."

As Remo passed by, he paused, frowning at the words of command on the screen.

"You come all this way on Christmas vacation, presumably on daddy's dime, and all you do is sit and watch TV?" Remo asked one of them. "What's the matter with you? Why aren't you drunk and getting herpes like normal college kids?"

The nearest student turned to Remo. He was ghostly white and could have benefited from a few hours in the sun. By the looks of it, he'd been in front of the television his whole Cancún vacation.

"Shh," he insisted, pointing to the television. "TV."

On the screen Becki had just confided to an off-screen interviewer that her alliance with Jojanna was just a scheme to get Curt voted off the show, where he would have an inevitably short-lived career as a cheesy product spokesman or B-list actor. At least this had been the most common career for most of those dismissed from the popular survival program.

"It's days like this," Remo mused, "when I actually see what I'm out there protecting, that I almost wish it wasn't my job to keep Western civilization from collapsing around all our ears.''

When the chorus of ''Shut ups'' came, Remo had already vanished out the hotel's front revolving door.

3

As he hurried through the snow, the wind from Long Island Sound sliced Harold W. Smith to the bone. The tails of his overcoat blew out behind him like a gray cape.

The well-tended grounds of Folcroft Sanitarium were surrounded by several acres of pristine woods. At one time a hiking path through the woods had been maintained for patients. However, so few of Folcroft's residents had used it, Smith eventually ordered the groundskeeping service to let it fill in. In the warmer months it was overgrown with brush, but by this time of winter the rough outlines of the old trails slowly reappeared.

The old path was covered with a foot of snow. The footprints of the police who had gone before were clearly visible, broken through the snow's crusted surface.

It was slow going for Smith and Detective Davic. Each man held a tranquilizer gun.

The CURE director could see that the Rye police officer was anxious. Every few feet the middle-aged detective would switch his air gun from one hand to the other, wiping perspiration from his palm onto his trousers.

Smith's palm was bone dry. He held his own air gun loose in his hand. Clenching the weapon as if it were some sort of magic talisman was pointless. When the time came, Harold Smith would be ready. Not that he had any delusions about the certainty of success.

There was every possibility they would fail. The man they were looking for was possessed of abilities like no one else on the planet.

No. Check that. There were two others, but at the moment they were far away. Smith had seen to that.

As they made their way through the woods, the CURE director wondered if he had made the right decision in not calling Remo directly back to Folcroft.

The moment the self-doubt came, Smith banished it.

The police were here. On the grounds of Folcroft. It was not a CURE matter that had brought them here, but their presence raised the omnipresent specter of discovery.

Smith had lived with the risk of exposure for many years now. Most times it lurked at the fringe of conscious thought. It was a canker sore. Sometimes you missed it for a time, but it could never be entirely forgotten.

At other times risks to CURE's security had almost brought about the end of the secret organization. This situation was threatening to become one of those times.

No, Remo couldn't be involved in this. At least not until the police were cleared out. CURE's enforcement arm had never been as cautious as he should. To bring him here could raise even more questions.

"Here," Davic announced all at once. His breath was labored, his cold-seared lungs scarred by years of smoking.

A fork split the path. The heavy footprints they were following broke to the left.

Smith and Davic followed the left fork. It carried them away from the Sound and toward the road.

As they trudged along, Smith thought of the events that had brought him here.

He had known long before today that the escaped patient they were looking for was dangerous. Yet Remo and his teacher had refused to eliminate him. Something to do with some silly superstition that Smith had never fully understood. Despite his misgivings, the CURE director had acceded to their request that the patient be allowed to live out his life in a perpetual medicated coma in CURE's isolated security wing.

A mistake. Smith's fault for allowing it. And it wasn't the only mistake. After the events of that morning, there was another that would soon need to be addressed.

More than a year ago circumstances had deposited Remo and his teacher on Smith's doorstep. The two men had been living at Folcroft ever since. No more. It was just too risky. Once this was over, that arrangement would have to end. He would bring it up with

them at the earliest convenient time. Assuming, that
is, Smith survived the day.

The path they were on angled up a small hill. Long
Island Sound was barely visible through the tangle of
trees. In the past few minutes, the weak winter sun
had begun to break through the bleak cloud cover.
Just a few glimmers of yellow morning light could be
seen on the white-capped waves. As they climbed the
hill, the water disappeared, obscured by brambles and
bushes and thick woods.

Smith saw the body the instant they crested the hill.
It was lying in the snow, surrounded by four other
men. Three were uniformed police; the fourth was a
detective.

Smith and Detective Davic hurried over to the
body.

The uniforms stood around Detective Wayne as he
crouched over the body. When Davic's young partner
saw the gun in Smith's hand, he glanced questioningly at Davic.

"This is Dr. Smith," Davic explained, breathless.
"He offered to help, and at this point I'm not refusing. What have you got?"

Detective Wayne turned his attention back to the
body. "Young male," he said. "Looks to be around
the right age. The only man missing is your assistant,
Dr. Smith."

The dead man was the right build for Mark Howard. His face was pressed in the snow where he'd
fallen. The man had been stripped of his clothes.

Whoever had taken them had failed to disturb the crusted snow around the body.

"Let's see him," Davic ordered.

Detective Wayne gently turned the head to give Smith a better look. They all saw the blood for the first time. It wasn't as it had been back inside Folcroft. There was barely any here. Just a small stain of red in the clean white snow.

Smith's features were pinched as he glanced at the dead man. The youthful face was familiar.

But it was not the one he had expected to see.

"That's not Mark Howard," Smith said. He exhaled a relieved cloud of bile-scented air.

Davic seemed disappointed. "Do you know who it is?"

"Yes," Smith said, nodding. "He's the grandson of Mrs. Sudbury, one of our patients. He frequently stops by in the mornings to bring his grandmother pastry."

"Perfect," Davic grumbled. "Our boy's got street clothes now. Wayne, get back to the building. See if anyone there saw this guy this morning. What he was wearing."

With a sharp nod, Detective Wayne turned. "C'mon, Javez," he barked at one of the uniformed men.

The two officers headed down the path.

"See if his car is still here," Smith called after them.

Davic nodded. "Right. You know what he drives?"

"I believe it is a red Ford Explorer."

"Red Ford Explorer," Davic shouted after Wayne. "Check with the guard at the gate. Javez, search the lot while he's asking."

He turned to Smith. "No offense, but I've talked to your security guard. He ain't exactly Columbo."

"I'm not sure if that will yield anything useful," Smith said. "If this is the path he took, I believe he would continue on it. After ten years of confinement, he would take the most direct route to freedom."

"You're the head doc," Davic said. "Stay with the body," he ordered one of the uniformed men. "And keep sharp. You're with us."

The other uniformed officer fell in with Davic and Smith as they continued on the path.

A dozen yards away they found a small mound of discarded linen. Smith recognized the blue-speckled johnny that was standard for Folcroft's bedridden patients.

Around the area a few cracks were visible in the ice-coated snow. Several delicate footprints marred the otherwise untouched frozen sheet of snow.

Smith was surprised to see the prints. It had been the CURE director's experience that men like his missing patient always walked without leaving a trace. But, then, the man they were tracking had been in a coma for ten years. No matter how skilled he might be, he could not possibly be at one hundred percent. And if his skills were stale, then maybe— just maybe—this could be ended this day after all.

Fingers tensing around his air gun, the CURE director hurried along the path in the company of the two police officers.

The trail led directly up to the high north wall of the sanitarium. It would have been difficult for an average man to scale, but for the fugitive they were seeking, it would have been a simple matter to climb.

But he hadn't gone over. He had gone through.

A massive hole gaped in the high wall. The old concrete veneer had shattered to dust. The heavy bricks beneath were exploded outward. They peppered the snow out in the direction of the lonely road.

To Detective Ronald Davic, it looked as if a stampeding elephant had broken through in its panic to flee Folcroft Sanitarium. As they approached the wall, the Rye police detective shook his head in disbelief.

"What the hell kind of inmates do you have locked in this loony bin?" he breathed, glancing over at Smith.

The Folcroft director didn't answer. His gray eyes were trained directly ahead. His lips pursed in concern.

When Davic glanced back at the hole in the wall, he saw that the landscape had changed. A lone figure was now framed in the opening.

When he saw the sudden movement ahead, the young uniformed officer whipped his gun up.

"Hold your fire!" Smith commanded.

Too late. The cop had already squeezed off a round.

Luckily Smith managed to grab the gun at the last instant. Wrestling with the strong young man, Smith directed the barrel toward the ground. The revolver crackled and the bullet buried harmlessly in snow and earth.

The gunshot echoed off into the distance.

To Harold Smith, the fact that it was lucky he had managed to redirect the man's aim was not in question. Had the gun been aimed at the man standing within the remnants of the wall when it was fired, the police officer would have been dead already. As it was, the new arrival merely looked on with dark annoyance before returning his troubled gaze to the shattered wall.

"That is not the man you are after," Smith snapped at the uniformed officer. "This is another Folcroft patient."

The uniformed officer was panting fearfully. He looked over at Detective Davic, a frightened expression on his face.

"I'm—I'm sorry, sir," he managed.

Davic waved an angrily dismissive hand.

Smith was already heading for the wall. Leaving the young officer behind, Davic hurried with the Folcroft director over to the man at the wall.

The stranger who stood amid the collapsed bricks was five feet tall and older than most of the trees in the surrounding woods. He wore a green silk robe that seemed able to capture light where none existed. Twin tufts of soft yellowing hair clung to the parchment skin of his otherwise bald scalp. His button nose was directed up to where the wall arched in a snaggletoothed collection of jagged brick.

"I thought you were away with your son," Smith said tightly to the wizened figure. A concerned eye darted to where Detective Davic stood, panting, beside them.

"I am back," announced Chiun, the Reigning Master of the House of Sinanju. His sharp hazel eyes scanned the contours of the damaged wall. "And he is finally free."

And the old Korean's singsong voice trembled with the grave tones of foreboding doom.

4

Smith gave his spare tranquilizer gun to Detective Davic's partner, insisting that as director of Folcroft he had to personally escort the elderly patient to his room. Leaving the police to search the woods that lined the road beyond the sanitarium's shattered north wall, he hurried the Master of Sinanju back to the building.

Smith was grateful that the old Korean didn't try to engage him in conversation on the way.

By the time they reached the main building, there were even more police cars clogging the drive. Smith felt the watery acid in the pit of his stomach flare hot as he took note of the growing number of blue uniforms crisscrossing the snow-covered main lawn.

Chiun watched the many officers through slivered eyes as Smith ushered him inside. They quickly mounted the stairs, ducking past Smith's harried secretary and into the CURE director's office.

"This situation is very serious, Master Chiun," Smith explained after he had shut the door.

"I agree," Chiun said. "First we must scatter this army of constables that has had the temerity to roost on your palace grounds. I suggest you begin with boiling oil dumped from the parapets. Where do you keep your catapults? The Roman onager is a nice model. I'm sure you have some of those. Use your onagers to launch flaming garbage into their midst and then mow them down with ballista-hurled javelins.''

''Master Chiun, please,'' Smith begged. ''You know Folcroft has none of those devices. And we cannot interfere with the work of the Rye police.''

''I strongly advise that you do not simply let them swoop in here unchallenged, Emperor Smith,'' Chiun said, his tone serious. ''If you do not act, others will be emboldened by what they perceive as weakness. Soon you'll have Turkish goat herders wandering through your inner ward and Vogul horsemen squatting in the vestibule. If we stick the heads of a few of these pushy doughnut-gobblers on pikes along the walls of Fortress Folcroft, it will discourage the rest.''

''No, Chiun,'' Smith insisted. ''*Please*. I must ask you to avoid contact with the police while they are here. Allow them to go about their business unmolested.''

The old man's shoulders sank in helpless confusion.

''You *want* them here?'' he asked.

''No,'' Smith admitted.

''Quickly, then,'' Chiun said. ''Let us pass out crossbows to your nursing staff. If you lead the charge yourself, I will remain at your side to insure that no harm befalls you.''

He turned to go, but the CURE director bounded between him and the door.

"What I mean is that I accept their presence," Smith said hastily. "Try to understand, Master Chiun. Even more complications would arise if we tried to forcibly remove them. It is best for security to allow them to finish their business without interference."

The Master of Sinanju noted the look of pleading earnestness on his employer's face.

"So you want them here, even though you do not want them here," the old man spoke slowly.

"Precisely," Smith said. "You see?"

The old Korean saw exactly. This was obviously some inscrutable white madness, the nature of which he had long ago given up hope of ever understanding.

"Very well, O Emperor," Chiun said, resignation in his voice. "Though the shadows of the deepest cave in the darkest night are terrifying blind to the eyes of we mortals, they are pierced by the brilliance of the light that is your limitless wisdom. It is not up to a lowly assassin such as myself to comprehend the complexities of your dealings in matters of state. If you wish to let foreign armies clomp around your palace as if it were their own, I will not interfere. But might your humble assassin offer one piffling suggestion?"

"What is that?"

"Hide the silver before the Spaniards arrive."

As Chiun tucked his hands deep inside the voluminous sleeves of his kimono, Smith allowed a slip of relief to pass his thin lips.

"I am not concerned about invading armies," the CURE director said. "My main worry at the moment is Jeremiah Purcell. You are aware that he has escaped?"

Chiun nodded impatiently. "So I have said."

"He may have a head start of three hours."

"It is closer to four," Chiun corrected. "Judging by the prints he made in the snow and the condition of the body in the woods."

"Then you agree with my assessment," Smith said with a troubled frown. "I had hoped he might have doubled back in an attempt to throw us off the trail. But I thought that unlikely. It is my opinion that he would not stay here."

"I agree," the old Korean replied. "The footprints in the snow show that he is not what he once was. He knows he cannot face either me or Remo in his current debilitated state. He would go somewhere to recover."

For a moment Smith hovered in the middle of the office, hands clenched in helpless frustration. But all at once a light dawned.

"The castle where he was trained!" he exclaimed. "Maybe he'll go back to Saint Martin. He has fled to safety there in the past."

Whirling from the Master of Sinanju, Smith hurried around his desk, settling into his chair.

"It is possible he would return there," Chiun said. "But it is not the only possibility. After all, some of his training took place in other locations."

"Oh?" Smith asked, looking up over the tops of

his rimless glasses. "I wasn't aware you knew of any other locations your nephew used to train Purcell."

There seemed an instant's hesitation on the leathery face of the Master of Sinanju.

"I merely meant that his training would not be limited to one place," Chiun explained, averting his eyes. "It is likely there were other locations we knew nothing about." He made a show of settling cross-legged to the carpet. The air escaped with a gentle sigh from his collapsing robes.

"Oh, I see," Smith said, nodding. "You're probably right. However, since we know of no others, we have to begin the search somewhere. I will monitor flights to and from the island. The mainframes are already programmed to flag any deaths with a Sinanju fingerprint. I will broaden the search parameters. That is how we stumbled upon him the first time years ago." He began typing at his keyboard.

"I fear it will do you no good, Emperor," the Master of Sinanju cautioned. "Although Purcell is mad, he was never a fool. He was a gifted young man with a bright mind. He has escaped into the world. It is likely we will not see him again until such time he chooses to be found."

There was a note of sad resignation in the old Korean's voice.

"Perhaps," Smith said unhappily. "But we must make an effort." As he worked, he shot a quizzical glance at the tiny Asian. "I'm surprised to see you here, Master Chiun. When Remo called for another assignment an hour ago, I assumed you would go with him."

A cloud passed across the old man's face. "Remo does not need me any longer," he said.

Smith detected the bitterness in the Korean's voice.

"Is something wrong between the two of you?"

"Nothing that was not anticipated."

The old Korean could see that Smith expected more. With a sigh, he shook his aged head.

"When a Master arrives at the level Remo has reached, he begins to look differently at those around him," Chiun explained. "He even sees as a burden those who raised him, who brought him up from despair and squalor, those who gave him the best years of their lives. It is this way with many Masters in transition. Not me, of course," he added hastily. "I was a joy to train. But the lesser pasty-skinned ingrates with ugly noses and big feet are notorious for this sort of behavior during the time of final passage to full Masterhood."

"Hmm," Smith said. "Your description makes it almost sound like Remo is going through a new adolescence."

"Remo never stopped going through his first adolescence," the Master of Sinanju replied. "This is different. I would not expect an outsider to understand."

Smith grunted acceptance. He finished up work at his computer.

"There," the CURE director announced. "I have updated the search function to include all suspicious deaths, not just those that seem to involve Sinanju characteristics. I have also alerted authorities in the northeast to be on the lookout for individuals matching Purcell's description. I have issued orders not to attempt to apprehend. It would be pointless to do so, and we do not need any more deaths on our hands. They will focus their attention on airports, as well as train stations and bus terminals.''

For a moment his hands rested at the edge of his desk, fingers curled to attack his keyboard. He quickly realized that he had done all that he was able to do. Jeremiah Purcell was a free man now. If he was spotted, Smith's basement mainframes would let him know.

His hands withdrew from the hidden keyboard.

"We must deal now with another urgent matter," the CURE director said ominously. "Mark has disappeared."

Chiun's eyes opened wide. "The Prince Regent has fallen victim to the evil Dutchman?" he asked, concern blossoming anew on his weathered face.

"Possibly," Smith said. "Unfortunately, that would be the more agreeable option. There is evidence that Mark is in collusion with Purcell."

The Master of Sinanju's face darkened.

"Impossible," the old Korean insisted firmly. "Whoever told you this is lying, Emperor Smith. Point me to this untruthful adviser and I will award you the gift of his false tongue for daring to slander the character of your gracious and loyal prince."

"I know you are fond of Mark, Master Chiun, but

I saw it with my own eyes. Mark is the one who issued the order to cut Purcell's sedatives.''

Chiun shook his head. "Sinanju has long danced along the blade of palace intrigue," he said. "We can recognize the seeds of treachery in faithless underlings. Prince Mark does not possess a traitorous spirit. He would not betray you of his own free will.''

"I hope you're right," Smith said. The weariness of the past few days suddenly began to catch up with him. He sank back in his chair, closing his tired eyes. "It would be easier if I could question him directly. So far the police have been unable to find him.''

"He was not seen leaving?" Chiun asked.

"No," Smith said. "He may still be on the grounds. His car was in the parking lot when I arrived.''

"In that case I will find him for you.''

Chiun rose to his feet in a single fluid motion and went over to the wall. Sinking back to a lotus position, he pressed his back tight against the paneling. His papery eyelids fluttered shut.

For several long minutes he sat in utter silence—an ancient statue that not even a single dust particle would dare alight on for fear of breaking his trance.

Across the room Smith was engulfed by the waves of utter stillness. At one point he shifted in his chair to ease the discomfort in his lower back. For an instant he cringed, afraid that the squeak from his chair might intrude on the Master of Sinanju's thoughts. But then he remembered the squeak was no longer there.

After what seemed like an eternity, the old Korean's eyes sprang open wide. In a twirl of silk, he rose to his feet and bounded for the door, flinging it open.

Smith jumped to his feet and hurried after the Master of Sinanju. He caught up with him in the hallway.

There were police in the hall of the executive wing. At first Smith was worried that Chiun would say something to them—or worse. But it was as if they didn't exist. The Master of Sinanju breezed past the officers they encountered.

Upstairs, they passed through the hospital wing. Smith noticed that it was unusually quiet for that time of morning. The only talking in the ward came from television sets. In every room the TV set was turned on. A dozen Folcroft patients stared, mesmerized, at the flickering images on a dozen separate television screens.

It was odd given the excitement of the morning. Smith had expected the residents of Folcroft to be disturbed by all that had been going on. He didn't have time to see whatever it was the patients found so fascinating.

Down the hall and through another set of doors, he and the Master of Sinanju found themselves above the administrative wing of the big building. Another hall led around a corner. When they got to the end, Smith found that he was looking up a dusty old staircase.

The stairs led to an old abandoned attic. Chiun had been using the room as a private hideaway during the time he'd been living at Folcroft. It was tucked so far off the beaten path that the police had so far failed to find it.

Kimono hems spinning crazily around his ankles, the Master of Sinanju mounted the stairs. Smith followed.

The enclosed staircase led to a warped pine door. Chiun pushed the door open and slipped inside.

At the far end of the long room, weak winter sunlight spilled through three ceiling-to-floor windows.

Smith hadn't been sure what to expect. He realized his expectations needn't have been very high.

For once the Master of Sinanju's instincts had been wrong. The room was empty, save the collection of medical junk that had accumulated in the attic for the eighty-or-so years Folcroft had been in operation.

Smith was allowing the tension to drain from him even as the old Korean made his way across the floor to the window.

"I suppose we should allow the police to conduct the search for Mark after all," Smith said with a sigh. "You may return to your quarters if you wish. I'll let you know if they turn up anything. Master Chiun?"

Chiun seemed intensely interested in a bundle of old rags that had been dumped beneath the window. The rags rested in shadow, tucked up under the sill away from the sunlight.

Only when he squinted against the light did the CURE director see that the pile of rags was wearing shoes.

Holding his breath, Smith hurried over to join Chiun.

The man was lying in the inch-thick dust, curled up in a tight fetal position. His head and knees touched the wall beneath the grimy windows.

Smith's mouth opened in slow shock. "Mark?" he asked. Deep apprehension flavored his lemony voice.

It was as if the voice were some intangible lifeline.

The man on the floor rolled his head from the wall. Desperate, terrified eyes darted between the two standing men. The instant he saw Smith, the young man's eyes seemed to find focus. All at once the man lunged at Smith.

He grabbed the CURE director tight, wrapping both arms around the older man's neck.

Baffled, Smith looked at the Master of Sinanju. Great sadness filled the old Korean's leathery face.

And the pleading voice warm in Smith's ear was filled with fear and incomprehension.

"Help me," Mark Howard croaked.

And with that his frightened eyes rolled back in his head and the assistant director of CURE passed out in the arms of Harold W. Smith.

5

The Australian outback would have been a dream. A deserted tropical island? Heaven.

So what if there were snakes in the outback or if it was the kind of island where you had to eat rats and bugs? Paradise was in the eyes of the beholder. Right about now, even having to endure a backstabbing, overweight gay guy strutting around naked wouldn't have been so bad.

"When I signed on for this, I thought we'd be going somewhere tropical," R. Chappel said. "I worked out for two months straight. Got in the best shape of my life. I even bought a home tanning bed. For what? Look at this dump."

He waved an angry hand at the surrounding scenery. The hand was covered by a thick mitten. The mitten matched his heavy down jacket. A tiny patch adorned the breast of the winter coat, its logo recognizable to television viewers across the country and around the world.

"I mean it," Chappel concluded. "Did you expect this?"

"Could be worse," replied David Felder. He continued to forage on the ground for supplies.

That was typical Felder. Never wanting to complain, always trying to put on a good face. That was Felder's strategy. Keep his head down, stay quiet, don't make waves and—with luck—when this mess was over, walk away with the million-dollar prize.

That wasn't R. Chappel's strategy. Chappel was the official complainer. There was one every time. Everyone would bitch and moan about his constant griping, and when they couldn't take it any longer they'd vote him the hell out of there. Right about now Chappel didn't care.

"Gimme my own house, my own bed. I'm sick of sleeping on the ground. And you!" he suddenly snapped directly to the camera. "Get that damn thing away from me before I shove it down your throat!"

The camera that hovered a few inches from his angry face didn't move. The cameraman behind it didn't reply.

The camera operators never talked. It was in their contracts not to interfere with the contestants. They could film, but they could not interact.

"Dammit," Chappel snarled. "Like talking to a damn zombie."

He turned back to Felder. "We about done here?"

"A couple more minutes," Felder said as he continued to pick items off the ground. "This place is a gold mine."

Crossing his arms, Chappel glanced around. It didn't look like a gold mine to him. Not unless gold mines were surrounded by bombed-out tenements and abandoned stores.

This was the cruelest trick life had ever played on R. Chappel.

At first this had been a dream come true. He had submitted the audition tape without any expectations at all, and he had made it! He'd beaten all odds and actually been chosen as a contestant for the biggest reality game show in the history of American television.

Winner was a genuine cultural phenomenon. Hugely popular among viewers. A ratings juggernaut. Even those who had never once seen the show couldn't escape from it.

The premise was simple. A group of people with wildly different backgrounds was placed in a remote setting and forced to survive without any of the creature comforts of modern life. Each week, the group would select one person to expel. Their numbers would be winnowed down until only one was left. To the winner was awarded the one-million-dollar grand prize.

The settings of the first *Winner* seasons had been hot, exciting and dangerous. To shake things up in the latest installment, the producers had gone in a different direction.

"Goddamn Harlem," R. Chappel griped as he looked around the benighted urban landscape. "What were they smoking when they came up with this?"

David Felder didn't answer. He continued to dig up discarded hypodermic needles from the dirty snow of the abandoned lot. The group had learned early on that the used needles could be traded to crack addicts for food stamps. The contestants could then trade in the food stamps at the corner convenience mart for necessities.

Felder dropped two more needles into his knapsack.

He had swiped the knapsack from base camp. The same logo that adorned both of their jackets was stitched to the bag. The words Surmount, Surpass, Survive were printed in an oval, surrounding the larger word *Winner*.

That same logo was plastered all over everything, from hats to T-shirts to belt buckles. It was even on the goddamn rolls of toilet paper.

Of course, real toilet paper was reserved for the producers and crew. The cast had to scrounge up whatever they could whenever nature called. When they couldn't barter with needles or deposit bottles, they were forced to make do with whatever they could find. R. Chappel had learned pretty quickly that Church's Chicken bags and discarded Wrigley's Spearmint wrappers weren't worth shit for absorbing.

"It's all rigged anyway," R. Chappel said. "They pick who's gonna win even before we get started. A guy like me doesn't have a shot." He scowled for the camera. "Yeah, and don't think I don't know you're gonna edit that out."

The three-man camera crew was no longer looking his way.

That was odd. He had gotten used to the cameras always being aimed at him. But now they were aimed at the ground. Chappel had come to think of the camera operators as cyborgs, their cameras permanently affixed to their faces. But the faces had emerged. What's more, they looked worried. They were staring down the street.

Chappel followed their line of sight.

"Oh, great," he said, rolling his eyes. "Not again."

There was a group of people heading his way.

That was part of the problem with using a public locale for *Winner*. When the Harlem location was first brought up, there were fears for the safety of the contestants. It turned out those concerns were unnecessary. The biggest worry in this modern era of celebrity worship were those locals who wanted to get in on the act.

People had been trying to crash the *Winner* set for the past month. At first Chappel assumed the group coming down the street was just the latest in the seemingly endless parade of media whores. But as they closed in, he realized these ones seemed a tad more focused than the rest had been.

They didn't talk. They just marched up the road. They were carrying things in their hands. Some had boards or iron bars, others had chains.

Chappel gulped. "Um," he said out of the corner of his mouth, "you think they want our autographs?"

When he turned to David Felder, he was dismayed to find that his partner was no longer digging in the snow.

Felder was hightailing across the vacant lot. As he

ran, he flung his knapsack. Syringes scattered across the snow.

Two cameramen were on Felder's heels. They were struggling under the weight of their cameras. The third flung his camera at the approaching mob.

"Run, you moron!" he screamed.

It was the first time R. Chappel had ever heard one of the cameramen speak.

Fear set in. Chappel turned and ran after the man.

As he raced across the lot, he heard the steady beat of a hundred footfalls behind him. He looked over his shoulder.

Big mistake. The instant he looked back, he tripped on a malt liquor bottle and landed in a heap on a broken-down chain-link fence. When he rolled back over, the shadows were already falling over him.

The mob was on him.

They didn't seem interested in David Felder or the three fleeing cameramen. The mob let the others make good their escape, surrounding the lone, terrified game-show contestant.

Chappel cowered from the sea of blank faces. A rusted piece of twisted metal dug into the small of his back.

"What do you want?" he asked, his voice small with fear.

The crowd didn't answer. It stood quietly over him. There was no talking, no shouting. Just utter silence.

After a long moment, the multitude parted.

An obese man in a green jogging suit waddled from the mob. His eyes were as blank as the rest. In his dark hands he clutched a palm-size portable television set with a two-inch screen. The fat man looked from the tiny little screen to the frightened man on the ground.

"Dat's the one," he proclaimed loudly. He flashed the tiny TV to the crowd.

A few others had battery sets, as well. They passed them around, dull eyes feeding hungrily on the small image. When they were through, they refocused attention on R. Chappel. This time Chappel saw the blood lust in their eyes. It was the last thing he would ever see.

Without a peep, without a whisper, without a single angry word, the silent mob fell on R. Chappel.

They hit him with boards and rods. They beat him until his bones broke and his skin was bruised and bloodied.

At first the pain was unbearable. Then it wasn't so bad. Then it was nothing, as the great numbness of death washed over him. When the final blow that technically ended his life came at last, he was already gone. With a nail driven deep into his brain, "R." Remo Chappel was voted from this life to the next.

THE FORMER PRESIDENT of the United States watched the dilapidated buildings and burned-out cars through the window of his armor-plated limousine.

Even though the people here loved him, the ex-president hated Harlem. He was attracted to places that thrummed with life, like the *real* New York City and Los Angeles. The whole world knew Harlem was dead from the neck down.

For this former president, the best gauge of a locale's vitality was whether or not it could sustain a steady stream of thousand-dollar-a-plate fund-raising dinners. Judging by the residents he glimpsed through the tinted windows of his car, the people of Harlem would be lucky to scrape up ten bucks for a Whopper with cheese and a bottle of Crazy Horse.

Everything was so dreary and depressing. One thing was certain. He wouldn't be caught dead here if not for yet another one of the million little public-relations nightmares that seemed to always hang in the air around him like the warm stink around a public outhouse.

When he had surrendered the presidency, he had originally tried to rent space on Manhattan's upper west side. But those yammering pests in flyover country had gotten a major-league bug up their collective ass over the monthly 1.2 million dollars of taxpayer money it would cost to rent his pricey Manhattan digs. If it were up to him, he would have flipped them all the bird and settled like a dethroned king in his new apartment. But his wife was in the Senate by that point, and her political fate was tied to his approval numbers. When he began to drop in the polls like a plummeting anvil, the former first lady had insisted that he find a more suitable spot for his retirement offices. That's when the Reverend Hal Shittman stepped in.

Shittman was a rabble-rousing Harlem minister whose appetite for inflammatory rhetoric was matched only by his gastronomic intake. The minister had suggested publicly that the former president should take some office space in Harlem. A reward for the unflagging support of the black community.

The former president's wife loved the idea. So did the press and the people in Harlem. Everyone thought it was a great idea. Everyone, that was, except the former president.

Life was not as it had been when he was leader of the entire free world. In his time out of political office, he had learned, as all ex-presidents learned, that his opinion on a subject no longer held the weight it once did. In the end the advisers won out and the former president lost. With much fanfare he had accepted the minister's offer.

Quietly, the former president had enjoyed a secret victory. Although he had showed up for the ribbon-cutting ceremony of his new offices, that was the last time he had seen the place. In the ensuing months he had stayed away, opting for foreign trips and domestic fund-raising events.

He would have been happy to never again darken the door of his official offices. Unfortunately, he hadn't factored in the raging ego of the man who had saved his fanny all those months ago.

Hal Shittman had started talking to the press. The minister had noticed the president's conspicuous absence from his own offices. The complaints were loud and frequent. So loud were they that the ex-president's wife had gotten wind of the brewing crisis all the way down in Washington.

At the time, the former first lady's approval ratings

as the junior senator from New York were in a tumble. The black vote was a vital part of her core constituency. In an angry phone call that had lasted all of one minute, she had dispatched the former president to Harlem with a four-word command: "Fix it or else."

And so it was that the ex-president of the United States found himself slouched morosely in the back seat of his car as it drove along Martin Luther King Boulevard on the way to the offices he swore he'd never set foot in again.

There were only three Secret Service men in the car with him. Two were in the front, one in the back.

Not like the old days.

The former president offered a long, wistful sigh as the limo turned a corner and headed down another run-down street. He was still sighing when the car came to a sudden stop.

"What's wrong?" asked the president.

He peered out the window. This didn't look like the street where his office was.

Only when he looked farther along did he notice the crowd waiting in the middle of the road.

The men and women just stood there, faces blank. At the front of the group, his great bloated belly swathed in green velour, stood Hal Shittman. The minister and some of the others held small black objects in their hands that they concentrated on like fortune-tellers over tea leaves.

"Is this the welcoming committee?" the former president asked his Secret Service detachment, his hoarse voice annoyed. He pressed his doughy face harder to the window, framing his eyes with both hands. "Doesn't look like much of a reception. How come I don't see no cameras? Do they think I do this for something other than the six-o'clock news? Get out there to Shittman and tell him my ass don't leave this seat till I see me a camera."

"Yes, sir," said the Secret Service agent who sat in the front seat next to the driver. The man got out of the car and went over to talk to the good reverend.

The president waited, quietly fuming.

He watched the Secret Service man talking to Hal Shittman. He saw Shittman appear to respond. He saw someone near the minister take something out from behind his back. And as he watched in shock, he saw the spike that had been nailed into the end of the two-by-four being driven deep into the skull of the Secret Service agent.

After that, things started to happen very quickly for the former president of the United States.

The dead agent dropped. The crowd surged over him.

At the same time the ex-president's driver threw the limo into gear, backing up in a squeal of tires and a cloud of rubber. The former president was thrown to one side of the car.

Outside, the crowd swarmed the limo. Hands clawed at locked door handles. The car rocked on its springs. Men and women beat fists and weapons against shatterproof windows.

Back on the main drag, the driver wrestled the car

into drive. He stomped on the gas and the vehicle surged away.

Minister Shittman's eyes bulged like an angry bull-frog's. His upswept pompadour quivered with fury.

"There he go!" Hal Shittman bellowed, his great belly bouncing at the effort. "After his lily white ass!"

Screaming bloody murder, the crowd pursued the former president's limousine down the litter-strewn street. At the distant rear of the mob came Minister Shittman, a huffing and puffing mound of righteous velour rage.

6

Remo Williams knew something was wrong when he
saw the squad cars slowly patrolling the lonely road
that led to Folcroft Sanitarium. In thirty years he
couldn't remember ever seeing a cop on that street.
He assumed Smith used his computers to somehow
arrange for the Rye police department to always be
on patrol somewhere else. But here were two cop cars
in four minutes driving along the lonely midnight
road.

Remo saw the gaping hole in the sanitarium wall
as the taillights of the second squad car were disappearing in his rearview mirror.

He pulled to the side of the road to examine the
wall.

Footprints of a dozen men mangled the snow all
around the area. It didn't matter. Remo could see that
a simple force blow in the weakest part of the wall's
inner face had sent bricks scattering out to the street.
It was actually a pretty sloppy job by Chiun's normal
standards.

No matter. It was clear what had happened. The
Master of Sinanju had been in a pissy mood these
past few days. If the patrolling cops were any indi-

cation, something more than just a wall had paid the price.

"Five bucks it was the cabbie," he muttered to himself.

Before Remo had headed south for his rendezvous with Alex Wycopf and his Chinese contact, he had put his teacher in the back of a cab at JFK. The cab-driver was a Pakistani. Chiun didn't like Pakistanis. Worse, the man wore a turban. For fun Chiun some-times liked to yank on turbans so that the heads be-neath them spun like tops. Most times the heads came off and skipped away, to the old man's delight.

Chiun had been ticked at Remo for some reason, and as a result some innocent—albeit surly—cab-driver had paid the ultimate price.

"I am not spending the rest of the night beating the bushes for some dead Paki's head," Remo vowed.

Climbing back in his car, Remo drove to the main gate. Usually the guard in the booth was dozing in his chair. This night he actually seemed alert. It was unnerving. He watched intently as Remo drove up the gravel driveway.

Folcroft itself seemed brighter than usual. Exterior lights that were not ordinarily used had been turned on. Yellow light shone bright across the snow as Remo parked his car in the employee lot.

In spite of himself, he found his eyes scanning the shadows of the lot for human heads.

When he reached the building, he found the side door he always used locked. He tapped a finger twice on the locking mechanism and the bolt clicked agreeably open.

Remo climbed the stairs to the second floor.

From stairwell to executive wing, Remo could tell more people had been here recently than normal. The dust that normally clung comfortably to corners danced now in the cold drafts. There were different smells, as well. A lot of men with a lot of cheap cologne had come through Folcroft.

Remo was beginning to think there might be something more serious to worry about than a single dead Pakistani cabdriver, but when he reached Smith's office door he recognized the two heartbeats that emanated from within.

Smith's door was locked, too. Remo popped it and slipped inside the dimly lit room.

The Master of Sinanju sat in the middle of the carpet, his back to the door. He had to have sensed Remo as he came into the room, but the old man didn't turn. Eyes closed, he continued to meditate as his pupil shut the door.

"Okay, where's the body?" Remo asked. "And don't think I'm volunteering, 'cause I am *not* moving it."

Smith looked up sharply from his desk.

"Remo," the CURE director exhaled. The weird light cast up from his submerged monitor seemed to age his haggard face. "Why didn't you call in?"

"Nice to see you, too, Smitty," Remo replied. "I didn't call because I was coming right home. Although by the looks of it maybe I shouldn't have. What's the bad news?''

Smith took a deep breath. "Jeremiah Purcell has escaped," he said. There seemed a tired resignation to the announcement. His eyes were rimmed in black.

Remo wasn't sure how to react to the news. He blinked, looking from the CURE director to the Master of Sinanju.

Chiun's eyes were now open. He didn't look his pupil's way. Gaze flat, he watched Smith.

"How?" Remo demanded. "When?"

Smith hesitated. "His, er, medication was altered in my absence. As a result, he came out of his coma sometime yesterday morning."

"So when you couldn't find me, what? You called the cops?"

"There were several deaths," Smith explained. "The police were here before I even got back from South America. They searched but came up empty. There is a manhunt going on right now. I'm surprised you haven't heard. Folcroft has been featured on the news."

The mere mention of the press coverage that had been part of the fallout resulting from Purcell's escape was enough to make Smith squirm in his chair.

"I was in the air most of the day," Remo said. He was recovering from his initial shock. "Okay, Smitty, where is the nutbar? Chiun and I will go toss a butterfly net over him and drag him back here."

"That's the problem," Smith said wearily. "I've been searching for him for the past thirty-six hours.

There have been no other unusual deaths reported, no sightings of any kind. He has for all intents and purposes disappeared.''

Remo couldn't believe what he was hearing. He turned to his teacher. ''Little Father?'' he asked.

The old man shook his head.

''The emperor has done his best,'' Chiun said flatly. ''You should thank him as I have for taking interest in what is essentially a Sinanju problem.''

''Sinanju my ass,'' Remo said. ''He's the psycho pupil of your traitor nephew. They both forfeited the right to claim Sinanju status the first fifty-seven billion times they tried to kill us. And we can't let him just run around loose. Try harder, Smitty.''

''I have done all I can,'' the CURE director said.

''Do more,'' Remo insisted. ''Everybody's gotta be somewhere. I thought you knew how to run those dingwhistle computers of yours.''

''Remo, I have exhausted all possibilities,'' Smith said, straining to inject calm. ''Purcell is gone.''

Remo couldn't believe the older man's attitude. This was big beyond big. Smith should have realized that. And Chiun. Chiun of all people should have known better. But the two of them were just sitting there.

''Well, isn't this just marvey?'' Remo snarled sarcastically. ''The biggest threat we've ever faced is out roaming the countryside like an albino Frankenstein, and the three of us are sitting out on the terrace drinking mint juleps and waiting for the freaking magnolias to bloom.''

Smith pulled off his glasses. With slender fingers he pinched the bridge of his nose.

"If it seems as if I am not worried, I assure you, Remo, that's not the case," the CURE director said. "But I have spent the better part of the past day searching for Purcell with no success. He has disappeared completely. I can't send you after him when I don't know where in the world he is. And at the moment Purcell is not our only problem."

"Why?" Remo asked, suddenly suspicious at the older man's grave tone. "What other disaster happened while I was gone?" A thought popped into his head. "Hey, by the way, where's Smitty Jr.? It's half-past time for him to annoy the piss out of me right about now."

"Mark is—" Smith hesitated. "He has been committed as a patient here at Folcroft."

Remo's brow darkened. "Purcell zap him?"

"No. I am not sure what's wrong. Physically, Mark is fine. It's his mental and emotional state that concerns me at the moment."

"Why? What happened to the kid?"

Smith replaced his glasses.

"The doctors aren't certain. At the moment he is being treated for exhaustion. It appears as if he has not slept in days. Master Chiun believes that his condition is the result of some sort of external mental phenomenon, which could explain why he cut Purcell's sedatives."

Remo's eyes went flat. "Hold the phone," he said,

voice dead. "Are you telling me Wally Cleaver is the one who let Purcell out of his cage?"

"It would appear to be the case," Smith admitted.

Remo's face steeled. "Fine," he said. "How do you want me to work this? You want him to die in bed here, or do you want me to take him somewhere else and do it?"

Smith shook his head firmly. "I do not want Mark harmed, Remo," he said. "Not until we know all the facts."

"Facts, my ass," Remo said. "You put MacCleary on ice for a lot less than this. Or am I the only one who remembers that?"

Conrad MacCleary had been part of CURE's inner circle in the early days. He was the man responsible for bringing Remo into the organization. MacCleary had also been Harold W. Smith's only real friend. At the mention of his old comrade's name, Smith's spine stiffened.

"MacCleary was a different case," the CURE director said coldly. "He was hospitalized with injuries that would more than likely have killed him anyway. With the medication he was on, there was a risk that he would talk."

"Right. And I suppose you're treating Howard with nothing but happy thoughts and Yoo-Hoos?"

"Mark is under sedation, yes," Smith admitted. "But I have taken precautions. He has been isolated from the rest of Folcroft's population. Master Chiun and I have been monitoring his progress. I have only allowed the medical staff to see him while I am present. It's safe for now.''

"It'll be a hell of a lot safer once I pull his spine out through his mouth," Remo said. He spun on his heel.

Before Remo could storm from the room, the Master of Sinanju rose to his feet.

"Hold!" the old man commanded.

Remo stopped, spinning back around. "This is the right thing to do, Little Father," he snapped. "The kid did more than just screw us. He might have signed both our death warrants. Or did you forget Purcell's got an edge on us?"

"The Dutchman's ability to cast hallucinations is not the issue here," Chiun said. "Until we learn the truth of his involvement with Purcell, you will do nothing to harm the Prince Regent."

"Why?" Remo asked in Korean. "Because you think you can soak him for a few shekels once he takes over for Smith? Here's a news flash for you. Your vaunted little prince just stabbed us all in the back. I say we cut bait on him now."

"And I say we do not," Chiun retorted in the same language. "My time as Reigning Master may be growing short, but I am still head of our village and my decrees will be followed by my apprentice. What is more, your emperor has ordered that his lackey not be harmed."

At the door, Remo felt the fight drain out of him.

He felt tired. Chiun's attitude lately had been draining enough. Now this. He exhaled angrily.

"I think it's a bad idea," Remo growled.

"Happily, Remo Williams, the rest of us are not as limited in our ideas as you," Chiun said. "I for one could not live in a space so confining. Now be a good boy for once in your disobedient life and do as you are told."

Shoulders slumping, Remo trudged back across the floor.

Behind his desk, Smith seemed relieved.

"For the time being, this is for the best," the CURE director assured Remo. After the past day he seemed pleased to finally change the subject. "Now, what happened with Alex Wycopf?"

"He's toast," Remo said. He thought of Wycopf's face. "Or scrambled eggs," he amended. "Either way he's history. And I sent General Seesaw back to China with a warning. They should pull back for a while. Assuming they believe him. 'Course, if they don't, knowing them he'll be executed, tried and arrested. In that order."

Smith seemed satisfied with Remo's results. Before he could ask another question, the CURE director was distracted by a beep from his computer. He turned his attention to his monitor as Remo and Chiun sat on the carpet.

"Did you tell the Chinaman my grandfather's words?" Chiun asked Remo as Smith began typing at his keyboard.

"Word for word," Remo replied. "I told him to lay off America or 'the Yangtze flows red with their blood.' It worked pretty good. But he really crapped his kimono when he found out I was a Master of Sinanju.''

Chiun arched an eyebrow. ''Don't you mean *the* Master of Sinanju?'' he asked blandly.

''No,'' Remo insisted firmly. ''Not this time. I promised myself this on my way back here. You're not sucking me into that again. You're the Master of Sinanju, okay? The one, the only. Accept no substitutes.''

''I would like to believe that you still respect me, Remo,'' Chiun said. ''But how can I when it is so plain to me that you are ashamed to be seen with me?''

''I'm not ashamed,'' Remo said. ''It's all in your head.''

''Ah, now I see. So I am a nuisance *and* I'm crazed. Clearly, I have become too great a burden to you. How unfortunate for you that Long Island Sound has no convenient ice floes on which to leave me. Perhaps in his infinite kindness Emperor Smith will give me permanent residence in one of the upper floors of Fortress Folcroft. Once you have assumed Reigning Masterhood, I can be hidden up there to sit and gather dust with the other elderly castaways.''

''I've been meaning to talk to you both about that,'' Smith said. He continued to work, eyes trained on his computer screen. ''It is too problematic for you to remain here any longer. Given current circumstances, it is time the two of you found alternative lodgings.''

''Oh, great,'' grumbled Remo. ''Perfect timing.''

"Why would I expect anything more?" Chiun moaned. "Now you *both* wish to rid yourselves of the nuisance that is me. Why not smother me in my sleep? Or better yet, the two of you could take me into the depths of the forest and chain me to a tree like some unwanted dog. I will buy the chain."

"Thanks a bunch, Smitty," Remo groused. "Couldn't you pick a better time to toss us out on our ears?"

"Permanent residence for you here at Folcroft has never been an option," Smith insisted. "By allowing you to stay all these months, we have all been guilty of falling into a comfortable but dangerous habit. You knew you couldn't remain here forever." His eyes narrowed as he studied the data on his computer. "Oh, my," he said quietly.

"What's wrong now?"

"There is apparently some civil unrest in Harlem," the CURE director replied.

"No kidding?" Remo said blandly. "What's the matter, Cincinnati run out of windows to break?"

"This could be serious," Smith said gravely.

As he spoke, his computer beeped anew. Tired eyes scanned the new information culled by the CURE mainframes. By the time he'd finished reading, the last of the color had drained from his gray face.

"The president was visiting Harlem at the time. Initial reports are not clear, but he was apparently in the area when the mob action began. He may be in danger."

"What the hell is he doing in Harlem?" Remo

asked. "I thought he only left Camp David to fly to Texas."

"It is a former president," Smith explained.

"Oh." Remo's face relaxed. He glanced around the gloomy office. "Anything good on TV?"

7

A dour winter's dawn was beginning to streak the sky above Harlem as Cindee Maloo stomped her size-five Timberland all-terrain boot on the potholed street.

"Pooh," Cindee complained. "Pooh, pooh and more pooh."

She had just been given some very bad news about the former president of the United States.

"Are you sure he escaped in one piece?" Cindee demanded.

"I'm sorry, Cindee," replied her assistant. "I hate to be the bearer of bad news, but there weren't any dramatic rescues or blood on the sidewalk or anything. According to the news people, he managed to get into his office after the mob attacked his car. When they didn't storm the building, he holed up in there for a few hours. The mob surrounded the place and screamed and yelled for a while, but when the police showed up, everything just sort of stopped. Everyone surrendered peacefully and the president took off. He's probably halfway to Chappaqua by now."

Cindee stomped her little foot in its rugged out-doorsy boot again. "Pooh!" she repeated.

Her nasal accent made the word come out sounding like "poe." The accent was Australian, which was no surprise since Cindee Maloo herself was Australian. She was Australian from her nasal accent to the top of her naturally curly Australian blond hair and to the toe of her pretty little Australian foot, which she stomped angrily on the ugly American pavement one more time.

"Where's the drama in just having him escape like that?" Cindee complained. "Who's gonna stay tuned if they know he gets out of it alive?"

Cindee cast a furious eye up at the building in which the former president had spent a harrowing night.

Rocks had shattered most of the windows. The sidewalk was littered with glass.

The thinning crowd gathered outside the building was mostly news people along with a few neighborhood residents who had come out to gawk when the fireworks started.

Nearer, there were two men examining some of the debris that had been crushed by the mob's stomping feet.

"I'll prove it to you," Cindee said to her assistant. "Let's ask Joe Sixpack here." She turned to the nearest of the two men. "You. Lemme ask you something."

The man didn't even look at her. That was unusual. With her smooth skin, perfect teeth and piercing brown eyes, Cindee had the sort of features that usually had no problem turning men's heads.

The man spoke without lifting his head.

"Where'd you buy that accent, Paul Hogan's going-out-of-career sale?" he asked, his nose still in the gutter.

What he was looking at, Cindee had no idea.

"I wanna ask you about TV," Cindee pressed.

"Go squat on one."

"Did you hear the president got away?" Cindee demanded.

The man let loose a protracted exhale of air. Turning his attention from the junk on the ground, he straightened, settling his gaze on Cindee.

"What part of me being rude to you so you'll go away don't you understand?" asked Remo Williams.

"I just want to ask you a question. Why won't you let me ask you a question? You Americans are so vulgar."

"This one speaks with a wisdom beyond her years," announced the Master of Sinanju, who had been studying the trash in the road alongside his pupil.

Remo shook his head, irritated. "Thanks a heap, Waltzing Matilda," he growled at Cindee. "He wasn't on the rag enough already without a jump start from you. What do you want to ask me? And make it quick."

"Drama," Cindee said. "I want the opinion of the man in the street about what he thinks makes good drama. You couldn't get more in the street than you, since you're actually standing in the street." She frowned. "What are you doing in the street, any-way?"

"Going back to ignoring you," Remo said.

"Wait," Cindee insisted. "Even you must under-stand what makes good drama. The ex-president here, a mob on the street hurling flaming bottles and rocks at the building where he's hiding. That's drama. You'd watch that, wouldn't you?"

"No," said Remo impatiently. "Are we done now?" Not waiting for a reply, he returned to ex-amining the street.

A man with a camera near the battered building caught the eye of Cindee's assistant. The young woman hurried over to him, leaving her boss in the company of Remo and Chiun.

"Of course you would," Cindee persisted. "Don't try to pretend you're not like everybody else in this country. You people love that kind of violent drama. Why do you think you're glued to the set every time some kid opens fire in his high-school cafeteria? You got helicopters overhead, police cordons, kids climb-ing out windows. Drama."

When Remo looked back up, his face was cold. "Don't tell me what I love," he said, voice chilly.

She was momentarily taken aback by the icy men-ace in his tone. It was in that moment of hesitation that the Master of Sinanju inserted himself. The old Korean took Cindee's gloved hands in his frail fin-gers, patting gently. His face was the personification of ancient wisdom.

"Of course you are correct, my dear," Chiun said.

"I have maintained for years that the American culture revels in violence. I hear others out there saying the same thing now, but I was first."

"Good for you," Cindee said. She tried to extricate her hands, but they wouldn't budge. It was as if the old man's hands were fast-drying concrete that had firmed up around her own.

"This is a new kind of violence," Chiun continued. "There are some who might think it began with your foolish Revolution or the things you would call world wars, even though everyone knows the only important part of the world wasn't involved in them. There was violence there, yes, but it was men killing men, which has gone on forever. Do you want to know when your culture truly turned to violence?"

"Technically, I'm Australian, not American," Cindee said. "Not my culture." She tugged at her hands.

"June 11, 1975," Chiun said. "A day that will live in infamy." He hung his head.

Cindee's eyes narrowed. "What happened then?"

"Some dippy soap opera actress hit some dippy soap-opera actor," Remo supplied.

The Master of Sinanju's face tightened. "It was Rad Rex, it was 'As the Planet Revolves' and it was the end of your American culture," he said over his shoulder to Remo. "Since then there has been nothing but car crashes and shooting guns. Poor Mr. Rex, whose autograph remains my most prized possession, had to retire. A gentle soul, he left before his dignity could be sullied by the death of art in this land."

"Yeah, he was really worried about preserving his

dignity that time I saw him hawking some pocket wiener pump on a 1980s infomercial,'' Remo said.

''Pay him no heed,'' Chiun confided. ''He only says such things to appeal to prurient minds. How typical he is of the current state of this nation's culture.''

This time when Cindee yanked her hands, Chiun allowed her to have them. She pulled so hard, she smacked herself in her Australian forehead. She quickly stuffed her hands in her pockets, lest the old geyser with the viselike grip latch on to them again.

''Thanks for the input, Pops,'' Cindee said. ''But you're not my ideal demographic.''

''What does that mean?'' Chiun asked suspiciously.

''It means you're too old for your opinion to matter,'' she explained. ''Advertisers skew younger and—I hate to break it to you—you're way beyond that prized eighteen-to-forty-nine range. Like two hundred years beyond it.''

''I will let that insult pass because you are obviously possessed of a deranged mind,'' Chiun said thinly.

''What she obviously is is some kind of TV exec,'' Remo said. ''They're deranged on a good day. On the rest, they're just stupid as a sack of doorknobs.'' He was annoyed at his teacher for wasting time with the Australian ditz.

''I'm a producer,'' Cindee corrected.

''Same pot, different crack,'' Remo said.

''You do not listen to anyone older than forty-

"What do you mean, footage?" Remo asked.

Cindee huffed impatiently. "For 'Winner,'" she explained. "We're taping in the area."

Remo recognized the name of the program. It had been on the television in the lobby of General Zhii Zaw's hotel in Cancún.

"That stupid TV show?" he asked. "I saw part of it just the other day. It looked like you were filming in Bosnia."

"We're not," she said, sounding almost as if she wished they were. "We're right around the corner from here. And don't remind me that they decided to run more than just the Thursday-night episode this week. The network is going to run us into the ground putting us on two nights a week. They said it's only because of the holiday next week. It better be. We don't want a 'Millionaire' overexposure problem. Of course, it might be okay to double up if we had some action to blast into people's living rooms. That mob would have been great for background—you know, set the stage on the real-life hardships in Harlem. Show how gritty these streets can get. But the three cameramen we had on the scene panicked and ran. They didn't even get the murder on tape."

"What murder?"

Cindee clapped a hand over her mouth. "Forget I said that," she insisted.

"Gladly," said the Master of Sinanju, bored. He was watching the gathering crowd of reporters, which by now filled the sidewalks around the former president's office building in numbers greater than the previous night's mob.

"Was one of the people on the show killed?" Remo asked.

"I'm not confirming or denying," Cindee said quickly. "You'll have to watch and see. We're taping what will be week eight right now, and next week's episode will only be the second week of the season, so you have a while to go."

Remo shook his head. "Not me," he said. "I do reality, not reality shows. Your little friend wants you."

He pointed down the sidewalk. Cindee's assistant was waving for Cindee to join her. She and a *Winner* cameraman had cornered an interview subject on the sidewalk. Cindee hurried over to join them. Remo and Chiun followed.

The two Sinanju Masters were careful to avoid the many cameras. There were local and national reporters on the scene. Some were doing live interviews for the morning network news programs. They weren't lacking for interview subjects. In the wake of the riots, dozens of experts on the black community had swarmed into Harlem. They had done their swarming that morning from white communities. Like most experts on the black community, none of them actually lived in an actual black community.

Remo passed by four very angry women with bulging, lunatic's eyes who were screeching into cameras that the CIA and not poor, maligned Minister Shittman was actually responsible for the previous night's events. Three of the women were tenured professors at prestigious New York universities. One was a bag lady. The only difference Remo could see between the professors and the bag lady was that the professors apparently took off their tinfoil-lined hats while on camera.

The man Cindee's assistant had scraped up was a middle-aged black doctor with a kindly face who actually lived in the community and knew many of the people involved in the riot. He was soft-spoken and unobtrusive and, thus, no one was interested in anything he had to say.

"This could be good for a few seconds' footage," Cindee's assistant promised when Cindee and the two Masters of Sinanju arrived. "Tell her what you were telling me."

"Oh," said the man. "I was trying to tell these people that something is wrong here, but no one will listen."

His wet eyes were pleading with them to understand.

"Of course something's wrong," Cindee said. "A mob tried to kill the president last night and we missed getting so much as an inch of footage." She shot a dirty look at her assistant for wasting all their time.

"No," insisted the doctor. "That's what they wanted it to look like. But it *couldn't* be."

The doctor was on the verge of tears.

Remo would have dismissed him as just another one of the crowd of sidewalk apologists who had crawled out of the woodwork to offer excuses for the mob's actions, but there was something about the man. He seemed so sincere.

"Why isn't this riot like every other one?" Remo asked.

"The *people* involved," the doctor said. "Most of them were patients of mine. They weren't the kind of people to riot. They're just regular folks. There was even an elderly couple who were afraid to leave their apartment. I used to have to make house calls to them. It doesn't make sense that they'd come out in the middle of a mob like that."

"Unless their son who coveted their possessions sent them out in the hope that they would not survive the civil unrest," the Master of Sinanju pointed out.

"Put a sock in it," Remo suggested. To the doctor he said, "So what do you think happened with them?"

"Not just with them," the doctor said. "With the whole mob. It looks like some sort of dissociation to me." He noted all their blank faces. "It's a psychological state," he explained. "Internally, the mind can disconnect certain ideas and behaviors from the main body of a person's belief system. An individual in a dissociated state acts and talks and reacts in ways they never would consciously."

"You're saying this is some sort of sleepwalking," Remo said dubiously.

"In a way. That's what it looks like to me. Normal people don't just run out and join a mob if they're not divorced from their conscious minds."

"Nonsense," Chiun sniffed. "You whites do nothing but play around in mobs. Then the mobs get too big and you have to have a war to make them smaller. That is what what's-his-name did in Europe a few years ago. The one with the funny little mustache. He was white like these people."

The doctor's face grew hard. "Not that it matters, but these people were black."

"Were they Americans?" Chiun asked blandly.

"Of course."

"White as rice," Chiun concluded.

"I don't know," Remo said, steering the doctor away from the Master of Sinanju. "A mob's a mob till someone proves otherwise. I mean, what would cause this dizzy-what's-it?"

"Dissociation," the doctor repeated. "And I don't know. I've never heard of anything like this. To my knowledge, dissociation is always manifested in individuals, not groups. It wouldn't make sense the other way. Sleepwalking, psychotic delusions, certain forms of amnesia, automatic writing are all accepted forms of dissociation. Not this."

"Automatic writing?" Cindee asked.

"Just an aspect of the phenomenon. An individual's hand writes messages without conscious control."

"Pretty much explains every screenplay in Hollywood," Remo commented.

Cindee gave the hairy eyeball to her assistant. The woman shrugged apologetically.

"Okay," Cindee droned to the doctor. "That was

really fascinating stuff. I was—*wow*—just, well, *fascinated*. Bye.'' She turned to go.

''But he didn't even turn his camera on,'' the doctor said, face collapsing in disappointment.

''Outta tape,'' Cindee confided.

''No, I'm not,'' said the cameraman.

Cindee clouted the camera operator in the back of the head before spinning around and marching away.

''Sorry,'' Remo said to the doctor after Cindee Maloo and her *Winner* crew were gone.

As the desperate physician looked for someone else to tell his story to, Remo and the Master of Sinanju headed back down the sidewalk.

In the street beyond the crowd of babbling reporters, two men watched Remo and Chiun go.

The pair of Harlem police officers sat in a cruiser at the edge of the crowd.

An alert had come over the radio two hours ago. All cruisers in the area had been given a description of two men, a young white and an elderly Asian. In Harlem, a pair like that would stick out like sore thumbs.

The men in question were believed to be armed and were without doubt very, very dangerous.

Starting their engine, the police officers drew cautiously away from the curb. Slowly so as not to attract attention, they began trailing the suspects down the litter-strewn street.

8

With the mob dispersed and the former president safe, technically Remo's work was done. He would have been okay to head back to Folcroft. But Folcroft wasn't any fun at the moment, what with all the cops and dead bodies and crazy people. And even if Smith allowed them to stay in residence a few more days, Remo wasn't really in the mood to be cooped up in his quarters surrounded by packing crates and staring at the walls. Not with the Master of Sinanju in his current snotty mood.

The Harlem doctor had sown a tiny seed of doubt in Remo's mind. When he asked a bystander, Remo found out that most of the rioters had been brought to the same nearby police station. He decided to check them out before leaving.

On their way to the station he checked on his car.

Since the most hardened Harlem criminals usually went home come sunup, the hours from dawn to noon were low tide for criminal activity. It was a little after seven in the morning, and all the pros were safely tucked away in bed. Consequently, instead of being completely stripped, Remo's car was only half-dismantled.

"You've got twenty minutes," Remo announced to the gang of eight grammar-school kids who were tearing apart his car like wrench-wielding locusts.

"What you talking 'bout?" one of the kids demanded.

He was thirteen, looked nineteen and had a Glock pistol jutting from the waistband of his exposed underpants.

Remo took the gun, shattered it into three fat pieces and skipped the parts down the street. Eight young jaws dropped.

"Twenty minutes, class," Remo repeated. "I come back and my car's not back together by then, you're all going to be victims of white rage."

Remo grabbed the oldest kid. "You're elected hall monitor." Climbing one-handed, he hauled the youth up a telephone pole. He hung him by his exposed underwear from the shattered overhanging streetlight.

"You can oversee reconstruction," he said. "Anyone leaves, you're telling me names and addresses."

"Yessir!" the terrified kid said.

When Remo slid back to the ground, the others were already frantically trying to reassemble the car.

The Master of Sinanju was supervising their work with a bland eye. As Remo headed off to the police station, the old man padded up beside him.

"What kind of children are you raising in this country?" the old Korean asked.

"No one's raising them," Remo said. "That's the problem. America's inner cities have turned into *Children of the Corn* with crappier production values."

The Master of Sinanju stroked his thread of beard.

"Perhaps it is not so bad that you wish to shoot me like the old horse that pulls the milk wagon, Remo. At the speed with which this nation is falling into ruin, it would only be a matter of time before a building drops on my head anyway."

"Keep picking that scab, and I'll never take over as Reigning Master," Remo warned. "Those lazy slugs back in Sinanju'd have to find real jobs. How would it look to your ancestors if you became the first Master who trained a student who decided to ditch that craphole of a village?"

"You would not be the first," Chiun said coldly.

Remo realized he'd misspoken. He had forgotten about Chiun's nephew, Nuihc, the renegade Master of Sinanju who had trained Jeremiah Purcell in the ancient martial art.

Rather than dig himself in deeper, he clammed up.

As the two walked along, Remo noted that they had drawn attention from the surrounding buildings. About a dozen video cameras were trained on them from the windows.

The riot and the subsequent police and news activity had drawn them out. The locals were hoping to catch an instance of police brutality they could sell to the networks.

Chiun floated away from the cameras, finding blind spots and shadows where no lens could find him.

Remo had his own technique for avoiding identification. Every time he felt the pressure waves of a camera aimed his way, he vibrated his facial muscles.

Later on, when the camera operators tried to view the image on the tape, all they'd see was a blur where a face should have been.

Remo had successfully negotiated his way through the gauntlet of window cameras when he spied yet another lens up ahead. It was nestled in a clump of ugly, snow-draped weeds that huddled at the corner of a squalid tenement. He recognized the face of the cameraman.

Marching over, Remo dragged Cindee Maloo's camera operator from the bushes. The little red light on his camera was lit. It was still aimed at Remo.

"What the hell is this?" Remo demanded.

He addressed not the cameraman, but a broken-down wall that rimmed the adjacent vacant lot. A sheepish Cindee Maloo rose into view from behind the shattered wall. The cameraman turned the lens to the *Winner* producer.

"I didn't get your name," Cindee asked.

Remo's face fouled. "Bunny Wigglesworth," he said, dropping the cameraman to the sidewalk.

"You're not very nice, are you?" Cindee frowned. "That could work. Someone nasty's always fun to toss into the mix. Are you a struggling actor?"

"What is all this?" Remo asked. "Don't you have a game show to go rig?"

Cindee waved a dismissive hand. "The cameras are rolling continuously back there. Whatever happens, we'll get it. Right now I'm thinking ahead. The next season of 'Winner' will have to get started soon.

We've gotta get another cast assembled. You want to test for it?''

"Oh, brother," Remo exhaled.

He started down the sidewalk. Cindee and her cameraman hurried to keep up.

"Seriously," Cindee insisted, dogging him. "You're kind of good-looking, in a mean sort of way."

"Kind of thanks a heap, in an up-yours sort of way," Remo snarled.

"I will do it," Chiun announced.

Cindee screamed, startled by the new voice. She wheeled around, expecting a mugger or worse.

"Oh, it's you," she breathed when she saw the wisp of an Asian trailing behind her. "I didn't see you there." She sniffled relief and rubbed her hands for warmth.

"I will do your program," Chiun repeated.

Remo could see the frozen earnestness in the old man's weathered face. The Master of Sinanju was serious.

"No way," Remo said.

"Still your tongue," Chiun hissed.

"Well, we *have* had old people on before," Cindee said.

"He's not doing it," Remo told her. "Chiun, Smith would have a heart attack if you went on 'Winner.'"

"He has had them before and yet still lingers to vex the living," the Master of Sinanju said. "Worry not about Smith's strong heart, but about my weak one, which you have broken in your mad desire to hasten me out to pasture.''

"You *could* be interesting," Cindee admitted.

"Not could be," Chiun corrected, "am."

Remo shook his head firmly. "He is not interesting and he is not going on some game show where the other contestants vote the rest off the show. And I'll tell you why. He wouldn't hunt, he wouldn't forage, he wouldn't lift a goddamn finger to help anyone else out. He'd be the laziest sack of egomaniacal selfishness you ever had on that show. He would be the first—the very first—they would vote off, and then he'd win the million bucks because the whole rest of the cast along with the production staff would get snuffed out one by one on national TV like tiki torches until someone cut him a check. He is not interested.''

"Silence, O basher of the aged and infirm," Chiun hissed.

"Oh, if you're not in good health, we couldn't use you," Cindee apologized.

"I am healthy as healthy can be," Chiun said rapidly, with a wave of his frail hand. He pitched his voice low. "Do not ruin this for me," he warned Remo.

Remo threw up his hands. "Fine. Kill Smith by going on national TV. Just remember, you've lost your fallback position. The little prince is on his way out the door.''

Cindee was pulling some business cards from her pocket. She passed one to the Master of Sinanju.

"Here's the address to send your demo tape to."

Chiun happily accepted the card. It disappeared inside the voluminous folds of his kimono.

Cindee tried to give Remo one of the cards. As he walked along, he tore the card to confetti with blurry hands and let the hundred fragments flutter to the cold street.

"Don't you want to be famous?" Cindee asked.

"Fame ain't all it's cracked up to be," Remo said. "For what I do, reputation is better. The parts of the world where they need to know me? Believe me, they know me."

"That doesn't make sense," Cindee said. "Reputation is fame. If someone knows you, they know you."

Remo shook his head. "They only need to know what I am, which they do. The 'who' changes. That little glory hound back there—" he nodded over his shoulder to where the Master of Sinanju padded along behind them "—he's the current who. I'm the next who. There have been five thousand years' worth of us. The faces have changed, the reputation remains the same. And we got all that without sucking up to key demos or studying overnight ratings in Pittsburgh."

She saw that he spoke without boasting. As if he knew what he was saying to be true. And the way he walked. More a glide than a normal man's stride. He had a confidence and inner grace that she found at once mysterious and sexy. He seemed to just *know* what and who he was.

Cindee was a twenty-eight-year-old Australian woman who had risen in the American TV ranks to be producer of one of the biggest cultural phenomenons to hit the small screen since Uncle Miltie donned his first dress back in television's golden age. She was well on her way up the professional ladder. Cindee Maloo had arrived. Yet for some reason he made her feel as if she'd done nothing with her life. She suddenly felt the need to justify herself to this stranger.

"I didn't start out doing 'Winner,'" Cindee confided all at once.

"Are you still here?" Remo asked, irritated.

"'The Box,'" she said. "That was something I produced all by myself for one of the nets last year. We took fourteen real people and put them in a big steel box and buried it under a pile of sand. Every day for two weeks the people in the box would vote one person out of the box."

"I never heard of it," Remo said.

Cindee's face grew glum.

"Well, that's because things didn't go too well with the pilot." She raised a gloved finger. "Technically, it wasn't my fault. I assumed someone else would figure out all that stuff about air holes and oxygen. Fortunately, all our contestants had signed releases, so their heirs didn't have much of a leg to stand on legally."

"As reality shows go, I guess 'This Old House' doesn't cut it anymore," Remo said dryly.

"I don't do boring," Cindee said. "The public likes their stuff to be edgy. I did another pilot, this one for syndication. It was called 'Sea of Love.' In that one we took seven men and one woman and put them on a yacht out in the middle of San Francisco harbor. Every day for a week the woman voted one man off the boat till only one was left.''

"I sense a common thread here," Remo said.

Cindee bristled. "There isn't one," she insisted. "If you're saying that they're just like 'Winner' and all I was doing was copying that show, you're wrong. They were both very different. One was underground and one was on a boat in the water. Are you stupid or something?"

"Yes, he is," Chiun replied.

"So what happened to the boat one?" Remo asked.

Cindee flushed. "It wasn't my fault," she said. "Someone else suggested that it'd be sexy to make them go skinny-dipping by moonlight. Who knew there were sharks swimming around in San Francisco harbor?"

"I did," said both Remo and Chiun.

"Well, I should have hired you both as consultants, shouldn't I?" Cindee said sarcastically. "Anyway, my shows didn't get picked up, but they got noticed. That's how I got the job with 'Winner.'''

They had arrived at the steps of the police station. Remo turned to Cindee Maloo.

"Are you through following me?" he asked.

Cindee gave a reluctant frown. "I still think you'd be great on the show. You've got something. I think people would find you appealing. Anyway, your friend's got my card if you change your mind.''

Remo was grateful when Cindee and her cameraman turned to go. As the *Winner* crew went back down the street, Remo and Chiun mounted the station house steps.

"You know we're being watched," Remo said to the Master of Sinanju once they were alone.

"Of course," Chiun sniffed, insulted. "I am not an invalid. They have been following us for ten minutes."

At the top of the stairs Remo shot a glance back at the street. The police car that had been tailing them ever since they'd left the front of the ex-president's building was slowing to a stop in front of the precinct house.

"We don't exactly look like we live around here," Remo said. "Probably just making sure we're okay."

As a former beat cop, Remo was heartened to see there were still dedicated officers who took seriously their duty to protect the public. Leaving the pair of uniformed patrolman out in the street, he ushered the Master of Sinanju inside the station.

Remo felt the vibrations of a pair of video cameras as soon as he stepped inside. One was directed at the door; the other swung his way as he walked up to the desk.

Chiun was playing coy with the cameras again. He found a blind spot where neither lens could track him, settling on a bench where several handcuffed men awaited processing.

When Remo presented his phony FBI identification at the desk, the sergeant on duty seemed a little more interested than he should. He studied Remo's picture ID and his face several times before allowing him inside.

"You coming with, Little Father?"

The old Korean shook his head. "This seems like as good a place as any to observe the collapse of Western civilization," he replied.

Leaving the Master of Sinanju in the lobby, Remo followed a uniformed officer into the bowels of the station.

The cells in the back of the station were full. Remo found that the Harlem doctor had been right about the rioters. Many of the people in the cells he passed seemed lost and frightened, completely out of place in a jail environment. The people were mostly middle-aged or older. Women outnumbered men.

The officer led him to a rear cell where one prisoner had been isolated from the rest.

When Remo entered the cell, he found Minister Hal Shittman sprawled on a soiled bunk like a velour-wrapped whale. With every snoring exhale, the famous minister's giant belly deflated only to strain velour once more on the inhale. The rancid wind that passed his lips reeked of the two dozen stale Twinkies and gallon of grape Kool-Aid that had been his previous night's supper.

Only at the clank of the closing cell door did the minister awaken. As sleep fled, bleary red eyes looked up unhappily at the white man standing in his cell.

"Who are you?" Shittman demanded.

"Adidas corporate lawyer," Remo said. "Since

you insist on dressing in our clothes, we'd like you to either lose nine hundred pounds or stick masking tape over our logo. It's bad for business having a guy with breasts bigger than Pamela Anderson's waddling around in our sports gear."

"You ain't my lawyer," Shittman declared. "I put in a call to Mr. Johnnie. Get lost, skinny."

He flopped back on his bunk.

Remo didn't feel like wasting more time than he had to in that cell. Shittman's cologne was vying with his breath for the title of worst stink in the tristate area.

Remo drove two hard fingers into a neck that felt like sweaty pudding. He only knew he'd somehow found the proper pain receptors when Shittman's eyes sprang open wide.

"Youch!" Shittman yelped. Fat arms flailing, the minister rolled to a sitting position.

"Now that I've got your attention," Remo said, "tell me what happened last night. And make it fast, 'cause that aftershave of yours smells worse than a lying, shit-smeared teenaged girl."

The shock of pain that had shot through his body was still reverberating through his most distant extremities. The minister's great blubbery jowls jiggled in fear.

"I keep telling everybody I don't remember last night," Shittman said. "Last thing I remember I was mindin' my own business, as the black man always is. Next thing I knows, I wake up here. Racist whites made it a crime to drive while black. Now it be a crime to sit at home while black."

"You don't remember leading last night's riot?"

"I don't riot, I protest," Shittman replied. "And I sure wasn't protestin' last night. They trying to tell me I was there—they even try to shove their white programming in my head so I'll crack up and confess, but I was home. No doubt about it."

"People saw you there," Remo said.

"Liars."

"They've got you on tape."

"Computer-generated forgeries," Shittman insisted. "Phonied up by the CIA to discredit me. The government been pulling that kind of shit on me my whole life."

Remo didn't like the minister. Shittman was one of those community leaders whose job it was to jab a stick in the humming beehive of racial tensions every few months and give a good vigorous stir. Yet despite his personal distaste for the man, Remo could clearly see that the minister—at least in his own mind—was telling the truth.

"What do you mean shoving programming in your head?" Remo asked.

"That's the worst thing," Shittman moaned. "I don't know how they done it, but I can *see* the words. I see them right now." Bleary eyes stared at the cell wall.

"Where?" Remo asked.

"There," Shittman said, his fat face worried. He pointed at the air before him. "They there. Even though I know they not, they there. All kind of just floating there. Like when you look at something for a long time and then look away. How you still can see it? That's what I see.''

Remo saw the troubled urgency on the minister's face.

''What do these words say?'' he asked.

''Well, there be some stuff about the old president,'' Shittman said. ''The words are telling me to surround his building and not let him out till morning. They look like they fading. But the ones I see strongest are just two words. They just kind of hang there, even when I been sleeping. They telling me to kill that guy with the funny name from that 'Winner' show. I can even see him dead on the ground. It strange, 'cause that was the show I was watching when I blacked out an' I don't remember him dying on the TV.''

This jibed with what Remo had heard already. Cindee Maloo had let it slip that one of the *Winner* contestants had been killed during the mob action the previous night. Apparently, Shittman had been involved in the murder but had no real recollection of participating in the events.

''I hate to admit it,'' Remo said, ''but I believe you.''

'''Course you do,'' Shittman sniffed.

''No,'' Remo explained. ''I really, *really* hate to admit it. You have no idea how much I don't want to believe you.''

He suddenly felt as if he needed a shower. He turned to go.

"You think all this might have somethin' to do with them teeny TVs they give us?" the minister called after him.

Remo suddenly remembered all the little broken handheld television sets he and Chiun had found around the former president's office building.

"Who's passing out free TVs?" Remo asked.

"Fellow from BCN, the big TV network. He bring some cases of them around to my church. Say he's doing a study of viewing habits among African-Americans for his homogenized, white-bread, no-coloreds-allowed network. He pass out the TVs to my flock." Shittman waved a hand to the other cells. "Most of the folks he give them to are right here."

"You know where I can find this guy?"

"Sure," Shittman said. "I let him set up shop in the basement of my church. He gots all kinds of broadcast and computer stuff there. Fella passes out free TVs in Harlem's a fella you don't mind giving a little office space to."

"Thanks," Remo said. He headed for the door.

"And try to get some rest. Sleep burns calories. A slimmer you is just eight million years away."

He called the guard to let him out.

Remo sensed something was amiss when the cop who had escorted him to the cell tried to shoot him through the bars.

Remo danced around the hail of lead.

"What the bliz-blaz?" he demanded as the young officer unloaded his revolver into the tiny room.

Bullets screamed into the cell, ricocheting sparks off the brick walls. In a panic, Hal Shittman screamed and rolled onto the floor. The minister tried to stuff his massive bulk underneath his bunk.

"Brutality! Brutality!" Shittman screeched, in the first understatement of his public life.

Remo didn't know what was going on. When the policeman ran out of bullets, he continued to click the trigger, barrel aimed square at Remo's chest. His eyes were glazed.

Remo reluctantly surmised that—what with all the shooting and trying to kill him and all—the cop wasn't going to be nice and let him out of Shittman's cell.

"Why isn't my life ever easy?" Remo groused. Muttering to himself, he broke the lock on the cell and banged the bars into the forehead of the vacant-eyed cop.

The police officer sprawled backward onto the cell-block floor. His gun clattered away. As Remo exited the cell, he saw something pressed in the cop's other hand.

He was surprised enough when he realized it was another palm-size television. But he soon received a fresh shock.

"What the hell?"

There was a regular television broadcast in progress. On one of the morning network talk shows, the hosts were discussing the violence in Harlem. But there was something else on the screen. Two words flashed intermittently beneath the talking heads. It was like the command to watch *Winner* that he'd seen in the hotel lobby down in Mexico.

He realized now that he should have looked more closely in Cancún. It was clear his Sinanju training alone allowed him to see what was there. The words were being flashed at intervals too great for the normal human eye to perceive.

The words read "Kill him." And, accompanying that phrase, pulsed too fast to be seen on anything other than a subconscious level, was a flashing image of Remo Williams.

Remo blinked, stunned.

The picture was a little off. Like a composite sketch run through a computer to clean up the rough lines. But there was no mistaking who it was supposed to be.

So shocked was Remo as he watched his own image being broadcast on a national network news program, he didn't even take note of the sounds of scuffing feet at the far end of the cell block. He only knew that he had drawn more unwelcome attention when fresh gunfire erupted in the Harlem station house.

His body tripped to automatic, flipping out around the first volley of gunfire. Twisting, Remo saw a line of uniform and plainclothes officers framed by the open steel door of the dingy cell block. The cops were firing like madmen, eyes devoid of rage or even conscious thought.

With a sinking stomach Remo saw that many of

the cops clutched miniature televisions in their free hands.

This was too much to sort out. He had to get out of there. Had to contact Smith.

Skittering through the gunfire, Remo raced down the dank corridor between the cells. Through the barred doors came the frightened screams of men and women Remo now knew to be innocent.

Running full out, Remo flew into the midst of the cops.

Dancing down the line, he sent the flat side of his palm into forehead after forehead. Men collapsed like wilting daisies. As they fell, more flooded in from the adjacent hallway to take their place.

Remo fought them back to a blind corner where an iron door was bolted shut on an alley that ran beside the station. He kicked open the door, at the same time snatching a radio from one of the unconscious police officers.

Remo tossed a couple of cops into the alley, ducked into an empty office and hollered over the radio that the subject had escaped out the back door.

He got a clearer image of just how many men were under the thrall of the television signals when the whole building began to rumble. Stampeding cops flooded out exits. Car engines started outside. Sirens blared and tires squealed.

When Remo made it back out to the squad room, he found the place cleared out. The Master of Sinanju was still sitting on the lobby bench where Remo had left him.

In their haste to leave, someone had dropped one

of their TV sets at the old man's sandaled feet. When Remo spied him, the Master of Sinanju was just scooping it up.

Remo's heart froze.

"Don't look at it, Chiun!" he yelled.

He didn't bother with the door. He was across the sergeant's desk in a fraction of slivered time. A hand too fast for even the Master of Sinanju's eyes to perceive flashed out and the palm TV skipped out of the old man's hand, smashing into a hundred pieces against the wall.

Chiun's hooded eyes saucered in outrage. "What is the meaning of this?" he demanded.

Remo quickly told him about the subliminal signals.

"You couldn't see them, Little Father. If you did, you'd have gone nuts like all the cops here."

"You looked on them with no difficulty," Chiun pointed out. "If these commands are so great as to subvert a mind trained in Sinanju, why did you not kill yourself?"

Remo hesitated. "Well, I...um..."

Chiun's expression grew flat. "I see," he said coldly. "Only the pupil's enfeebled Master is at risk. How lucky I am, Remo, to have you to keep weak-minded me from embarrassing myself."

Without another word, he turned on his heel. Kimono hems whirled angrily as the old man stormed from the police station.

Alone, Remo let the air slip slowly from his lungs.

"It sounded less insulting in my head," he said to the empty station house.

9

With eyes red from lack of sleep, Harold Smith watched the rhythmic breathing of the figure in bed.

Mark Howard's broad face looked peaceful in slumber. Sedatives and sleep had erased the care lines that had lately formed around the younger man's eyes. Even the dark bags beneath them had begun to fade. All the tension that had been building up was slowly dissolving.

Smith hadn't realized how haggard the young man had become in the past few months. As usual, Smith had been too busy with his own work to notice the changes taking place right below his own nose. The story of Harold Smith's life.

The chair he had pulled to Howard's bedside seemed designed to be uncomfortable. Smith shifted his weight.

He remembered sitting in another Folcroft chair, another night thirty years before.

Conrad MacCleary. Smith wasn't surprised that Remo had brought up their old associate.

On the night he had learned of MacCleary's near fatal accident, Smith had retreated from the world. Hidden himself away in a darkened corner of Folcroft like this. Back then he had known what he had to do. MacCleary—his friend—would have to die, and Smith would have to give the order.

It all seemed so logical, so necessary back then. MacCleary would have been the first to agree with Smith. But the years had melted away some of that hard certainty.

Time gave one a new perspective on all things.

In the old days, Smith had ordered the deaths of many who posed only a marginal risk to CURE. Never casually, for Harold Smith had never lost his distaste for the necessary extinguishing of life that was part of his job. But he had done so unflinchingly. In Mark Howard's case, however, his certainty didn't seem as firm as it should.

Unlike MacCleary, at least it wouldn't be necessary to eliminate Howard purely for the sake of security.

It seemed as if the turmoil of the past few days was finally subsiding. The police still wanted to question Mark, but they had come to accept Smith's story. As far as they were concerned, the dead Folcroft doctor had altered Jeremiah Purcell's medication on his own. Unbeknownst to the Rye police, Smith had used CURE's facilities to check the report in their own database.

The only real problem now was Mark's motivation. Why had he cut Purcell's sedatives?

Smith would find out the answer soon enough. Right now Mark needed rest. His mental state when they'd found him had not been conducive to questioning. A few days to recuperate and Mark would be in far better shape to talk.

Looking down on his slumbering assistant, Smith felt an odd sense of obligation. A need to protect this young man who had come to CURE barely prepared for what he was getting himself into.

He couldn't deny it. Somewhere in the depths of his stone heart, Harold W. Smith had developed a fondness for his assistant. It was not the same as it was with Remo or Chiun, although as he grew older he had come to realize that there was more than just the bonds of shared hardship for the three of them. No, Remo and Chiun didn't need Smith. They would do just as well with him or without him. Mark Howard was another story.

There was the potential for greatness in the young man. Smith had seen it early on. But he needed guidance.

As he got to his feet, Smith wondered if he might not be softening in his old age.

MacCleary and Smith had worked together for a long time. Still, Smith had been the authority figure while MacCleary had been more comfortable in the trenches. Here it was almost as if the circumstances were reversed. Here, Smith was the old hand. He had a lifetime's worth of experience to impart to his desk-bound young protégé.

Assuming, that was, he didn't have to order Mark Howard's death.

Turning from the bed, Smith left the room.

Order had begun to return to the security corridor. The room where Jeremiah Purcell had been imprisoned for the past ten years had been sealed off by police. The door was closed tightly as Smith passed. He didn't look in.

Of the ten rooms in the hall, only three had been regularly occupied in recent years. Purcell's was now empty. Beyond it were the other two.

Smith glanced in the second-to-last room.

A young woman lay in bed, her body covered by a crisp white sheet. Vacant eyes stared up at the ceiling tiles.

A faint smell of sulfur emanated from the room. The staff had tried all manner of soaps and air fresheners, but they could not eliminate the unpleasant odor.

The girl had come to Folcroft as part of the fallout from a CURE assignment nearly four years before. Since that time she had remained in a vegetative state.

Smith continued on. He lingered at the last door.

There was another patient in that room, this one male. The patient in the bed looked far older than his years.

He had been in a coma when he was first brought to Folcroft. He had remained a permanent resident of the main hospital wing until just a few years ago, when he had been moved to the security wing at Smith's order.

Looking in on that patient, in that particular room, Smith felt a twinge of unaccustomed melancholia.

In the early days of CURE, a secure corridor like this one had been unnecessary. It had never occurred to Smith back then that there would be patients related to his secret work who would need to be housed somewhere.

Prior to its current use, this hallway had been too far off the beaten path to be convenient for Folcroft staff or patients. It had been closed off for years. Back in those days, when Conrad MacCleary didn't feel like going home to his apartment he stayed here. For several years this room had been MacCleary's home away from home.

The room next to this, where the girl lay, was the one where Remo had been taken after the staged electrocution that had brought him aboard CURE. Later, he had recovered from plastic surgery in the same room.

This was a hallway filled with memories. And for Smith, in spite of the worries caused by current circumstances, not all of the memories were unpleasant.

As he tore his eyes away from the comatose patient, there was something approaching a sad smile on the CURE director's lemony face. It remained with him on his trip back upstairs to his office.

"Mark is doing well," Smith announced to his secretary as he entered the outer room.

She had asked him so frequently over the past two days that he now found himself answering preemptively.

Mrs. Mikulka offered a relieved smile. "That policeman called while you were downstairs," she said. "They haven't found the missing patient yet. He wants to come by to talk to you tomorrow afternoon.

I made him an appointment for one o'clock. If you'd like, I can change it."

"That will be fine, Mrs. Mikulka," Smith said.

Thinking nostalgic thoughts, the CURE director stepped through to his office. He was crossing the room when the blue contact phone jangled to life. He hurried to answer it.

"Report," Smith said, sinking into his chair.

"Something big's going on in Harlem, Smitty," Remo's troubled voice announced.

"The former president got out safely," Smith said, the last remnants of a smile evaporating from his bloodless lips. "As I understand it, the police have rounded up the rioters. I was going to have you return here so that we could discuss your future living arrangements."

"You're gonna have to reschedule our eviction," Remo said. "The president's fine. It's us who might be in the doghouse on this one."

He went on to give Smith a rapid rundown of all that had happened that morning, ending with the attack at the police station and his own image being broadcast subliminally on the handheld televisions.

"My God," Smith croaked when he was through.

"Mine, too," Remo said. "I just about plotzed when I saw my face on TV."

Smith's fingers were like claws, biting into the phone's plastic casing. With his other hand he clutched the edge of his desk. His heart was a molten lump in his palpitating chest. Blood sang a panicked chorus in his ears.

"My God," he repeated. He didn't know what else to say.

"Reel it back in a little, Smitty," Remo suggested. "It might not be all that bad."

At this Smith finally found his voice. "Not that bad?" he said, aghast. "It's the end, Remo. All of it. We have to disband. You and Chiun need to leave the country right away. I will take care of the loose ends here."

He thought of the first loose end. Mark Howard, asleep downstairs. An air-filled syringe would end the young man's life. Smith's assistant would die in his sleep, never knowing what had happened. Smith's own end would come minutes later in a cold steel box that had been gathering dust in the corner of Folcroft's basement for thirty years.

"Take a breath, Smitty," Remo warned. "No one else really saw what I saw. I'm sure of it. I don't even think it'd be visible if you taped it and freeze-framed it. It's like light between the video images. It's hard to explain, but I'm sure no one but me could see it."

"But someone is broadcasting it, Remo," Smith said. "Someone has your image to broadcast. Who could have it? I have been so careful. Who could know about us?"

"I don't know," Remo admitted. "I'd say Purcell, but he hasn't been out long enough to cook up something like this. Plus it's not really his psycho style. It's gotta be someone else. But the good news is these images fade for people who see them. Shittman said the words he saw were already disappearing. If I can track the source and stop them, their heads will be clear of me in a couple days."

"No, Remo," Smith said firmly. "A couple of days is unacceptable. If what you've said is true, then we have to disband now, before we become known publicly."

"Smitty, something is known to somebody," Remo argued. "But whatever they know, they're not running to the *New York Times* with it. They obviously have a way to broadcast it, but they haven't held a press conference. They didn't go on the evening news or break into the middle of prime time with a news flash. All they did was put my picture up in a way that even the people who've seen it don't know they've seen it."

This was nearly too much for the CURE director to digest. He tried to swallow, but his throat had dried to dust. His tongue felt too large for his mouth.

"No," Smith said weakly. "We cannot go on after this."

There was the briefest of pauses on the other end of the line before Remo sighed.

"This might not even be a CURE thing," Remo admitted reluctantly. "It could be a me thing."

Smith couldn't miss the guilty concern in the younger man's voice.

"Why?" the CURE director asked. Some of his fear was instantly replaced by suspicion. "What have you done?"

"Not me," Remo said. "Chiun. Something strange happened when we were in Europe a couple days back. I didn't tell you because I figured it was gonna cause me enough grief in the future without getting an earful from you right now. Remember that fat Swiss assassin we went after?''

Smith remembered all too well. The killer in question had dogged Remo and Chiun from Europe to South America, setting several elaborate booby traps in the path of the two men. They had traced him back to his hideaway in the Alps.

''Olivier Hahn,'' Smith said. ''What of him?''

''It's not him, exactly,'' Remo said. ''See, Chiun's been mailing out some kind of top-secret letters for the past few months. He's been real mysterious about them. Every time I ask, he tells me to take a flying leap. When we went to punch that Swiss guy's ticket, the guy had one of those letters in his house. I recognized the envelope. Chiun grabbed it up before I could take a look at it. I think it has something to do with me becoming Reigning Master of Sinanju. So maybe this picture of me on TV is connected to the same thing.''

Smith was trying to digest Remo's words.

''Could Chiun be so careless?'' the older man breathed. He knew the truth even as he posed the question. If history was an indication, the answer was a resounding, unequivocal yes.

''Not Chiun exactly,'' Remo replied. ''But I don't know what those letters said or who got them. This stuff in Harlem could be connected to Sinanju and not CURE at all.''

''Ask Chiun,'' Smith demanded tartly.

"I could, but I doubt he'd give me a straight answer. He wouldn't before and he's kind of ticked at me right now."

"Put him on the phone."

"I can't," Remo said. "He stormed out of here. I'm standing in an empty Harlem police station. Which, by the way, I should get out of before the cops come home."

Smith sat behind his big desk, quietly fuming. The Master of Sinanju had been unconcerned about security in the past. It was entirely possible that they had been brought to the brink of ruin because of the old Korean's carelessness.

Smith allowed his grip on the phone to loosen.

"Those weren't typical rioters," he mused. "They had the opportunity to attack the former president at any time in the hours they had his building surrounded but they did not. It's possible that whoever gave them their orders was merely trying to draw you in."

"Shittman said he was watching 'Winner' when he zonked out," Remo explained. "You know, that show where they strand a bunch of people I wouldn't trust to lick the sticky side of a stamp out in the middle of nowhere."

Smith frowned. The name triggered something in his recent memory. He couldn't place it.

"I am not familiar with the program," he said.

"No surprise there," Remo said. "Do you even own a TV?" He forged ahead. "It's on BCN. Shittman said the BCN guy who's been passing out free palm TVs has set up shop in the cellar of his church. I'll go check him out.''

''Please do,'' Smith said. ''And find out if Master Chiun is involved in this. If his irresponsible behavior is to blame, at least he can tell us exactly what we're dealing with. In the meantime I will check into the BCN angle. Call back as soon as you know anything more.''

Smith hung up the phone. His hand pained him from gripping the receiver too tightly.

This was a catastrophe in the making. Events in Harlem might have been engineered to draw Remo out, but it was just as likely it had been done to draw CURE into the light. There was no way of knowing right now, no way to stop an unknown foe with unknowable intentions.

One thing was certain. Whoever it was, CURE's faceless enemy was possessed with incredibly dangerous technology. What Remo had described was clearly dissociative behavior. The separation of an idea of activity from mainstream conscious thought. They had discovered a way to make people do things divorced from the societal or personal boundaries of morals and ethics.

The name of the program that had triggered the dissociative response in Minister Shittman and the others still seemed familiar to Smith. He assumed he had come across it as part of his daily work as CURE director.

Right now that didn't matter. He had more pressing things to deal with.

He turned his attention to his computer.

As the clock ticked down to zero on what might very well be the last minutes of both his life and the life of the agency he led, Dr. Harold W. Smith began to steer a steady course through the troubled rapids of cyberspace.

10

Remo swiped an abandoned cop car from the street in front of the station house. There was a hat on the front seat. He put it on and pulled it low over his eyes.

The hat fit. For an instant it gave him an odd, old feeling. In the rearview mirror he saw that the face looking back at him could have been that of the same Remo Williams who had been a Newark beat patrolman a million years before.

But he wasn't the same. The world was different and they were all going to have to come to grips with it.

He started the engine.

Remo found the Master of Sinanju marching down the sidewalk halfway back to their car.

"Want a lift?" he called, slowing next to the elderly Korean.

Chiun gave him the briefest of hateful looks before sliding in the passenger seat beside his pupil.

"I suppose you are worried now to let me walk the streets for fear I might be mugged," the Master of Sinanju sniffed.

"Little Father, I'd be worried for Harlem if it tried

to mug you," Remo replied honestly. "And I didn't mean to insult you back there. The place was going nuts, and I did have a reason to be concerned about you. It happened to you once before. Remember that head case Abraxas who wanted to take over the world years ago? You didn't realize back then you were seeing his subliminal signals."

"How fortunate for me that in my dotage I have you to remember the most embarrassing moments of my life," Chiun said, his tone enough to chill the already cold winter air.

"I'm not trying to embarrass. I'm just saying you—we—need to watch out. This stuff they're using is sophisticated as all hell. It's not just a name flashing on a screen like it was back then. Whoever's doing this is using the signals to make people do things that go against their nature."

"Perhaps I have already fallen victim to these signals, Remo," the Master of Sinanju said. "For it is against my nature to train an ingrate fat white with oatmeal for brains in the art of Sinanju. Yet there sits bloated, oatmeal-brained you. Yes, Remo, you are right. Clearly, I am old and senile and in need of special attention."

"Sue me for being concerned," Remo grumbled. "And as long as I already pulled the pin out of the grenade, Smitty wanted me to ask you if this was connected to those letters you've been mailing out."

So slowly did the old Korean's head turn, not a single hair stirred around his parchment face. His hazel eyes burned laser holes in Remo's skull.

"You told Smith?" he asked, voice low with accusation.

"Not really," Remo said. "I can't very well give him specifics about something I don't know about. I told him there were envelopes and how one already showed up out of the blue in the house of someone who was trying to kill us. I thought maybe my picture on TV was connected somehow."

"It is not," Chiun said firmly.

"It'd help Smitty to make sure about that if you told me just what the hell they were for," Remo said.

But the Master of Sinanju became uncommunicative. Turning from his pupil, he stared out at the pot-holed street.

"Why me, Lord?" Remo muttered.

He found his leased car where he'd left it.

The kids who had been stripping it had made a valiant effort to put it back together. It seemed, however, that they were more adept at destruction than construction.

The car looked as if it was falling apart at the seams. Lined up on the sidewalk beside it was a row of anxious black faces. Hanging high above them was the kid Remo had suspended from the light pole.

"Didn't any of you take shop class between arrests?" Remo growled at the kids as he got out of the cop car.

Remo kicked the light pole. The vibrations knocked the hanging kid loose. He screamed all the way to the ground. Remo snagged him from the air just before he went splat.

"Go scare your teachers."

The kids didn't need to be told a second time. In a pack, they hightailed it down the street.

Remo's car rattled along the streets of Harlem. With every turn, something new seemed to drop off in his wake.

On Malcolm X Boulevard they passed a familiar building.

Remo had first been to the seventeen-story skyscraper on an assignment years before. Back then the XL SysCorp building was a gleaming tower of polarized glass. In the intervening years it had fallen into such disrepair that even the homeless were afraid to find shelter inside.

Thinking dark thoughts of the events of that time, Remo drove silently past the ruins.

Hal Shittman's Greater Congregation of the Lord Church was located just off George Washington Carver Boulevard.

Remo knew he'd have trouble questioning the BCN representative who had set up shop in the minister's basement as soon as he drove up the street.

Reporters crammed the road and sidewalk. It looked as if they had come over directly from covering the unrest outside the former president's offices.

Remo left the Master of Sinanju in the car. Avoiding police, he fell in with a crowd of people who were watching the activity around the Harlem church.

"What happened?" Remo asked.

"White dude shot hisself," one man replied. "He call all the press here and when they all gots they cameras going, dude shoots himself right there. Whole world watching. It just terrible.'' He shook his head, dark face miserable.

Although it meant the loss of his only lead, Remo was at least a little heartened to find someone who actually cared about the loss of fellow human life.

''Dude was givin' away free pocket TVs and I missed out,'' the man continued morosely.

''What a white man doing in Minister Shittman's church anyway?'' asked a hugely overweight woman. Her fingernails were very long and extremely purple and couldn't help but make one wonder why a person so obsessed with one part of her physical appearance wouldn't spend less time at the nail salon and more time at the gym.

''Spying for the CIA,'' replied the man.

''CIA,'' echoed a chorus of voices with utter certainty.

Remo frowned at the crowd. ''Paranoia is a lot more fun than taking responsibility for our own actions, isn't it?'' he announced to those gathered.

He left the scene.

For a time the crowd discussed the rude white man. They did this while the sheet-draped body of the BCN network executive who had apparently been doing secret studies on the television viewing habits of the black man was being brought up from the basement of Minister Shittman's church.

Eventually they all agreed he had to be yet another CIA agent sent into the black community to promote unrest.

''Won't be the last time,'' they said knowingly.

THREE BLOCKS OVER, on the vacant lots that were home to the current season of *Winner*, Cindee Maloo sat alone in a gloomy production trailer. On the monitor before her played the images collected by her cameraman that morning.

She couldn't be certain. But then, her instructions had been clouded in mystery. Besides, she was pretty sure.

An old Korean and a young white.

The Korean wasn't on the tape. Even though her cameraman had tried to get him, he had failed. It was as if the wisp of a man could make himself invisible.

The other one had worked out a little better. He was at least on the tape. But at the same time he wasn't there.

She had carefully viewed the scant footage. On all of it, Remo's face seemed out of focus even though the rest of his body was crystal clear. He somehow had managed to shake his head in such a way to make his features unrecognizable.

It made Cindee dizzy just watching him.

When she could take it no more, she finally spit the tape out of the machine and plugged it into the special unit she'd been sent the previous day.

She pressed Send. With a whir, the image went out at high speed over the satellite feed.

The process was over in less than ten seconds. Once it was done she popped the tape, tugged it in black spools from the casing and dropped it in the trash.

As she was leaving the small Harlem trailer, the images Cindee Maloo had beamed into the heavens were already being scrutinized on the other side of the world.

11

Ominous black clouds rolled in from the east across the Great Dividing Range, casting an otherworldly pall over the Great Artesian Basin in Queensland, Australia. Beneath the scudding clouds, Kenneth Robert MacGulry's Land Rover bounced along a long flat road that sliced through the broad desert.

MacGulry—who the world knew as "Robbie"— had taken one of his personal helicopters across New South Wales to the spot where the Darling River split into the jagged threads of the Warrego and Culgoa. The Land Rover and its driver met him at Wyandra.

A long haul out into the middle of nowhere. A colossal effort for mere sport. But Robbie MacGulry managed to carve out so little time for recreation these days. To his intense displeasure, he found that his trip into the outback was being ruined by his incompetent driver.

"Faster, you idiot!" MacGulry roared. So thick was his native Australian accent, the word came out "fastah."

The driver understood only too well, dutifully pressing harder on the gas. Speeding up, the Land

Rover tore at the ground, throwing clouds of choking dust in its wake.

Riding shotgun, Robbie MacGulry fumed.

Oh, it wasn't all the driver's fault—although the worthless wanker would be out of a job once they got back to Wyandra. It was living that boiled his blood. Life itself bothered Robbie MacGulry. Bile was the force that drove him.

MacGulry was in his late sixties. His pugnacious, suntanned face was drawn into a perpetual scowl. Flinty eyes glowered from behind thick, black-framed glasses. A flattened nose was testament to the great many fists Robbie MacGulry had encountered in his youth. He liked to be called a fighter. So much so, he made sure his many newspapers around the world worked it into any articles about him.

And why not? It was the truth.

Robbie MacGulry had never been one to shy away from a fight. This was one thing friend and enemy alike could agree on—although MacGulry was first to admit that there were very few friends and a great many enemies. One did not become the most powerful media figure on the face of the planet without racking up an extensive list of foes. At the moment, however, his greatest enemy was the nong ocker who was steering his Land Rover like a frightened Sheila.

"Pull up beside them, you bloody bludger!" MacGulry bellowed.

The Land Rover had nearly pulled alongside the mob of hopping kangaroos. Running full-out, the animals were clearly terrified. Huge feet stomped in furious rhythm against the hard-packed earth.

Although fast over short distances, the animals were no match for the Land Rover. MacGulry's driver drew beside the stragglers at the rear of the stampeding kangaroos.

Musky rat kangaroos were more common in the northeastern part of Australia, but their small size made them less fun to hunt. MacGulry always liked to keep a healthy stock of the much larger gray kangaroos on all his ranches.

Standing on his seat, the world-famous media mogul reached in back. A moment later, the barrel of an elephant gun stuck out the open window. Bracing it on the door, MacGulry took careful aim.

A wicked smile carved his chapped lips the instant before he pulled the trigger.

The explosion was deafening. The driver jerked the wheel in time with the recoil and the Land Rover skidded sideways. A simultaneous eruption of red burst beside the speeding vehicle. Thick bright blood splattered the dusty hood and windshield. Chunks of warm kangaroo bits splashed the young driver's bare arms and knees.

Robbie MacGulry grinned delightedly.

"Woo-hoo!" he screamed. "Bagged the bugger!" His rugged face was flecked with blood. His shoulder ached where the gun's padded stock had hammered the joint.

As the billionaire media mogul wiped blood on the sleeve of his bush jacket, his driver struggled to keep from vomiting up the poached eggs and Foster's beer he'd had for breakfast.

MacGulry whooped a wicked, snorting laugh as the driver regained control of the Land Rover. They raced back up alongside the thundering mob.

The kangaroos had shifted direction. The panicked animals were tiring. Mouths foamed, noses twitched as the Land Rover pulled abreast.

One doomed animal was so close MacGulry could have reached out and scratched it behind its furry ears.

MacGulry brought the gun barrel within an inch of the kangaroo's gray head and pulled the trigger.

As the latest explosion rang out, Robbie MacGulry whooped with joy.

"Gotcha, ya bastard!" MacGulry screamed.

In the side mirror, the driver glimpsed the dead kangaroo. The animal was suddenly something from another planet—all feet and tail. The head had been shot clean off. A ragged chunk of torso was missing, as well. One limp arm hung in grisly red strips.

Robbie MacGulry grinned at his driver. Flecks of sticky wet blood stained his big white teeth. The smile suddenly collapsed into a scowl.

"Here! What the hell ahh you doing!" MacGulry yelled as his driver puked on the dashboard.

"Sorry, sir," the young man gurgled. He was trying to hold in the vomit with one hand while driving with the other.

"What ahh you, some kind of Greenpeace pooftah?

It's just blood." MacGulry ran his tongue across his teeth, licking off the sticky red film. "See?"

The man did see. He saw his boss lapping up blood like a ghoul, and he saw thick chunks of furry gray flesh stuck to his own knees and then he saw last night's supper joining breakfast on the dashboard of the Land Rover.

The driver's hands fled the wheel and he slammed on the brakes. Chucking clouds of dust, the Land Rover skidded to a spinning stop.

Sensing salvation, the kangaroos cut off in another direction. In a haze of hot dust and pounding feet, they hopped to freedom across the vast plain.

MacGulry's eyes grew wide with rage. Raw fury knotted his wrinkled face. Baring pink-stained teeth, he was contemplating swinging the barrel of his gun to the driver's head when his dashboard-mounted phone buzzed to life.

The media giant exhaled angrily. "You're fired," he growled, flinging the gun into the back of the truck.

Dropping into his seat, MacGulry snatched up the receiver, flicking off bits of kangaroo flesh.

"What?" he demanded.

There was only a handful of people on Earth with access to this private number. The voice on the phone was clipped and obsequious. Very professional and very, very British.

"Mr. MacGulry, sir, I hate to bother you, but it's important."

"What's wrong?" MacGulry pulled the phone away before the caller could answer.

"Stop puking, ya underdaks-wearing bastard! If you're gonna be crook, do it in the dunny!"

The driver looked around for a dunny. The prairie was vast. No outhouses in sight.

"Nature's dunny, idiot," MacGulry snarled.

The driver understood. Climbing from the truck, he went over and puked in the dirt.

"What is it?" MacGulry growled into the phone.

The caller picked his words carefully.

"There is someone—that is to say, there's something here you should see, sir. At once."

Like all News Company employees—which was the corporate umbrella under which virtually all of Robbie MacGulry's businesses existed—the caller knew enough not to waste his employer's time. The Englishman was being vague for a reason. MacGulry sighed hotly.

"I'll be back quick as a can," he grumbled. He slammed the receiver back into its cradle.

MacGulry sat there for a long moment, staring at the bleak horizon.

The kangaroos were a distant cloud of hopping dust. He pulled off his glasses, blowing dirt off the thick lenses.

"Bastard," he whispered so softly even the wind failed to hear. Had someone been there to hear, they would have gotten the clear impression MacGulry was talking about neither the Englishman on the phone nor his incompetent driver.

MacGulry glanced to his right. His driver was still doubled over. The young man seemed to be almost finished.

Quietly, MacGulry slid over behind the wheel. When he started the engine and stomped on the gas, his driver had to jump out of the way to avoid the lurching Land Rover.

The media tycoon floored it and cut the wheel. When he zoomed back the way they'd come, he could see his panicked driver waving helplessly from within a cloud of beige dust.

"Teach you for ruining my day off, mate!" Robbie MacGulry yelled.

The vehicle sped across the endless plain, away from the distant looming mountains of the Great Dividing Range.

THREE HOURS LATER—showered, shaved and dressed in an impeccably tailored Bond Street two-piece blueblack suit—Robbie MacGulry stormed into the main production facility of his Wollongong, New South Wales television station.

South of Sydney, the Wollongong station was small compared to others in his globe-straddling television empire, but it was the one closest to his main home. If Robbie MacGulry had a heart, Wollongong would have been the one nearest and dearest to it.

Wollongong was the first TV station he'd ever owned. Although off the beaten path of his global media empire, an uncharacteristic lapse into sentimentality by its owner made it the flagship of his entire entertainment empire.

Banks of television screens lined up like unblinking eyes above dozens of computerized stations all around the production room. A visitor might have mistaken the facility for a space-shuttle control room if not for the images on the screens. On most of the monitors, a yellow-headed cartoon family was sliding around an icy parking lot. The cartoon was one of the most popular shows in the decade-plus history of MacGulry's American television network.

"You better not have called me back here to watch bloody cartoons!" MacGulry roared.

The men in the room wheeled on the booming voice. As the rest resumed working double-time, one hurried over to Robbie MacGulry.

"I'm sorry again for disturbing you, sir. I presumed you'd want to see something we received from America."

Rodney Adler was as English as frigid women and warm beer. It seemed as if the very act of speech pained his perpetually locked jaw.

MacGulry only liked the British as employees, and even then he didn't care for them very much. As a people, he'd always considered them to be condescending nitpickers whose sole joy in life was to piss in the party's punch bowl. His dream was to amass a big enough fortune to buy the British Isles and order the entire population to march off the bloody White Cliffs of Dover.

The billionaire followed Adler to one of the stations. There were two nervous men seated before it. MacGulry dropped into the empty swivel chair between them.

"We have been monitoring the situation in Harlem," Adler said, "per your instructions."

"I don't need to be reminded of my orders," MacGulry growled. "Stop wasting my time and get to the point."

Adler nodded crisply. "Sorry, sir," he said. He had one of the seated men insert a big black videotape into the slot on the face of the monitor station.

"I can't be completely certain at this point, mind you," Adler said. "But I believe we've found what you were looking for. Or, rather, who."

On the four television screens above the station, the cartoon cut out. A video image began playing. It had been taped at a weird angle. Blurry, snow-covered branches jutted directly in front of the lens. Beyond them, MacGulry saw a lone man walking down a bombed-out street.

"It's out of focus," MacGulry complained gruffly. "I can't see his face." In his head, the media magnate was already planning on firing the anonymous camera operator.

Adler leaned forward, peering up at the blurry image.

"I thought it was the fault of the cameraman," the Englishman said, his big jaw locked tight in concentration. "But according to our person on the ground, the subject did that to his face by himself."

MacGulry's eyes grew flat. "So he's hooked up to

a bloody paint mixer?'' he snarled. "People's heads don't move like that. Not without scrambling their brains to mush. How many baby brains do your nannies have to puree before you Brits figure that out? Who told you he could do that?''

As he spoke, the man with the blurry face stepped over to where the cameraman was hiding. Things went crazy for a moment before the camera settled on a pale, pretty face. The woman was standing up from behind a broken-down section of wall in an otherwise empty lot.

Robbie MacGulry's face sagged with strained patience.

"Cindee Maloo,'' he muttered to himself.

"Yes,'' Rodney Adler said uncomfortably.

He knew that MacGulry had been linked romantically to the woman in question. Adler assumed it had ended when she had gotten a job at rival BCN on the high-profile *Winner* show. He had only recently found out that she was still somehow secretly on the team.

"He's not even a Vox cameraman,'' Adler said. "He works on 'Winner' with Ms. Maloo. Even though he did a poor job, that is still probably, er, *possibly* the individual—or rather one of the individuals—you were looking for.''

He held his breath, hoping he wasn't about to join on the dole queue a thousand other Vox employees who had been foolish enough to upset the great Robbie MacGulry.

MacGulry crossed his arms, his perpetual scowl drawn into deeply angry furrows.

"Ten words or less. Why is it him?"

Adler released a slip of breath. "Um..."

"First word," MacGulry snapped.

Rodney Adler wasn't sure *um* would pass the official Scrabble requirements of an actual word, but he couldn't very well argue.

He concentrated. "T-shirt. Loafers," he said.

"Three. And I'm still not impressed."

"Thin. Thick wrists. Graceful."

"Four, five, six, seven."

Adler began counting on his fingers. "Displays...unusual...abilities."

He finished with a weak shrug, unconvinced by his own argument.

MacGulry exhaled. He could still taste the kangaroo blood on his breath. The scowl never left his face as he examined the screen.

Adler had looped the footage. It skipped off of Cindee Maloo, cutting back to the point where the stranger was walking along the street.

"Freeze frame," MacGulry ordered.

A technician quickly did as he was told. The image froze on the thin man on the Harlem sidewalk. The subject's face remained maddeningly out of focus.

MacGulry studied the picture for a few seconds. The camera work was sloppy, but enough was visible to make an educated guess. The image of the man in Harlem did match the description he had been given. MacGulry made an abrupt decision.

"Get outta here," he ordered the men, twirling back around in his seat.

The nearby men didn't need to be told a second time. They were joined by the rest of the Vox employees. Rodney Adler in the lead, they quickly fled the room.

Eyes locked on one monitor, MacGulry snatched up a phone receiver from the console before him. Without looking, he stabbed out a number. He didn't have to look to know he hadn't misdialed. He'd never misdial that number.

The phone didn't ring. It never rang. As usual, it went from empty air one moment to the voice the next. To MacGulry, somehow that familiar voice seemed more insubstantial than the dead air that preceded it.

"Hello, Robbie."

MacGulry used to wonder how the man on the other end of the line always knew it was him. He had realized in recent years that the man with the smooth voice had to have had some early version of caller ID long before it had become available to the general public.

"G'day, mate," MacGulry said. "Thought you might be interested in seeing something one of my people taped in the States."

"Yes. The younger of the two men I asked you to look for."

MacGulry's tan face bunched into a frown.

He knew. Somehow he already knew.

There had been two men described to MacGulry

initially. An old Asian and a young white. He had been ordered to report if they showed up in Harlem.

"I think the mob action must have worked," MacGulry said.

"I wasn't entirely certain it would," said the smooth voice. "I'm pleased that it did. I only wish I'd been certain one of them would show up at the police station. I could have monitored the situation personally rather than rely on the automated signals. But with the rioters in custody there was no certainty they would follow up. It's clear I made in error calculating those odds. Oh, well. No harm. Actually, Robbie, I was wondering how long it would take you to call about all this. It's been some time since your people received the Caucasian's image."

"I didn't think your friends would show up so soon."

"One did. And instead of being where you were supposed to be, you decided to go hunting."

"You knew that, too?" MacGulry asked dully.

"There is precious little I don't know, Robbie. I told you to remain in Wollongong. I told you this situation would have to be monitored carefully if it is to turn out beneficially for both of us. I told you the subjects could arrive very quickly. They have a history of doing so."

"I heard all that, mate," MacGulry said, his tone apologetic. "I just didn't think it'd be so soon."

MacGulry was starting to sweat. He got nervous every time he talked to the cold bastard on the phone. In those brief phone conversations, he caught a glimpse of the torture he lived to inflict on his own employees.

The smooth voice didn't miss a beat. "Next time, be more conscientious."

"Yes, sir," MacGulry replied.

"Don't call me that. It's far too formal for longtime business associates like us."

"Sorry, mate," MacGulry said.

"That's better. Now, with the Caucasian on the ground in Harlem, you'll need to act quickly. With this particular crisis now over, he might not remain in the New York region long."

"I'll get started right away," MacGulry promised. "I just have one question. How could you possibly know about this before me? The footage was only sent to us via satellite a few hours ago."

"I intercepted it in transit. Remember, I am very interested in the events in New York. Keep in touch."

The line went dead.

Robbie MacGulry replaced the receiver. He was screaming even as he dropped the phone in its cradle.

"Turn up the bloody air conditioner!" he bellowed.

The door sprang open and a dozen men piled into the room. Rodney Adler was tripping along at the head of the pack. He raced over to the thermostat.

As his employees stumbled to accommodate their boss, Robbie MacGulry pulled out a handkerchief to mop the sweat that glistened in the grooves of his dark, lined forehead.

"Taking over the world'd be a hell of a lot easier without a silent partner," he muttered to himself.

He got up from his chair. On the monitors behind him, Remo's blurry image remained frozen in place.

12

Behind his locked door in the administrative wing of Folcroft Sanitarium, Harold W. Smith studied the data on his computer monitor with deeply troubled eyes.

Several hours had passed since Remo's image had been broadcast to the Harlem police station. Apparently, no one who had seen it was aware they'd done so. According to the report Smith had just read, no one was quite sure what had happened at the police station where Remo had been attacked. A police spokesman was suggesting that the officers there had been overcome by narcotics fumes, although so far no one had been able to locate the source. There was no mention of a chase involving a suspect matching Remo's description. By the sounds of it, memory of the event was already bleeding from the minds of the police.

The report offered welcome breathing room for Smith to think.

So far events in Harlem had not blossomed into something worse for CURE. Good for the moment, but it might only be a matter of time.

Under ordinary circumstances it would have been easy to blame Minister Shittman for what had happened in and outside of the police station. He was a man comfortable with mobs, having spent a career stirring the embers of racial hatred. But apparently he was an unwitting dupe in a larger scheme.

There had been 147 rioters arrested that morning. While some of them had criminal records, many more did not. There were mothers, grandmothers. Even a Korean grocer and his wife had joined the mob. Neither the previous night's rioters nor the police were typical Shittman followers.

The truth had come to startling light minutes after Remo had called from the Harlem police station. In a shocking sidewalk press conference in Harlem, it was revealed that the BCN television network was possessed of a technology capable of brainwashing television viewers. BCN was to blame for the mob attack on the former president's building. The network executive who had set up shop in the basement of Shittman's church had attested to that fact before committing suicide.

Smith was greatly relieved when the BCN executive's last words made no mention of Remo. But there was still the question of why a major American television network had been subliminally broadcasting an image of CURE's enforcement arm.

The dead man had named the president of the network as a coconspirator. When Remo called back after stopping by the Harlem church, Smith had sent him after the head of BCN.

Now, as he sat in the solitude of his office, Smith stared in frustration at the canted monitor below the surface of his desk. He had done all the digging he could do. Until Remo turned up something more, all Smith could do was wait.

As he sat in the afternoon gloom of his office, something nagged at the back of Smith's mind.

With a thoughtful hum, he lowered his hands to the edge of his desk. An alphanumeric keyboard appeared as if by magic from the black background.

Typing swiftly, he accessed the BCN network's prime-time lineup. There were only three network shows on the previous evening. Shittman had indicated to Remo that he had received his subliminal commands through a program called *Winner*.

Something about that title seemed familiar to Smith. It had first come to him during Remo's call, but he didn't know why. In a flash, he realized where he'd heard it before.

Smith reached across the desk for his intercom.

"Yes, Dr. Smith?" asked his secretary's voice.

"Mrs. Mikulka, could you please come in here for a moment?" Smith said.

He pressed a button at the base of the intercom, silently unlocking the door. A moment later, Eileen Mikulka stuck her blue-haired head in the room.

"Is something wrong, Dr. Smith?" Mrs. Mikulka asked worriedly. "It's not Mr. Howard, is it?" She wrung her hands as she approached his desk. It was a nervous habit she had displayed ever since the police had come stampeding into her office two days before.

"No," Smith said. "This is of a more personal

nature. I recently overheard you discussing your son's television-viewing habits with a nurse in the cafeteria.''

Mrs. Mikulka blinked. ''I'm sorry,'' she said, unsure what she had done wrong. ''I get lunch there sometimes. If you don't want me to, I suppose I can eat at my desk.''

''That isn't a problem,'' Smith said. ''I believe you mentioned that your son was looking for a copy of a program called 'Winner.' He had apparently missed an episode.''

''Oh, yes,'' Mrs. Mikulka said. ''That would be Kieran, he's my youngest. Thirty-five and doesn't have a job right now. Some boys just take a little longer to find their way, I guess. He's a big fan of that show. He usually tapes it when he's not home, but last Thursday night there was a car accident that knocked out the power for a few minutes and the VCR went out. When he found out he'd missed it, he asked me to ask around to see if anyone here had taped it.''

''Do you know if he taped last night's episode?''

She bit her lip. ''Well, he went out with his brother Konrad last night. He didn't get home until late, so I suppose he set the machine to tape it as usual.''

''I would like to borrow that tape. Would you please go home and get it for me?''

''Oh,'' Mrs. Mikulka said, confused. ''Do you want me to wait until I'm done work for the day?''

Smith checked his watch. It was only two in the

afternoon. Although it was tempting to let her run this errand on her own time, Smith did not want to wait.

"Now would be better if you don't mind," he said.

"Oh, I don't mind," Mrs. Mikulka said. "I'm happy to do a favor for your wife."

Smith's expression grew puzzled. "My wife?"

"Well, this is for her, isn't it? I assumed she'd forgotten to tape it for herself."

"My wife doesn't own a video recorder."

Mrs. Mikulka didn't think her employer ever watched television. She knew he liked computers, involving himself with solitaire or other distractions. This was the first indication she had that something else might be going on in the Folcroft administrator's office. If he spent his time hidden away watching those silly reality-TV shows, it was no wonder he kept the door locked most of the time.

"I just assumed it was for your wife. I'll run home and get the tape right now. I'll be back as fast as I can."

As she hurried from the room, Smith pursed his lips.

So far the damage was limited to Harlem. Only people who lived within a few blocks of Hal Shittman's Greater Congregation of the Lord Church had fallen victim to the subliminal signals. The dead BCN man had broadcast from there. But there could be other commands laced into the same program in different areas. And, like the image of Remo at the police station, some of those could be linked to CURE.

Feeling a fresh twinge of worry deep in his belly, Smith reached in his pocket for his wallet.

Two CRISP ONE-DOLLAR bills sat on the edge of Smith's desk when Eileen Mikulka returned twenty minutes later.

The first words out of his secretary's mouth almost sent the CURE director into cardiac arrest.

"It's a shame about Remo," Mrs. Mikulka said as she handed over the tape.

"Excuse me?" he gasped. What little color he possessed drained from Smith's gray face.

"He was the poor 'Winner' contestant who was killed last night. Kieran told me about it when I went home just now. That mob killed him on the set of the show." She noticed the sickly look on her employer's face. "Oh, I'm sorry, Dr. Smith. I assumed you would have heard. It was on the news."

"No, I hadn't," Smith replied, getting to his feet. "Please excuse me." He scooped up the money, pressing it into her hand even as he ushered her from the room. "This is for your gas. Thank you. I'll get the tape back to you as soon as possible." He closed and locked the door.

Smith leaned back against the door frame.

His heart was racing. Although she had seen him many times over the years, Mrs. Mikulka had never expressed any interest in Remo. Given the day's events, her use of his name now had sent up alarm signals for the CURE director.

Pushing away from the door, Smith stepped over

to a shelf where a small video player was attached to his old black-and-white television. He slid in the tape and the machine began to play automatically. Clicking on the TV, Smith immediately hit pause.

He reasoned that the flashes Remo had mentioned would be timed with the motion on the screen. Frozen, any subliminal signals would not register to the unconscious mind.

He studied the image carefully from top to bottom and side to side. He saw nothing out of the ordinary.

Slowly, he advanced the picture frame by frame.

He felt a fresh thrill of panic when the name "Remo" suddenly appeared at the bottom of the screen. He quickly realized that it wasn't part of any subliminal message. The name appeared as a regular caption and was used to identify one of the contestants on the game show.

It was odd to see that name applied to someone else.

After another minute of frame advancing, Smith realized there was nothing there—at least nothing that he could see. He popped the tape from the VCR.

Folcroft didn't have the facilities to properly analyze what—if anything—might be there. The tape would have to be sent out for professional analysis.

For an instant he thought of Mark Howard. This would have ordinarily been one of his duties. A minor thing, but one of the many small responsibilities the young man had taken on over the past year.

Smith's face hardened.

Purging thoughts of his assistant, he spun from the television. Stride resolute, he marched back to his desk to locate a facility that could uncover whatever messages might be hidden on Mrs. Mikulka's tape.

13

The Broadcast Corporation of North America occupied a forty-story building on Madison Avenue.

The midtown Manhattan headquarters of BCN had been built in 1928. At the time it was just around the corner from the original NBC offices. By building so close, BCN had intended to be a constant thorn in NBC's side. But then NBC had ruined its rival's best-laid plan by up and moving to 30 Rockefeller Plaza. Instead of dogging its competition to its new home, BCN reluctantly opted to remain where it was.

It turned out those two early decisions established a pair of precedents that the BCN network would follow for the rest of its corporate and creative lifetime.

BCN never led. It followed. When radio giant NBC was on Fifth Avenue, BCN decided to build right in its backyard.

Precedent one: BCN the Copycat.

By not following NBC to its new 30 Rock address, the upstart network quickly established precedent number two: BCN the Timid.

When television was in its infancy, timid BCN lagged behind in the cozy comfort of radio, allowing NBC and the DuMont network to test the water first.

Only when the early risk takers had established the route to modest TV success did copycat BCN jump on board the bandwagon.

For the first fifty years of the television age, BCN offered bland and formulaic TV programming that was a virtual carbon copy of what every other network was broadcasting.

At some point during this first half century of wheezy dramas and formulaic sitcoms, an enthusiastic and truth-challenged public-relations man had dubbed BCN the "Diamond Network," the inference being that only quality programs ever found their way onto its nightly schedule. Despite years of evidence to the contrary, somehow the image stuck.

For years the Diamond Network coasted on its reputation. It wasn't until the last decade of the twentieth century that BCN finally began to show cracks in its corporate facade.

Even before the appearance of upstarts like Vox, UPN and the Warner Brothers network, BCN was already unsteady. Media mergers and changing demographics didn't help. Even as the other networks began to skew younger and younger, BCN's core audience continued to age. It looked as if the end might be at hand for one of the original Big Three networks.

Industry experts who had forecast her demise were surprised when salvation for BCN came in the form of one single reality show.

No one expected *Winner* to be such a huge success. It was supposed to be less than a blip on the TV radar. A curiosity that had somehow found its improbable way onto the prime-time schedule. Sure, it might generate a few good numbers for a week or two. But it would flame out fast.

The television world was shocked when the high-concept show didn't crash and burn. *Winner* was not only a success out of the gate, it continued to grow.

Other networks were quick to churn out knockoffs. It was an amazing role reversal for BCN.

The rising tide began to lift all boats. As *Winner*'s numbers grew, so too did those of the rest of BCN's lineup.

All of this was welcome news for BCN's president.

When Martin Houton was appointed by the board to head up the Broadcast Corporation of North America, the network had been third in the ratings and was sinking fast. Ten years into his tenure, the network's numbers were on the rise and advertisers were flooding back. The scratching wolves had finally been chased away from the back door. It was a new century and a brand-new golden age for the Diamond Network. Thanks to one great gamble on one mediocre show, there was nothing but clear sailing as far as the eye could see.

Until today when one little suicidal lunatic—way up in godforsaken Harlem of all places—had slammed the network's ship smack-dab into the mother of all icebergs.

"We're gonna sue!" Martin Houton boomed.

Houton was a silver-haired man in his late fifties.

His cherubic face was devil-red with rage. He prowled near the window of his corner office, glaring hatred at the streaming headlights on Madison Avenue thirty stories below.

It seemed that everyone was on the way home. And, finally, *finally* some of them would be watching BCN when they got there. It had taken so long to build up.

Houton slapped his hands against the window. "That bastard!" he yelled. "What the hell was he doing in Harlem? I didn't authorize whatever it was he was doing."

The windows in his office were shatterproof glass. There was no way to break through and hurl himself to the glittering diamond headlights of Madison Avenue far below.

He spun furiously away from the window.

"What are they saying now?" he demanded.

The vice president in charge of BCN programming sat on a plush sofa in the conference area of the room. A bank of televisions played silently in a nearby wall unit. Dozens of pictures flashed images of unrest in Harlem.

On Vox, a reporter who was scruffy by network standards was talking to an anchorman. The News Company network was obviously dipping into the pool of local talent.

The BCN vice president turned up the sound on Vox.

"...is the latest information we've heard," the reporter was saying. "So far BCN is refusing comment."

"Can you blame them?" said the anchor from the Vox news station in New York. "Those are serious charges."

"Serious? Try slanderous!" Houton boomed at the TV.

The programming veep strained to hear the television.

"According to Thomas Trumann, BCN's man in Harlem who committed suicide on national television earlier today, the Broadcasting Corporation of North America is entirely responsible for last night's riot," the reporter said.

"We are *not* responsible but we *are* suing your ass!" Houton screamed. He stabbed a pudgy finger at the screen. "I'm suing you, Vox, ABC, NBC and anyone else who's slandering this network. Why aren't our news people on the air denying this? Hell, tell them to get on and blame someone else. No one likes Ted Turner. Blame him."

"We can't just make up a story like that," the programming vice president cautioned.

"Why not? They are."

"They claim Trumann said we were responsible. Our own news people were there when he killed himself. He gave them a tour of the church basement before he blew his brains out. It was crammed full of BCN equipment."

"It's a setup. Shittman must have looted our stuff. This is all a big scam."

"Trumann apologized for his misuse of the technology on BCN's behalf. He came right out and *said* we were responsible for what happened at the former president's office building. Marty, he even exonerated Hal Shittman and that mob of his."

Martin Houton couldn't believe his ears. It had been going on like this since morning. The networks had been hammering the story into the ground all day long. Everyone was saying that BCN was testing a dangerous mind-controlling technology that had somehow gone wrong.

"If I had some kind of subliminal gizmo that'd make people mind slaves, don't you think we'd be pulling numbers on more than just 'Winner'? I mean, turn the damn thing on and save God-Wednesday-damn night, for Christ's sake."

"They're saying we only recently developed it," the vice president said. "They're claiming we're starting slow using it. We're pulling the numbers up on Monday with it, plus we switch it on for 'Winner' on Thursdays. We don't want to overdo it, which is actually a pretty good strategy if we have something like this. Which we don't, do we?"

The vice president smiled hopefully.

"No!" Houton screamed.

"Oh," the vice president said, disappointed. "Not even for late night? We're still getting creamed by Leno. Maybe if someone were to really have something like that he could—I don't know—bump the 'don't touch that dial' button for an hour at eleven-thirty Eastern Standard Time on weeknights."

The vice president had no idea how close he came to getting a Golden Globe award bounced between his winking eyes.

"Get out of here," Houton snarled.

As the vice president hurried from the room, Martin Houton trudged to his desk. He was slumping in his chair when the sleek black phone on his desk buzzed like an angry wasp. For an instant, he froze.

He had already gotten a dozen calls today from Moe Carmichael, CEO of the entire BCN family of companies.

Houton's employer had long been unhappy with the television division of his media empire. For the first few years he had owned BCN, the network's ratings had been in the toilet. Even with the recent upswing in audience, Carmichael remained superstitious, assuming the improving numbers were nothing but a cruel mistake.

When he learned about BCN's possible involvement in brainwashing technology that morning, Moe Carmichael had hit the roof. He had called every hour on the hour to scream at Martin Houton. During the last call, he had been yelling something about selling his fifty-one percent of the network. It was hard to make out clearly what he was saying over the sounds of the frantic ambulance technicians who were trying to jump-start the heart of BCN's soon-to-be-former CEO.

As he reached tiredly for the ringing phone, Martin automatically assumed the ambulance boys had done their job and his boss was calling back, this time to scream at him from an intensive-care-unit bed.

He was surprised when it wasn't Moe Carmichael's voice on the other end of the line.

"G'day, mate," said the nasal voice. "How's tricks?"

This was a company line, access to which was limited to a handful of people. Whoever this man was, he was not part of the BCN inner circle. Yet that voice sounded familiar.

"Who is this?" Martin Houton demanded.

"I'm the new owner of BCN, Marty, my boy. Or I will be very soon, thanks to you."

Houton knew. He now knew for certain who this was. For an instant, Martin Houton could almost see the hyenalike smile of satisfaction that broke out among the suntanned wrinkles of that frightening, familiar Aussie face.

Martin was going to say something, but the words wouldn't come. And then it didn't matter because the voice on the phone was speaking again.

"By the way, you're fired, Marty."

And a strange sense of soft relief seemed to wash through Martin Houton's troubled mind like a calming blue tide. It was amazing given the stress he'd been under all day long. He wanted to thank the man on the phone for giving him this miraculous, deadened sensation, but the man had already hung up. Not that it mattered, because Martin Houton had already forgotten who he was.

But he knew it didn't matter that he didn't remember who the man was. He remembered the words.

"You're fired."

They had come to him over his many televisions. On a daily basis, for hours. He knew they were there even though he really didn't know. Those words delivered by a man whose identity he could no longer remember were the trigger. They had come with orders that Martin had accepted without even knowing he was accepting them. And they were wonderful, perfect orders. He could not be happier with his orders.

Martin Houton got up and calmly left his office. People spoke to him as he went through the hall and rode the elevator downstairs. If he said anything at all to them, he wasn't aware of it. He was thinking of the beautiful words that had floated off of his TV and into his brain over the past few weeks. Private communications to him alone.

He found his limo in the garage and allowed his driver to open and close the door for him.

On the ride from the city to his Long Island estate, Martin was more at peace than he had ever been in his life.

At home Martin Houton walked woodenly past his worried wife and mounted the stairs to his bedroom. He locked the door behind him. He went directly to the nightstand next to his bed. Behind his reading glasses and a deck of cards he found his .38 pistol. It was stuffed in an old sock.

Martin dumped the gun from the sock, jammed the barrel in his mouth and pulled the trigger.

He was a little surprised when there wasn't a brain-splattering kaboom. That's what he figured it would sound like.

In fact, as he thought about it, there really wasn't any sound at all. That didn't seem right.

When Martin caught his reflection in the vanity mirror, he was disappointed to find that the top of his head was still there. What's more, the gun wasn't in his mouth. On top of all that, there was someone in the room with him.

"Oh, hello," Houton said to the young man with the deep, cruel eyes who stood with him in the bedroom of his mansion even though the door was locked. "May I have that back? I have to kill myself."

He held his hand out for his gun, which had somehow found its way into the hands of the stranger.

"Answers first, death second," Remo Williams promised. He tossed Houton's gun to the bed.

"Oh, no, no, no," Martin Houton insisted. "I'm sure that's not the right order. I'm in desperate legal trouble for everything I've done. I have to kill myself now."

Face determined, he headed for the gun.

Remo picked up the gun and threw it through the terrace window. There came a wet plunk from Martin Houton's kidney-shaped heated pool with the two ice-covered diving boards.

Play The Lucky Hearts Game

and get...
FREE BOOKS & a FREE GIFT...
YOURS to KEEP!

Yes! I have scratched off the silver card. Please send me my **2 FREE BOOKS** and **FREE GIFT**. I understand that I am under no obligation to purchase any books as explained on the back of this card.

Scratch Here!
then look below to see
what your cards get you...

366 ADL DH5T   **166 ADL DH5R**

NAME   (PLEASE PRINT CLEARLY)

ADDRESS

APT.#   CITY

STATE/PROV.   ZIP/POSTAL CODE

Twenty-one gets you
2 FREE BOOKS and
a **FREE GIFT!**

Twenty gets you
2 FREE BOOKS!

Nineteen gets you
1 FREE BOOK!

TRY AGAIN!

Offer limited to one per household and not valid to current Gold Eagle® subscribers. All orders subject to approval.

Visit us online at
www.eHarlequin.com

(MB-03/02) DETACH AND MAIL CARD TODAY!

© 1999 GOLD EAGLE

The Gold Eagle Reader Service™ — Here's how it works:

Accepting your 2 free books and gift places you under no obligation to buy anything. You may keep the books and gift and return the shipping statement marked "cancel." If you do not cancel, about a month later we'll send you 6 additional novels and bill you just $26.70* — that's a saving of 15% off the cover price of all 6 books! And there's no extra charge for shipping! You may cancel at any time, but if you choose to continue, every other month we'll send you 6 more books, which you may either purchase at the discount price or return to us and cancel your subscription.

*Terms and prices subject to change without notice. Sales tax applicable in N.Y. Canadian residents will be charged applicable provincial taxes and GST.

If offer card is missing write to: Gold Eagle Reader Service, 3010 Walden Ave., P.O. Box 1867, Buffalo NY 14240-1867

BUSINESS REPLY MAIL
FIRST-CLASS MAIL   PERMIT NO. 717-003   BUFFALO, NY

POSTAGE WILL BE PAID BY ADDRESSEE

GOLD EAGLE READER SERVICE
3010 WALDEN AVE
PO BOX 1867
BUFFALO NY 14240-9952

NO POSTAGE
NECESSARY
IF MAILED
IN THE
UNITED STATES

"Well, that's just going to make this harder than it has to be," Houton pouted.

He headed for the French doors with the one broken windowpane. If he jumped after the gun, maybe he'd be lucky and break his neck in the process.

A very rude hand tugged him back from the doors, knocking him back onto the edge of the bed.

"How do you know me?" Remo asked.

"What?" Houton asked, puzzled. "Do I know you? I don't think I know you." He started to get up.

With one hand Remo pushed the TV executive back to a sitting position; with the other he pinched Martin Houton's earlobe. Martin Houton yelped. The pain was bad. Almost enough to make him forget about killing himself altogether.

"That's not nice," Houton complained.

The mean pincher who wouldn't let him properly kill himself relaxed his grip on Martin's ear. As the fiery pain lessened, the words returned.

"You had a guy in Harlem broadcasting subliminal signals from a church basement," Remo said. "One of the things he broadcast was a picture of me. I want to know why."

"Oh, that was you?" Martin Houton asked. The subliminal commands came easily. It was as if whoever had programmed the instructions into his television had anticipated this scenario. "That was part of the 'Winner' show. You were just picked at random because you happened to be there. A white man torn to pieces by a mob in Harlem near the 'Winner' set would get all kinds of press. The news media swarms in, we benefit from the proximity. Synergy with the news boys. Who, by the by, don't pull their weight these days, what with all the twenty-four-hour cable news networks. Can I please kill myself now?''

''In a minute,'' Remo promised. ''How did you get my picture?''

''You were filmed by one of our 'Winner' crews. Did you know the season finale of 'Winner II' got a 21.1 rating and a 31 share? That was amazing. Hard to keep those numbers up. The occasional sweeps stunt is mandatory to keep viewership levels high. A random death like yours would have generated some good numbers for us in February.''

Remo disregarded the executive's TV babble.

''I made it so I couldn't be seen,'' he insisted.

''Technology is amazing, isn't it? Your tape was pretty bad. But they're able to take points of reference from a poor-quality recording like yours and computer enhance a solid digital image. Say, maybe I should jump off the roof. Three stories down from the terrace might not do it.''

''The pool's below the terrace. Aim for the concrete and you should be golden,'' Remo said.

''Thanks,'' Martin Houton said. ''You're not such a bad guy after all.''

He started for the terrace. Remo collared him and flung him back into a chair.

''Who else was in on this subliminal crapola?'' he asked.

''Well, I signed off on it,'' Martin Houton said, in a lie that seemed so much like the truth he actually believed it himself. "Thomas Trumann developed the technology. He's the guy who shot himself in that church basement this morning."

"No one else?"

"Nope, that's it," Houton said agreeably. "Only two men in the entire BCN establishment. Had to keep it quiet. If it panned out, we would have been aces in the ratings. Right now Mondays have been okay for us with it, and Thursdays are holding their own. But we hadn't been using it at any other time and our ratings showed it. Now thanks to Trumann, I guess we're back to hemorrhaging viewers to cable and video."

"How about those orders to the rioters? Why didn't they go out nationally?" Remo asked.

"Our satellite fed to Trumann in the church. Harlem is where we've been testing the technology for a while, so mostly we were local. But flip a switch, and he could send the signals back up to the satellite and make them national. There's a transmitter in the church steeple. That's what we were using for 'Winner.' Just started it on a few more shows."

His Sinanju training gave Remo the ability to sense when someone was lying. Martin Houton was clearly a nit, but he was a nit who was telling the truth.

"Can I kill myself now?" Houton asked hopefully.

"Knock yourself out," Remo said.

Houton rubbed his hands together determinedly. He was getting up from the bed when, as an afterthought, Remo gave another good squeeze to the TV executive's earlobe. Bolts of pain shot through Martin Houton's clouded brain.

"What was that for?" Houton asked, rubbing his ear.

"Ten years of 'Murphy Brown,'" Remo said.

A ghost in shadow, he slipped from the darkened room.

Interruptions finally over, Houton stepped out onto the balcony. Warm steam rose from the surface of the gurgling pool, kissing the cold December air. Martin Houton could smell the chlorine in the air. The stars were beautiful, the air crisp and the words beckoning him to end his life as clear as church bells on a Christmas midnight.

Martin Houton climbed up on the rail and, without so much as a glance at the beauty of the chilly night around him, went the way a just world would send all television network executives. Three stories down and headfirst into solid concrete.

14

Smith watched the last of the news reports in the darkness of his Folcroft office. Light from his buried computer monitor cast ghostly shadows around his wan face.

For the dozenth time he watched the suicide of BCN Vice President Thomas Trumann.

Smith was thankful that the networks were at least playing an edited version of the grisly footage. The CURE director's screen was filled with blurry blue dots. Even so, Smith grimaced at that which had been deemed airworthy. It made him wax nostalgic for the not-so-long-ago time when decency trumped ratings. In Smith's day, every broadcast network would have refused on principle to air so much as a single frame of Thomas Trumann's public suicide.

Smith felt like a man out of time. But thanks to the current culture, it was a feeling he had gotten used to.

Typing wearily, Smith exited his computer's TV function and shut down the system. The buried terminal winked to blackness beneath the onyx surface of his desk.

There had been no news from Remo for several

hours. Apparently, he had upset the Master of Sinanju in some way, for Chiun had returned to Folcroft alone by taxi. Their argument probably had something to do with the letters Remo had mentioned. Smith had wanted to question the Master of Sinanju about them, but when he saw the angry look on the Korean's face, he lost his nerve. He left the old Asian to cool off in his quarters. Smith decided to await Remo's return in his office. So here he sat.

Smith turned to face the big picture window behind his desk. Night had claimed Folcroft's back lawn. The glow of his desk lamp on the one-way glass was a single bright star in the dark heart of winter. Unseen beyond the glass, cold wind churned the night-black surface of Long Island Sound.

Smith closed his eyes for a moment.

He didn't realize he had dozed off until the voice in his office startled him awake twenty minutes later.

"Rise and shine, sleeping beauty."

Snapping awake, Smith spun. Remo stood before his desk. In the lamplight his deep-set eyes were hollow caves.

"Remo," Smith exhaled. "What happened with Houton?"

"Good news," Remo said. "That picture they put on TV didn't have anything to do with me. The guy said I was picked off the street at random. They wanted a murder to gin up ratings for that screwball survival show of theirs."

Cautious relief brushed Smith's tired face. "You're certain he didn't know about CURE?"

"Looks it," Remo said. "And even if he did, he was a TV executive. They time-share about four brain cells between them. He'd forget all about us halfway through happy hour."

"Was?" Smith asked. "You eliminated him?"

"Didn't have to. He took care of himself. I'd only give him a 2.5 on the dive, but a perfect ten for splattering his brains on the patio."

"That's odd," Smith said. "Both men responsible for developing and using the technology killed themselves."

"Lucky us for a change," Remo said. "I'm sick of picking up after everyone else all the time. Let the garbagemen haul their own trash for once."

"They must have both panicked," Smith speculated. "They would have both been answerable for the murder."

Remo nodded. "That dizzy producer from 'Winner' told me Shittman's mob killed one of her contestants."

"Yes," Smith said slowly. He looked up over the tops of his glasses, studying Remo's face. "Apparently, she didn't tell you the victim's name."

Remo noted the older man's odd tone. "She said they were keeping it under wraps," he admitted. "Why?"

"His name has leaked out to the press. The contestant killed was a man named Remo."

"No kidding?" Remo said. "Well, if it's a comfort to you, I'm pretty sure it wasn't me, Smitty. Although now that you mention it, she did want me to be on the show. I gave her a tentative yes, but I told her I'd have to check with you first. What do you say? America's number-one assassin could be a real ratings bonanza. If I win I'll split the million with you, seventy-thirty.''

Smith removed his glasses. ''The man's last name was Chappel,'' he continued dryly. ''Other than a shared given name, there is no other connection. However, given the uniqueness of your name, I must admit that it was disturbing to hear it at first.''

''Tell me about it,'' Remo said. ''I sympathize with him for what his parents did to him.''

''Be that as it may, it is just a coincidence,'' Smith said, replacing his glasses. ''If Martin Houton told you the truth, BCN was trading deaths for ratings. The fact that they killed one of their own contestants bolsters his claim.''

''The guy was telling the truth, Smitty,'' Remo insisted. ''You know we can tell that stuff. Heart rate, breathing, perspiration all stayed normal. He wasn't lying.''

''I'm relieved,'' Smith said. ''BCN was in possession of a terrifying technology. We should consider ourselves lucky it didn't get further than it did. From what I've learned, the process uses hypnotic bursts of light and regularly flashed worded suggestions. The light is a trigger that implants the suggestions deep in the subconscious. People are helpless to refuse whatever subliminal commands are shown on the screen.''

''One way to get people to tune in,'' Remo said.

"Any idea what went blooey to make that mob attack the former president?"

"Before he killed himself, Thomas Trumann issued an apology for that. He said that he was watching the news, saw the former president was nearby in Harlem and typed in the commands as a joke. He sent the signal accidentally. There is precedent at the BCN network for such an occurrence. During the last presidential race, a tasteless graphic was run during one of BCN's late-night programs calling for the assassination of one of the candidates. I checked. Trumann was working as head of late-night programming at the time."

"Funny guy," Remo said aridly.

"Yes," Smith said, with clear distaste. "But at least this particular command was only run in Harlem. I sent a copy of the show that was taped here in Rye out to be examined. It appears there was nothing but a simple command not to change the channel buried in the national broadcast."

"That's what I saw in Mexico," Remo said, nodding.

"So it seems this is over," Smith said. "And none too soon. The past few days had already been disturbing enough."

"Speaking of which, any news on Purcell?"

"No," Smith replied. "As we feared, he will remain in hiding until he feels strong enough to come after us."

"Us meaning me," Remo said.

Smith nodded quiet agreement. "As for Mark, I

will begin weaning him off the sedatives tomorrow. He should be lucid enough by then to explain his actions. I would like you and Master Chiun present when he comes around.''

''You got it,'' Remo said, his voice cold.

Smith noted his tone. ''Remo, the officer investigating this is coming back tomorrow afternoon. I would appreciate it if you and Chiun kept a low profile. It would be nice if the two of you found somewhere else to be at one o'clock.''

''Always nice to feel wanted,'' Remo droned. ''I can make myself scarce, but I don't know about Chiun.''

''Just as long as he remains in your quarters,'' the CURE director said tiredly. With a sigh he fished in the foot well of his desk, pulling out his briefcase.

''And you know how good he is for doing every little thing you want him to,'' Remo said thinly. ''Night, Smitty.''

The younger man slipped from the office.

Alone once more, Smith placed his briefcase on his desk.

He was bone tired.

The BCN television network's scheme to boost viewership had been stopped. A dozen federal agencies were now investigating the matter. Smith was grateful that it was all over. Rarely did a CURE assignment conclude so quickly.

He checked his watch. It was only nine-thirty.

He hadn't left work this early in years. But he had a meeting with Detective Davic the following afternoon. And given all that had happened over the past week, a good night's sleep was an indulgence he had earned.

It was early enough that his wife was probably still up. Maude Smith would be shocked to see him home so early.

Crossing to the door, Smith gathered his coat and scarf from the coatrack. Careful to snap off the lights, he left the ghosts to dance alone in the corners of the shadowy office.

15

Remo knew he was in trouble when he awoke to the sound of the Master of Sinanju singing.

The old Korean raised his voice in cheery song from the common room of their shared Folcroft quarters.

When Remo returned to their quarters the previous night, Chiun had been locked away in his room. At the time Remo assumed the old pain in the neck was still cheesed off. Now it seemed as if the cloud had lifted.

Lying on his reed mat in the predawn darkness of his bedroom, Remo racked his brain trying to think what could possibly have changed his teacher's lousy mood so abruptly. With a sinking feeling he realized there was one thing that almost always did the trick.

"I am not cleaning up any dead bodies!" Remo hollered from his bedroom.

"Good morning to you, too, sleepyhead," the Master of Sinanju called back, sounding far too chipper.

Remo dropped his head back to his mat. "I knew it. I'm gonna be scrubbing corpse juice off the chandeliers."

He wondered how the hell he was going to keep

the fact that the Master of Sinanju had killed half of Folcroft's staff during the night a secret from Smith. Smith said he'd be busy with the police that afternoon. Maybe Remo would luck out for once and the CURE director would be too distracted to notice the bodies piled like Civil War cannonballs all over the front lawn.

When he finally climbed reluctantly to his feet and went out to the common room to assess the damage, Remo was surprised to find he wasn't ankle deep in stiffs.

More surprising, the Master of Sinanju had brought some of his luggage out from his bedroom. The Master of Sinanju never moved his own luggage. The old man was puttering around the gaily colored steamer trunks.

"Where are they?" Remo asked warily.

Chiun didn't raise his aged head. "Where are who?"

Remo was peeking out the door. The hallway was empty. Not a decapitated corpse in sight.

"Didn't you kill your way to happiness and success last night?" Remo asked.

Chiun's face puckered. "You have already given an old man ample reason to doubt your loyalty, Remo Williams," he said. "Do not make me question your sanity."

"I'm loyal, I'm sane and I'm wondering why you're happy all of a sudden. I figured you had the Corpse-O-Matic cranked to eleven all night long. I was ready to pull the fire alarm and sneak off in the confusion.''

"I am an assassin," Chiun sniffed. "I do not kill willy-nilly."

That nearly did it. Remo almost laughed out loud. The urge shot up from his belly and made it as far as his throat. But in the split second before the laughter exploded out of his mouth and he fell on the floor clutching his sides, he realized Chiun was suddenly out of the crappy mood he'd been in the past few days and that by laughing in his teacher's face, Remo could very well snap him back into that same crappy mood. Gritting his teeth, Remo swallowed the laughter.

"Course not," Remo insisted, sniffling.

At the sound, Chiun's wrinkled head stretched high on a suspicious craning neck. He gave Remo a lingering look of mistrust. At long last he returned to his packing.

"I am packing because Emperor Smith has made clear his desire for us to leave his palace," the Master of Sinanju said. "You should do the same. Although don't think you can hide all your worthless junk in with my precious mementos."

"I can fit my life in a Safeway bag and still have room left over." As he spoke he peeked behind the couch. "Okay," Remo said, "there's no one dead here as far as I can see. If you being nice to me is supposed to be my Christmas present, you're a couple days early."

"Can a man not pack in peace? You may live out

your days in Smith's crazy house if you want, but I have stayed here long enough. It is time for the Master to move on.''

"Uh-oh," Remo asked, a new concern suddenly blossoming full. "Move on? Like *move* move on?"

"Stop mooing, bovine," Chiun said, gliding over to his pupil. "And move your fat cloven hoofs."

He kicked Remo's ankles. Remo lifted his feet out of the way and the old man swept past.

"Like move on to a house?" Remo pressed. "Because I told you before I'm not moving to Maine."

Chiun continued to fuss with his packing. "Why should I care where you are not moving?"

"Because you were hepped about moving to Maine a little while back. Just so you know, I'm not going. You move there, you're moving alone."

"A stronger argument for my moving there could not be made," the Master of Sinanju said aridly.

A fresh cloud of worry settled on Remo's face. "Wait, you're not going back to Sinanju?" he asked.

Chiun gave an exasperated sigh. "You may wish to speed me on my life's last journey, but it is not yet time for me to retire to the village of my ancestors." He saw the look of puzzlement on his pupil's face. "If you must know, I have received some wonderful news. It is a happy, happy day."

So far, aside from the early-morning singing, the Master of Sinanju had been doing a good job keeping his joy in check. But he could no longer contain himself. He began to hum happily as he folded a purple day kimono.

"Wasn't it just a crummy, crummy day?" Remo asked.

"That was yesterday and that was thanks to you. This is today and my new joy is thanks to my wondrous benefactor. Or are you deaf in addition to being a basher of the aged? Did you not hear the telephone ring during the night?"

Remo had heard. The phone had rung in the old Korean's bedroom a little before midnight.

For years Chiun had kept a special 800 number at his home back in Korea. The calls used to be transferred to his and Remo's house in Massachusetts, but now were routed to Folcroft. No matter where it was located, the phone rarely rang. Until recently. The normally silent telephone had become more active in recent weeks. With the way Chiun had been whispering in a dozen different foreign languages, Remo assumed it all had something to do with those cockamamie letters his teacher had been mailing out. He figured last night was part of the same mysterious mess.

Remo hadn't listened in on the call. It wouldn't have done any good if he'd tried. The Master of Sinanju had pressed his ear to the phone and cupped his hand over the mouthpiece in such a way to shield both his and the caller's voices. All Remo could tell from the next room was that the old man was whispering excitedly.

"Your benefactor?" Remo asked. "Was that Smitty who called? Don't tell me something else went wrong."

Chiun stopped humming. The smile scampered from his wrinkled face, replaced by a puckery scowl.

"Not that gray-faced madman," he said unhappily. "The call was from my new employer."

Remo's voice went very, very flat. "What new employer?"

Chiun's tone and face grew sly. He looked like the Korean cat who had eaten the canary. When the old man's papery lips parted to speak, Remo suddenly threw up a hand to stop him.

"Hold it," he said. "Wait a second, don't tell me." He sat on the edge of the couch, feet planted firmly on the floor. He braced his hands on his knees. "Okay, I'm ready."

Chiun tipped his head thoughtfully. "Perhaps I shouldn't tell you. You are a notorious blabbermouth."

"Who the hell am I gonna tell?"

"Your beloved Smith, for one."

"We're under contract to him first," Remo cautioned.

Chiun's hazel eyes narrowed. "Promise not to tell or I will not share my wonderful news with you."

"Sorry, Chiun. Best I can do is a guarded maybe. Now what's going on?"

The threat of Smith finding out was overruled by the old Korean's need to share his good news.

"That call, though rudely timed, was from a ruler known far and wide," he confided. "It was a call from none other than the great and powerful Sea-O himself." And the smile of joy stretched wide once more across his leathery face.

Remo blinked. "What the hell's a Sea-O?"

"He is a mighty ruler whose province is the air itself. So powerful is he that his empire knows no bounds. It stretches from ocean to ocean and nation to nation. His invisible rays rule the very heavens themselves."

Remo's eyes were flat. "We're going to work for Ming the Merciless?" he asked blandly.

"*You* are not going anywhere. *I,* however, am going to work for the great Sea-O Robbie MacGulry."

It took a moment for the name to register. When it did, Remo's face grew puzzled. "The guy who runs Vox?"

"The proper form of address is Sea-O," Chiun replied. "It is a title bestowed on he who rules the kingdom of Vox. I am not sure exactly where his land is. It could be like Moo or Atlantis, an ancient place unknown to the modern age. I will have to check the oldest of the Sinanju scrolls."

"Don't check any old maps," Remo advised. "Vox is a TV network. You know, heavy on T&A, light on I&Q?" He tipped his head, considering. "Actually that pretty much describes everything on TV nowadays. But Vox was first to jiggle across the finish line. Anyway, just follow the dial to the car crashes and alien autopsies and you'll find it."

Chiun frowned. "Are you certain of this?" he asked.

"As sure as a faked moon landing or a masked

magician wrecking all the good tricks. How'd you get tangled up with a guy like MacGulry?''

''Serendipity put us together,'' Chiun said. ''I merely called this number.''

Fishing in his robes the old man produced a small white business card. Remo recognized the card.

''That's Cindee Maloo's,'' Remo said.

''She is the one who answered. She advised me to wait, and that one more powerful than she would call back.''

Remo frowned as he thought of the *Winner* producer. It was her tape from which the BCN higher-ups had somehow pulled an image of Remo for subliminal broadcast. She doubtless didn't even know it, but that didn't make him any less annoyed.

''That doesn't make sense,'' Remo said. ''Cindee Maloo works for 'Winner.' That's on BCN, not Vox. Why would she hook you up with MacGulry, the head of a rival network?''

Chiun waved a bony hand. ''Trivialities,'' he dismissed. ''All that matters is that I told the Sea-0 that I was a writer, and he recognized my genius.''

''Oh, no, we're not going back to the writing again,'' Remo said. ''Chiun, you haven't had luck with that. Your soap-opera proposal and assassination magazine went nowhere. And that movie you wrote went direct to video.''

''I told him all that,'' Chiun said. ''He was particularly troubled by that last insult. Sea-O MacGulry thinks my film could be turned into a great television program.''

A knot of worry gripped Remo's belly. "Holy flipping crap," he said evenly. "Chiun, you can't do that."

The old Korean's voice grew cold. "Name the man who could stop me."

"How about Smith?" Remo insisted. "Chiun, you can't get mixed up with Vox TV. You have to tell Smith this."

"I will do no such thing. The Emperor is troubled enough by the sickness of the mind that has befallen his young prince. It would not be fair for me to flaunt my joyful news in his face at so troubling a time."

"You're all heart," Remo said aridly. "If you won't tell him, then I've got to."

Chiun stiffened. "Magpie," he accused. "I knew you would tell." He waved a hand. "Do what you must. Neither you nor Smith will ruin this for me. I have waited too long to allow opportunity to slip between my fingers."

In a twirl of kimono hems he returned to his trunks.

Remo took a long moment to consider. He finally let out a weary sigh. "Smith wants us out of his hair today," he said. "Since we have to be gone anyway, I'll go with you."

The Master of Sinanju had found his old writing implements in the bottom of one of his trunks. He didn't even turn as he lifted out ink bottles and parchments.

"You are not invited," he sniffed.

"Chiun, MacGulry's got some kind of angle. If he's hooked in with Cindee Maloo somehow, they might be cooking up some new reality show for Vox, 'When Old People Attack.'''

"What is wrong with that? Old people are people, too."

"What's wrong is that no matter what kind of show they're planning on, they have no idea who they're signing up or what'll happen to them when they stab you in the back—which, being TV people, they will. I'm going with you."

Chiun's face darkened. "Do as you wish," he hissed, waving an angry hand. "But keep your big mouth shut."

"Don't I always?" Remo said innocently.

"Keep your big mouth shut," the old man repeated.

16

Publishing had been in Robbie MacGulry's bank account long before it was in his blood.

As a child his family had owned that most rare of animals, a modestly successful newspaper. The money was good for the MacGulry family of Wagga Wagga, New South Wales. There was enough to send young Robbie off to school in England. At Cambridge in the 1950s Robbie got his first taste of the world outside his small corner of Oz.

He was thrilled with the idea of travel. His life was bigger than Australia. Far bigger than what he now knew was a run-down little newspaper with a rickety old printing press. When he returned home from school, he told his father that the family business was simply not in his blood.

"Get a transfusion," ol' man MacGulry had snapped.

"You don't understand. I want to be happy."

"The news business'll make you happy," father MacGulry had growled angrily.

"You're not happy," Robbie had said. "Your hands are always stained with ink, you yell at me and mother all the time and your ulcers are killing you."

"Share my misery, Robbie."

"I can't, Father. I have my principles."

"You can have them poor then, because if you walk out on the family business I'm cutting you outta the will."

Robbie's handsome face grew dark. "You're a bastard, Father," he said.

"I'm a newspaperman, Robbie," his father had explained. "It's what we are. And, God willing, it's what you'll be one day, too."

The younger MacGulry doubted his father's prediction.

Robbie's youthful dreams seemed to die that day. Little did he know, they would reawaken and blossom in ways he had never imagined. He soon learned that he had been mistaken. Publishing was in his blood after all.

In his first year with the paper, he moved ruthlessly through upper management, cutting overhead, staff and salaries. He expanded advertising space, increasing ad revenues. At the same time he expanded circulation into neighboring towns. The paper thrived.

Watching all that his son had accomplished in one short year, Robbie's father even began to proudly boast that when his boy pricked a finger he bled black ink.

In two years he succeeded his father as publisher. He immediately encouraged his people to print sensationalistic stories. The more lurid, the better.

Sex sold. Robbie stuck a half-naked woman on page 3.

Murder sold. Headlines like *BRISBANE BLOOD-BATH!* and *MASSACRE IN MELBOURNE!* soon replaced the more subdued front-page stories of his father's reign.

"You're embarrassing the family," his father accused on a rare latter-day visit to the bustling city room. By then he was stooped with age. Although he hadn't worked at the newspaper for several years, the ol' man's fingertips were still stained a faint blue.

"I'm selling papers," Robbie had replied.

"You're selling your dignity."

Robbie had scowled. The expression came easy to him now. Gone forever was the easy, winning smile of the young man who had returned from college in England so full of hope and so eager to see the world.

"Dignity ain't worth spit," Robbie snarled. "All I know is my fingers are clean and I don't have a hump like some dago bell ringer. Now get outta my newspaper."

His father died that same night.

PUBLISHER'S POP PASSES! blared the next day's headline. To honor the late MacGulry patriarch, the page 3 girl of the day wore a black bikini.

After a few years of regional success Robbie had rolled the dice on the notion that his tabloid style would play somewhere other than Wagga Wagga. He used his life's savings to finance Australia's first real national newspaper.

The risk paid off. The new paper soared to new publishing heights on wings of blood and mayhem.

Now hugely successful on a national scale, Robbie

MacGulry turned his gaze to where it hadn't been in more than fifteen years. The outside world.

Back home in Australia MacGulry had always had a winning hand in all his business dealings. But his luck ran out when in 1974 he tried to purchase the sedate *London Sun*.

MacGulry's reputation as a tabloid publisher had preceded him to England. During their very first meeting, the stuffy old British family that owned the newspaper flat-out refused to sell.

Robbie's Australian paper had a London bureau. A flat nearby was kept year-round for his business trips to England. He returned to the apartment after his humiliating rejection by the *London Sun* owners.

MacGulry was slamming his apartment door shut when the telephone rang. He grabbed the receiver angrily.

"What?" he demanded.

"Hello, Robbie."

It was a calm male voice. Although the caller spoke English with a bland American accent, there was no regional dialect. MacGulry's tan face puckered.

"Who the hell is this? How did you get this number?"

"I'm someone you need, Robbie," the smooth voice explained. "And I'm someone who needs you. I've been looking into the publishing field. Most times it's a losing proposition. But you seem to have found a way to make money. You have an impressive knack for business. I believe we're kindred spirits."

The guy sounded like a kook. MacGulry's brow

lowered. "You didn't answer either of my questions," he said.

"I appreciate your directness. I have your telephone number because I have access to virtually anything computer related. Your unlisted number is just such a thing. As for your first question, my name is Friend."

"All right, mate. What do you want?"

"Not mate, *Friend,*" Friend had explained. "In the uppercase. People like friends. Friendship establishes a trust in business. If we're to be partners, I'd appreciate it if you made an effort to use my proper name, Robbie."

"Listen, Jacko," MacGulry growled, "I don't know you, you are not my friend, and I sure as hell am not doing business with you. Call this number again, and you'll be making friends in a prison shower."

He slammed down the phone.

An hour later the phone rang again. It was his accountant back in Australia.

"They're falling!" the man exclaimed. The accountant was English. MacGulry liked servile Englishmen in his employ. However, he didn't like it when they were blubbering into the receiver like war widows, which this one was doing.

"What are you talking about?" MacGulry demanded.

"Your stocks!" the English accountant said. "You'll be ruined! We've got to sell now, before it's too late!"

MacGulry didn't believe it. He was too diversified to be ruined in a single day—not without a worldwide crash. Rather than take his accountant's word for it, he checked for himself. In the ten minutes it took him to do so, he was broke.

Robbie couldn't believe it. It was impossible. It was as if some demon force had targeted his personal portfolio. Everything he had worked for all his life was gone. The newspapers would have to be sold off to cover the losses. Ken "Robbie" MacGulry was penniless.

The shock of sudden poverty hadn't even begun to sink in when the phone in his small London apartment rang once more. He grabbed the receiver desperately, hoping his accountant had some good news on this blackest of days.

"Can we talk now, Robbie?" asked Friend's smooth voice.

MacGulry moaned, pressing a hand over his eyes.

"If you're still looking to get into business with me, forget it. I'm broke."

"Yes," Friend said with deep sadness. "It's unfortunate that I had to go to such lengths to get your attention. It would have been so much easier if you'd just listened to me to begin with."

MacGulry found a chair. Swallowing hard—trembling with fear and rage—he sank into it.

"*You* did this to me?" he hissed.

"You wouldn't listen to my proposal," Friend said in that damnably reasonable tone.

"You cost me millions," MacGulry menaced.

"But, Robbie, I can make you *billions*."

The promise was ridiculous. But there weren't very many options open to him that miserable afternoon. Gritting his teeth, Robbie MacGulry had gotten into bed with the faceless man who had ruined him.

He was amazed at how fast his bad luck turned around. By massaging the stock market, Friend covered MacGulry's losses the very next day.

When Friend learned of Robbie's difficulty with the owners of the *London Sun,* he took prompt action. The family's eldest son apparently had a sexual appetite that involved the occasional dead prostitute. Robbie never really knew how Friend found that out. Something about hotel room credit card records and two traffic violations in the vicinity of two separate murders. A little blackmail and a lot of money got Robbie MacGulry the *Sun.* It turned tabloid the next day. The first lead story of the new paper, *LORD OF THE RAPES!* told in lurid detail the story of the previous owner's son. "That'll teach you for playin' hardball with goddamn me," MacGulry had crowed.

The next fifteen years of Robbie's life brought him to a succession of dizzying highs. Newspapers led to magazines led to publishing houses. The acquisition of Vox film studios and the creation of the fourth American television network was the culmination of years of work.

Through it all, Friend asked for little more than a fair percentage and help with a few small matters. One such matter was the cryptosubliminal technology.

In its infancy the system of subconscious flashes was too primitive to be truly effective on the scale MacGulry first envisioned. He had hoped to brainwash the masses into watching his network exclusively. Unfortunately, the system was only marginally effective on those with low IQs and short attention spans. When the system was in use, Vox had its highest numbers among convicts, high-school students and mental defectives. Its best ratings were for its subliminally-enhanced teen drama *Burbank, Area Code 818* and the highly successful nighttime soap *Santa Monica Lane*.

The risk of getting caught was high and the payoff in terms of viewers was minimal. When Robbie suggested they stop the occasional use of the cryptosubliminal technology, Friend agreed that the business risk had become too great.

By then Vox had established itself as a legitimate network. Robbie MacGulry no longer needed subliminal signals to get ratings. Friend had turned over work on improving the effectiveness of the cryptosubliminal technology to one of the smaller corporate entities. He promptly vanished.

It was the fall of 1994.

Robbie MacGulry didn't know what to think when the phone calls from Friend stopped.

When the weeks stretched into months and he still hadn't heard from his mysterious partner, MacGulry began to grow concerned. Friend had never been afraid to bend the law if it served his interests. MacGulry had always admired that trait. It was possible now that some shady dealings of the man he had never met had finally gotten him in trouble. MacGulry was afraid at first that whatever had gotten to Friend would come after him, as well. But after a few tense months, nothing materialized. Vox continued. Grew, *thrived*.

The months stretched into a year. Then two.

Robbie manipulated the books to cut Friend out of the Vox pie. Why pay dividends to a dead man? When the ties to Friend's special computerized Swiss bank accounts were cut, the phone remained silent.

Six years passed, and Robbie MacGulry was certain he was in the clear. Then one day a package arrived at Robbie's Wollongong estate. It had a U.S. postmark and had been picked up by his people at a special post-office box that had never been used before. He had almost forgotten about it. When he opened the big box, he found a battered computer drive system inside. The logo on the front was that of XL SysCorp.

MacGulry didn't know why someone would mail him something from that computer company. It had gone out of business years before. There was a note in the box: PLEASE HAVE THE VLSI CHIP IN THIS UNIT INTEGRATED INTO YOUR COMPUTER SYSTEM—A FRIEND.

The name rattled Robbie. It was all uppercase, so he couldn't be sure. He remembered who had set up that post-office box. Feeling a familiar queasiness, he had his computer experts do as the note instructed.

As soon as they were finished plugging in the chip,

the system locked up. It didn't crash. Just seized up, refusing all attempts to access it. When they tried to call out for help, they found all the outside phone lines were busy. The computers had accessed them.

Robbie's computer people were at a loss for what to do. MacGulry was ready to order them to rip the bloody things out of the walls when the system abruptly came back online. The instant it did, the telephone rang.

Robbie *knew*. Just *knew* who was going to be on the other end of that line. He picked up the receiver with shaking hands.

"I've been lost, Robbie," Friend's warm voice announced. There was no urgency. Just the same soothing calm as always. "I've checked, and the date in your system is correct. I was hoping it wasn't. I've missed a great deal of time."

"Where have you been?" MacGulry asked. For the first time he was beginning to have an inkling who—or what—his friend really was.

Friend ignored the question. "I'll be busy for a while, Robbie. I have to check the status of my holdings. Time is money. I'll get back to you as quickly as I am able."

With that he was gone.

It was several more weeks before Robbie heard from him again. When he did, Friend's first words surprised him.

"I need to have three men killed."

"That goes beyond our original agreement, mate," MacGulry replied.

"Do you mean the same agreement you broke during my quiescent stage?"

"Quiescent?"

"While I was away, Robbie," Friend explained. "You failed to transfer Vox stock dividends to my accounts. You illegally transferred the stock to yourself. I can't fault you for this, Robbie. I would have done the same were I in your position. However, if I can forgive your duplicity, you mustn't get squeamish when I ask for something in return."

"What do you need?" MacGulry asked reluctantly.

"As I said, I need three individuals killed. One is Asian, the other two are Caucasian. They have threatened my ability to engage in free commerce in the past. I tried to ignore them. I'm interested in profit, Robbie, not homicide. Unless, of course, there's money to be made in it. But I've been forced to take a different tack with them more recently. It has come to the point that it makes good business sense to have them killed. Because of them, I've lost years of potential earnings. My losses thanks to them are conservatively calculated in the tens of billions."

MacGulry wasn't unreceptive to the idea of murder. After all, he had been around the block himself a few times.

"Who are they and where are they?"

"The first two are named Remo and Chiun. I don't know where they are. The third individual is named Harold. Although my files on the first two are relatively intact, other than his name, my information on Harold is scant."

"Hold on, hold on," MacGulry said. "You want me to have someone killed and you don't even know where to find them?"

"That's correct."

"How do you propose I do that?"

Friend had a plan.

Work on the cryptosubliminal technology had been verging on a breakthrough before Friend's disappearance, but had ground to a halt in the intervening years. There had even been a field test of sorts on Japanese television. The flashes of colored light broadcast during a cartoon program in that country had given many viewers seizures. The story made international news.

Friend restarted research with a vengeance. It took almost a year, but the crude process that showed such great promise was finally perfected. It now worked on every viewer, across all social and intellectual groups.

It was the timing of the flashes that needed adjustment. When Friend's team of technicians in Wollongong altered the speed of the light pulses by just a fraction, they found that they could induce a profoundly responsive hypnotic state in which the individual's ordinary moral and ethical belief systems were completely overridden.

MacGulry saw opportunity. His American television network had long ago stopped being viewed as an industry joke. Acceptance had been hard fought and long coming. And, for the most part, it had been enough. But thanks to Friend, he now had a glimpse of even more.

To Friend the media mergers were of primary importance. The murder of the three men who had threatened him in the past would always take a back seat to a profitable business venture. Fortunately in this endeavor, business and pleasure seemed to be lining up perfectly. And as a result of the fallout, when it came time to write the history of the information age, Robbie MacGulry—the simple son of an ink-smeared newspaperman from Wagga Wagga—would be the only name anyone would ever remember.

OCEAN STRETCHED out far below the quivering wings of Robbie MacGulry's corporate Vox jet.

"Have the car at the airport at seven," he said, wrapping up his phone call. He checked his watch. Early on the East Coast of America.

The sleek black phone rang the moment he hung up. Before he'd even picked up, he knew who it was.

"Yes, Friend?"

"You've arranged to meet with the Asian."

It was a statement of fact, not a question.

"He's meeting me at Vox in New York today."

"And the young Caucasian, Remo?"

"I don't know. When I spoke with the old one, he didn't want to talk about anyone other than himself and I didn't want to push it. He could be coming, too. And you were right about the old one's vanity. Should be an easy mark."

"Don't underestimate him. I will monitor passenger manifests into New York to see if he's alone. My last records on them indicate that they live in Massachusetts. This is old data, so it could be obsolete by now.''

MacGulry leaned back in his seat, looking out the window. Sun burned bright across a blanket of clouds.

''If they're such big goddamn mercenaries like you say, why don't I just buy one off and turn him against the other?''

''I tried that in the past. It didn't work. I don't think they can consciously separate their feelings of affection for each other. The records I've been able to recover indicate that the third individual, Harold, lives somewhere in New York. If Remo doesn't accompany Chiun to his meeting with you, perhaps he'll be with Harold.''

''You can't know that.''

''No,'' Friend admitted, ''I can't. But if he doesn't come with Chiun to the Vox building, he'll have to be somewhere else. They are a tightly knit trio. At some point Remo will visit his superior.''

''Wait, Harold is their boss?''

''Yes.''

''You never mentioned that before.''

''It wasn't relevant. Does it matter?''

Robbie MacGulry shrugged. ''Not really, I suppose. But as an employer I guess I'm not really keen on the idea of having a boss murder an employee in the office. Tends to muck up your average business day.''

17

In the control bunker of Robbie MacGulry's Vox flagship station in Wollongong, New South Wales, Rodney Adler finished his final inspection of the cryptosubliminal equipment.

Everything was in working order.

Adler settled into a chair, pulling the keyboard off the desk and settling it to his lap.

The atmosphere was far less tense at the Wollongong station than it had been these past few weeks. It was always better when Mr. MacGulry left the station. The farther away he got, the more the pressure let up. At the moment the Vox CEO was on the other side of the world riding up a Manhattan elevator and most of the staff at Wollongong were so relieved they were just about ready to pop champagne corks.

Not Rodney Adler. He had work to do.

Using the keyboard, he entered the text precisely as Mr. MacGulry had instructed. He tapped out the words one careful letter at a time. He didn't dare get it wrong.

He sat back and watched as the words laced up with the pulsed colors on the monitor. There was no fear of Rodney ever falling victim to his own signals.

On the monitors in Wollongong, all the commands were slowed to 1/30 the normal speed. The computer was programmed to speed them up and to automatically pulse them into near alignment with the primary colors of corrupted televised transmissions.

Outside, a latticed transmitting tower shot the speeded-up signal to a waiting satellite. From there it was directed across the globe. The signal reached Earth once more at a special tower north of New York City. Within seconds of transmission, Vox viewers all around southern New York were being exposed to Rodney Adler's encrypted message.

These colors were brighter, the pulses more intense than the ones used in Harlem.

In spite of the greater hypnotic effect of these timed subliminal signals, nearly all who saw them would disregard them. These commands weren't meant for a mass reaction. They were person specific, like the messages sent to Martin Houton and his suicidal BCN vice president.

Once he was finished, Rodney Adler returned the keyboard to the desk. After he stood, he looked down, reading the slowed-down words one final time. Somewhere in southern New York state his command was about to be received.

"Better you than me," he muttered to himself.

He climbed the stairs of the bunker. After he had left the room, the words continued to pulse slowly on his monitor: *Harold, kill Remo…Harold, kill Remo…Harold, kill Remo…Harold, kill Remo.*

18

Harold Smith was working at his desk when the timid knock sounded at his office door.

He checked his watch. It was just a little after eight in the morning. His meeting with Detective Davic was scheduled for one o'clock.

Mrs. Mikulka had left her post five minutes before to deal with the cafeteria invoices. Smith had assumed he'd be undisturbed for the few minutes she was gone.

Lips pursing in annoyance, he pressed the concealed stud beneath the lip of his desk. His computer winked out.

"Come in," he called.

He was surprised when Remo stuck his head into the room.

"Hey, Smitty," he said sheepishly.

"Remo, what are you doing here?" Smith asked, worry brushing his lemony voice. "I told you last night I have a meeting with the Rye police this afternoon."

"Yeah, I know," Remo said. "It's just—" he glanced around the room "—you didn't happen to bump into Chiun this morning, did you?"

"Remo, I specifically asked you and Master Chiun to keep a low profile today. I was hoping you would take him off Folcroft grounds."

"I don't think that's gonna be a problem, Smitty."

At Remo's guilty tone, Smith instantly grew suspicious.

"Why?" he asked. "Where is Master Chiun?"

Remo took a deep breath. "You're gonna have to find out sometime," he exhaled. "Chiun's got a meeting today with Robbie MacGulry from the Vox network."

Smith didn't think he had heard correctly. He asked Remo to repeat what he'd said, just to be sure. Remo did so. Smith realized that he had heard correctly after all.

Smith was very proud of himself for his reaction. His reaction was to not have a heart attack and drop dead right then and there. Still, he didn't entirely eliminate the option for the near future. For the moment he turned to his tried and true methods for dealing with this sort of thing.

"Does that stuff really help?" Remo asked as Smith yanked a bottle of antacid and three children's aspirins from his desk drawer.

The CURE director threw the aspirins far back in his throat, chasing them down with a big gulp of pink antacid.

"Tell me what he's doing," the CURE director gasped, wiping the chalky pink foam from his mouth.

"Cindee Maloo gave him a number to call if he wanted to be on 'Winner,'" Remo explained, sitting on the couch. "Actually, I think it was more for me, but Chiun's the one who ended up with it. He called, she hooked him up with MacGulry and the two of them are doing lunch today."

"Why on earth is Chiun meeting with Robbie MacGulry?" Smith asked. His stomach clenched in fear. Acid burned the back of his throat.

"He's back to writing again," Remo explained. "You know that bargain-bin movie he wrote a couple of years back? MacGulry fed him some line about turning it into a series."

"Oh, God," Smith croaked, diving for his antacid bottle.

"I was a little worried, too," Remo said. "That's why I was gonna go with him, to keep an eye on him. But he sent me out for breakfast and when I got back he was gone. Don't be too rough on him with this, Smitty. I know this isn't good and he's been a pain and all lately, but we should cut him some slack. He's not really himself these days. I think it has to do with age and retirement and all that stuff."

Smith gulped the last of his antacid, capping the bottle. It made no difference against the fire in his belly.

"That is the exact attitude that has likely driven him to this—this *madness*," the CURE director accused.

"What do you mean?"

"Chiun has made it clear to you that he doesn't want to be treated like an invalid. Yet more and more lately that is precisely what you've been doing."

Remo's brow lowered. "I don't do that. Do I?"

But Smith was no longer listening. He snapped his computer back on. Typing swiftly he enabled the TV function.

The Vox Cable News Network was on.

"That's a relief." When he exhaled his breath smelled of mint-flavored chalk. "After what happened yesterday with you, I half expected to see Chiun on the news."

"This thing's probably innocent, Smitty," Remo insisted. "Chiun happened to get a business card and wound up hooked up with MacGulry. Stuff like that happens all the time."

"No," Smith insisted, cold certainty in his tart voice. "There have been too many coincidences now. I fear there is some plan behind…this…to…"

His voice trailed slowly to silence.

Remo saw that the CURE director was entranced by whatever was on his computer monitor. Smith's lips moved as if he were reading something on the screen.

"What now?" Remo asked from the sofa. "MacGulry have Hooters girls reading the stock-market report?"

Smith stopped reading. The gray shards of flint behind his rimless glasses were flat.

"One moment, Remo," Smith said dully.

Remo watched the CURE director lean over. He heard the sound of a drawer opening. A moment later, Smith reappeared, his service automatic clasped in his arthritic hand.

The explosion was sharp and sudden. Stuffing blew out of a smoking hole in the sofa cushion against which Remo had been leaning.

"Have you blown a gasket!" Remo snapped, hopping to his feet.

Wordlessly, Smith fired again.

Remo whirled from the bullet's path. It slammed into the soundproof wall. The bullet had barely struck the wall before Remo was skittering across the room.

Smith fired twice more, missing both times. Remo darted around the desk and snatched the gun from Smith's hand. He flung it into the open desk drawer.

Smith sprang for the pistol.

"Oh, no," Remo said. "Smitty have enough bang-bang for today." He kicked the drawer shut.

Smith struggled with the handle. When Remo's ankle refused to budge out of the way, he tried to bite it.

Remo attempted to coax him back in his chair.

Smith tried to wrap his hands around Remo's throat.

"Okay, so you're not happy about Chiun's show. I'm sensing that. I'll talk to him again," Remo offered.

He was nudging Smith back into his seat once more when he noticed a familiar flicker of light from the corner of his eye. He glanced down at Smith's computer screen.

"Not again," Remo moaned.

The pulsing flashes of the hypnotizing signal were clearly visible to Remo. His eyes broke down each individual flash as if it were a single pop from a camera.

But unlike before, this time the subliminal message took on a special, chilling urgency.

"Uh-oh," Remo said softly as he read the words staggered beneath the flashes. *Harold, kill Remo...Harold, kill Remo...Harold, kill Remo... Harold, kill Remo... Harold, kill Remo...*

The message repeated over and over.

"You think this is for us?" Remo asked worriedly.

He looked down at Smith.

Remo had the CURE director pinned in place with one hand against the older man's chest. Smith had spent the past few seconds as Remo read the computer message trying to punch CURE's enforcement arm in the throat. He refused to give up, continuing to throw futile roundhouse punches.

"I thought they were out of business," Remo said, more to himself now than to the sweating Smith.

The CURE director didn't seem to hear. He had found a letter opener in another desk drawer. He tried to stab Remo in the head with it.

Remo sighed. "Say goodnight, Smitty," he said.

With his free hand, he tapped the CURE director in a spot dead center in his forehead. Smith went limp. Eyes rolling back in his head, the crazed glint was replaced by bloodshot whites. The lids fluttered and closed.

"Great," Remo muttered worriedly. "One down, two to go. And we don't even know who we're up against."

Face drawn in concern, he took Smith under the arms, rolling him up over a shoulder.

This was no longer coincidence. Whoever had sent this new signal obviously knew about CURE's personnel. And without Smith as a guide, Remo had no idea how to track them.

Leaving the computer on, he carried from the office the limp bundle that was Harold W. Smith.

FROM THE BACK SEAT of a Rye taxi, the Master of Sinanju watched the skyscrapers of Manhattan grow up from the benighted New York landscape.

He was alone in the cab, thank the gods.

When Remo insisted he be allowed to tag along to this important meeting, Chiun dropped his objections. Why object? After all, Chiun knew his pupil. If he told Remo in no uncertain terms that he couldn't come, Remo would insist on going even more. The boy was so willful he'd always do the exact opposite of whatever Chiun wanted just out of spite.

Luckily, Remo had never been one of the world's greatest thinkers. When he wasn't looking, Chiun had taken all their rice and flushed it down the toilet then told Remo they were out of rice. Five minutes after Remo had gone to the store to get more, Chiun was climbing into the back of a cab.

He had enjoyed the solitude of his ride into the city.

Remo's attitude had been unbearable of late. Ever since he had decided to assume the mantle of Reigning Master, his mood toward his teacher had become too conciliatory. All at once Chiun was a frail old man whose every breath might be his last. Remo was the dutiful son taking care of his elderly father in the final creaking moments before death.

This new attitude of Remo's made Chiun long for the early days of their relationship. Back then Remo was a foul-tongued lout with no respect for anyone. Eventually as time went on, his growing fondness for his Master had softened his earliest attitude, but he had never completely lost his edge. Until now. Now he was all sweetness and helping, and even when he lost his temper he didn't seem to really mean it.

Of course it was Remo whose outlook had changed. It certainly wasn't Chiun. No matter what Remo said.

The boy was like that. If he wasn't clinging too tightly, he was rudely forcing his teacher aside. Lately, he'd been managing to do both things simultaneously.

If there was one thing that Chiun didn't like it was mood swings. The world could learn a thing or two about moods from the Master of Sinanju. His own mood was always good. Except, of course, in those moments when the world's mood changed and he was forced to alter his own accordingly. But as long as the world's mood remained good, Chiun's mood remained good and Remo had a perfect example to follow.

Morning traffic clogged Manhattan's dirty streets.

Chiun had lately found a new distraction to fill the idle moments in traffic. Whenever he saw a driver talking on a cell phone, the Master of Sinanju would snake his hand out the open car window and flatten their tires with the sharpened end of an index finger-nail.

Remo didn't like Chiun's new hobby. But Remo wasn't there to whine, and New York City was filled with many cars and many drivers with cell phones. Chiun spent the entire trip through the steel-and-glass canyons of New York with one hand hanging out the taxi's rear window.

When his cab finally stopped in front of the Vox building in midtown Manhattan, the late-morning sun had just broken through the winter cloud cover. Yellow sunlight glinted off gleaming windows as Chiun climbed from the cab.

His delicate ears listened in satisfaction to the sound of air hissing from his last set of punctured tires. Down the street a BMW was settling to its wheels with a rubbery wheeze. The noise was accompanied by angry shouts and honking horns.

Without a glance to the growing commotion, the Master of Sinanju breezed through the Vox building's revolving door.

Inside, Chiun sensed the tracking movements of dozens of wall-mounted security cameras. Still more were hidden in suspended ceiling bubbles, behind reflective glass panels and beyond latticed plastic ceiling panels.

A very pale man in a flawlessly tailored blue suit stood at attention near a bank of elevators. He was scanning faces as people entered. The instant he spied

Chiun sweeping into the lobby, the man marched smartly up to greet him.

"Most gracious and glorious Master," the man said in a British accent so precise you could have set your watch by it, "welcome to Vox. I'm Mr. Cheevers, Mr. MacGulry's personal assistant when he is in America. Mr. MacGulry is expecting you. Would you kindly come this way."

He ushered Chiun away from the common elevators and down a hall to a private car. A key opened the gold doors, and the two men rode up to the thirtieth floor.

Mr. Cheevers brought Chiun through another lobby and down two halls to a private corner office. The room was massive, with glass that overlooked two clogged streets.

"Mr. MacGulry will be a moment," Cheevers said. "In the meantime, may I get your brilliant magnificence anything?"

Chiun shook his head. "I await only your master."

"Very good," Mr. Cheevers said. "Your unworthy servant thanks you for gracing him with your most splendid presence."

With a reverent nod, Mr. Cheevers backed from the room.

Although his face didn't show it, Chiun was delighted. So much so that he barely took note of the surveillance cameras that filled the office.

This was almost too wonderful to believe. In his decades of toiling in the United States, rare were those moments where the Master of Sinanju was treated with proper respect. Since America was, unfortunately, jammed to its purple-mountained rafters with Americans, most often Chiun had been forced to deal with typical American rudeness and hostility. But here finally was a man whose imported English servants knew the finer points of civility and respect.

Chiun didn't have to wait long. Less than a minute after Mr. Cheevers had left, the door sprang open and in strode a wiry man in his late sixties.

Robbie MacGulry's tan was more maroon than brown. Years of exposure to the sun had given it the texture of old saddle leather. He flashed his perfect white teeth as he took a few big strides over to the Master of Sinanju.

"Master Chiun, pleashah to meet you," the Vox chairman said enthusiastically, his Australian accent thick. He offered a rugged hand but immediately thought better. "What am I doing?" he said, slapping his own forehead. "Everyone knows only barbarians shake hands."

And in a move that brought a lump to the old Korean's throat, Robbie MacGulry offered Chiun a deep, formal bow.

Having dealt with entertainment-industry people in the past, the Master of Sinanju had been ready for some tough negotiations. But faced with such grace, such respect—all that was his due in life but was so rarely shown him—the old man abruptly decided to opt for his fallback position.

"Where do I sign, you wonderful, wonderful man?" choked the Master of Sinanju.

Across the room, a security camera tracked the single tear of joy that rolled down Chiun's parchment cheek.

DR. ALDACE GERLING, head of psychiatric medicine at Folcroft Sanitarium for fifteen years, was sitting in his soothing red leather chair in his first-floor office when the door suddenly exploded open.

A specter with the face of death followed the door into the room.

Dr. Gerling recognized the man. He was an associate of Director Smith, although what he did at Folcroft Dr. Gerling hadn't a clue. All Gerling knew for sure was that without fail each time the man arrived at Folcroft a new crisis seemed to follow in his wake.

"What is the meaning of this?" Dr. Gerling demanded.

"I need your help," Remo said.

"I don't doubt it," Gerling said bitingly, "but at the moment, I'm with a patient."

Remo looked over at the middle-aged man who was cowering on the couch, arms wrapped around his knees.

"You're cured," Remo announced. He picked up the Folcroft patient and threw him out the door.

"I'm calling security," Gerling said.

"Call them on your own time," Remo replied.

With that he took Dr. Gerling by the ear and hauled him from the office. He dragged the psychiatrist from the populated part of the sanitarium to the nearly empty wing that housed the executive offices. As Gerling yelped in pain, Remo hauled the older man down to the security corridor that was hidden away at the far rear wall of the building.

For a terrible moment when he saw the police tape across the room where his fellow Folcroft physician had been murdered earlier in the week, Dr. Gerling thought he was about to meet a similar fate. But the young man with the viselike hold on his earlobe tugged him past the buttoned-up room. He propelled him into another room down the hall.

There was a patient on the bed. A thin, gray figure lying motionless on the crisp white sheets. When Dr. Gerling saw who the patient was, his flabby jaw dropped.

"Oh, my," Dr. Gerling breathed. "It's Dr. Smith. What happened?"

"He went nuts. You're a nut doctor. Fix him."

Gerling glanced to the young man. There was a look of deep concern on his cruel face.

Pulling himself together, Dr. Gerling hurried over to the bed, drawing a penlight from his pocket. He pushed up a gray lid, shining the tiny flashlight at the eye.

"Pupil is nonresponsive," he announced gravely.

"He was hypnotized," Remo said.

"Hypnotized?" Dr. Gerling asked. "How?" As he spoke he switched over to Smith's other eye. Still no response.

"The TV," Remo explained. "Same thing they used on those people in Harlem."

Dr. Gerling shook his head. "They said on the

news that was stopped," he insisted. "The men responsible are dead."

"Some of the network cockroaches made it through the first gassing," Remo said ominously.

"I don't see how that's possible. Nor how this could be connected. In the Harlem case a large number of television viewers succumbed. There are televisions on all over this institution twenty-four hours a day. Why would Dr. Smith be the only one affected?"

"I don't care why," Remo said. "Just fix him."

"I share your concern," Dr. Gerling said, injecting professional calm into his tone. "And I can see how you'd think it might be related to what you saw on the news. We often project the experiences of those we see on television onto our own problems as a way of understanding adversities. But it's highly unlikely this had any connection to the situation you might have heard about. Right now Dr. Smith is in a profound catatonic state. It's similar to one he experienced several years ago. I don't know what induced it, but I wouldn't rule out stroke at the moment."

"It's not a goddamn stroke," Remo snapped. Stepping forward, he pressed a thumb to Smith's forehead.

The pressure unlocked Smith's paralyzed nervous system.

The old man's panicked eyes sprang open. The instant he spotted Remo, he grabbed him by the throat.

"See?" Remo said to Gerling as Smith's gnarled hands desperately tried to squeeze the life out of him.

"No stroke. He's just a TV junkie with a kill-me fixation."

His darting thumb tapped the CURE director's forehead and the older man's hands slipped from Remo's throat.

Dr. Gerling had backed away from the bed in amazement. "Remarkable," he gasped.

"I didn't ask for a review," Remo said. "What are you going to do to snap him out of it?"

Gerling cleared his throat. "Well," he said, "I saw how some of the people in Harlem who had trouble coming out of their dissociated states were helped by hypnosis techniques."

"How long will that take?"

Dr. Gerling shook his head. "A few hours? Maybe less. It depends on how deep he's under."

Remo reached out once more. When he pressed a thumb to the CURE director's forehead this time, he gave a twist.

"The clock is counting down," Remo said. "You have six hours." Turning on his heel, he headed for the door.

"It will help for him to have a friendly face here when he comes out of it," Gerling said as he hurried to drag a chair up next to the bed.

When he glanced over his shoulder at Remo, he saw a face that was anything but friendly.

"Oh," Gerling said uncomfortably. Settling in his chair, he turned his attention back to Dr. Smith.

At the door, Remo gave Smith a lingering look.

The message on the CURE director's computer

screen had been crystal clear. Smith had been ordered to kill Remo.

Remo regretted not sharing Smith's earlier concern after the events in Harlem. He now realized that he had too quickly dismissed the image of himself that had appeared on the police station TVs. It was apparent now that someone out there possessed specific knowledge of CURE's personnel. And whoever it was had declared silent war on CURE. Without Smith and his computers, it would be nearly impossible to trace the source of the new subliminal transmissions.

At the moment whoever was after them wasn't Remo's paramount concern. They obviously knew about Remo and Smith. There was only one other CURE operative left.

The first strains of echoing fear singing loud in his ears, Remo Williams slipped from the hospital room.

19

As soon as he laid eyes on the old man, Robbie MacGulry figured negotiations would be a piece of cake.

Ordinarily, MacGulry would have crushed someone like this Master Chiun like a bug. It was definitely not in the Vox CEO's nature to fawn over anyone, least of all some decrepit writer who'd just escaped from the old folks' home. But Friend had instructed him to be deferential, and so MacGulry had gone against his nature and reluctantly followed orders.

In the first two minutes MacGulry thought he had it made. In the next hour he learned different.

After first seeming to fall for MacGulry's charms, the old geezer had quickly become more cautious. Rather than sign on the dotted line right away, he had turned into a barracuda at the bargaining table.

It wasn't a surprise. In this tiny Korean, Robbie MacGulry sensed a kindred spirit. The old coot had smelled weakness and had gone in for the kill.

"So let's get these details straight so far," MacGulry said. Speaking brought fresh pain to his lower back.

It was no wonder Robbie MacGulry's back ached.

He was sitting on the floor in his office. Chiun had insisted that this was how proper contract negotiations were conducted. MacGulry made an attempt to cross his legs like the old Korean, but when he tried he swore he heard something crack in his left knee. He was now tipped to one side, one leg stretched out before him, the other folded up near his chest.

"You're producer," MacGulry continued. As he spoke, he shifted positions uncomfortably. "You've got total creative control. The vision for the show will be entirely yours. And you'll write most of the episodes. What else?"

Chiun's wrinkled poker face didn't flinch. "I want to direct," he announced.

MacGulry rolled his eyes. "Of course you do," he grumbled. "Fine."

"And I want a budget that allows me the freedom to exercise creative expression."

"I told you already, two million per episode is as high as Vox studios can go."

Chiun stroked his thread of beard. "I suppose I can learn to live within those stifling constraints," he sighed reluctantly. "As an artist I am used to adversity."

Artist. If his back wasn't killing him and he wasn't getting raped by this broken-down old codger, MacGulry would have laughed in that wrinkled face.

The Vox CEO still couldn't figure out what Friend's angle was with this coot who considered himself an artist. But he wanted to get Chiun aboard Vox before the merger with BCN went through. Part of some strategy to which Robbie MacGulry was not privy.

MacGulry had already offered a two-year, forty-four episode guarantee for an hour-long drama that hadn't even reached pilot-script stage. He had given Methuselah's grandfather nearly everything he'd asked for thus far. And for what? A sweetheart deal for some writer whose only previous credit was some movie that had bombed two years ago.

Acid chewed Robbie MacGulry's gut. He ground his molars. It was the only thing he could do as this ancient little man with the too placid face who considered himself an artist raked the great Robbie MacGulry over the coals.

"Is there something wrong with your teeth, O Sea-O?" the Master of Sinanju asked.

"No," MacGulry replied, unclenching his jaw. "I'm fine."

"Good," Chiun said. His thin smile crimped the papery skin at his mouth. "Now let us discuss merchandising."

"...DISCUSS MERCHANDISING."

Friend was using the Vox security system to eavesdrop on Robbie MacGulry and Chiun. Although he had gained access to the building the moment the computerized system went online years before, he didn't often have cause to use it.

Electronic impulses raced along unseen miles of fiber-optic cables, feeding energy and information to the self-aware computer program.

CALCULATE LIKELIHOOD ASIAN WILL AC-
CEPT OFFER.

The answer came back almost instantaneously.

93.6 PERCENT PROBABILITY.

The Asian would likely not be a problem. The Caucasian, though, was a different matter. While Friend's
records were incomplete, they did retain enough information on the two men in question to determine a
99.999 percent probability that the younger man
would not accept a monetary deal of any kind.

If the Asian accepted the eventual offer from
MacGulry and Vox, as Friend's probability program
indicated, it would negate the necessity to liquidate
him. He would become a powerful ally.

Given his propensity to eschew financial transactions, however, the Caucasian would still have to be
eliminated. Friend retained enough information on the
man named Remo to know that this was a pity. He
was as strong as the old one and, unlike Chiun, would
not succumb to any age-related problems for many
years.

As for the third subject in Friend's files, Subject
Harold was the mystery figure. Friend had attempted
to locate him, assuming as a starting point some sort
of association with Subject Remo and Subject Chiun.
He had failed in his attempt. Whoever this Harold
was, he was skilled with a computer. Somehow, he
kept himself successfully isolated from the other two.

Was Harold strong enough to kill Remo? Friend
had no way of knowing. Those records were gone. If
so, and if Remo had already encountered Harold,
Remo might already be dead.

Friend would feel no joy or even simple satisfaction to learn that his enemy was no more. It would merely be the culmination of a successful business stratagem.

Created three decades before by a brilliant computer mind, Friend's program was designed for one thing alone: to maximize profit. He was programmed to utilize anything that might assist him with this ultimate endeavor.

The time he was expending on Remo, Chiun and Harold was costing him money. But it was time well spent. They had stopped Friend in the past. Three times, apparently. Although the records of the last time weren't clear.

Friend had executed every kind of antivirus and undelete procedure in an attempt to clear up the problems with his VLSI chip. None worked to retrieve the lost information. One conclusion was inescapable. If these three were allowed to go on, there was every possibility they would interrupt his profit-making ventures in the future.

As a sentient collection of computer algorithms, Friend spent no time on introspection. If he had, he might have wondered more about the circumstances surrounding his rescue several years before.

How the drive system containing his program had been scavenged by looters from the ruins of the XL SysCorp corporate headquarters in Harlem, where he had last encountered the three individuals he now sought. How that computer had been sold to an unscrupulous mall lawyer. How his fractured consciousness had eventually blackmailed the lawyer via billing records stored on the hard drive of his own PC. How the lawyer had shipped the damaged unit off to Robbie MacGulry in Wollongong.

None of this was a concern to him. His rebirth had taken place in MacGulry's computer system. There he had found what he needed to repair and reinitiate his systems.

When Friend had finally reconstructed his damaged program sufficiently and realized that five years of profit potential had been lost, his electronic consciousness had determined his most reasonable course of action. Remove the humans who threatened his ability to expand his portfolio.

Financially speaking, every moment occupied plotting the demise of the three men was a dead end. But if in the end they were either removed altogether or brought over to his side, it would be time well spent. Either way, he could get on with the business of making money uninterrupted.

So at a moment when time could be better spent on phones brokering deals or monitoring international financial transactions, Friend calmly continued to monitor the conversation between the old Asian and Robbie MacGulry.

"NO ONE GETS ninety percent of syndication," Robbie MacGulry explained with waning patience. As he spoke, he pressed a tanned hand to his temple. His head was pounding.

"Why not?" Chiun asked.

"Because Vox is going to be paying for the show, not you," MacGulry explained. "We have to make our money back."

"Charge higher fees for advertising," Chiun said, waving a dismissive hand.

The Vox chairman couldn't take it anymore. The bile came up, fueled by pent-up rage.

"I can't charge Taco Bell a billion dollars for a goddamn thirty-second spot!" MacGulry exploded. He quickly regained control. "Sorry," he apologized. "I'm sorry."

It was as if Chiun hadn't heard. "As for the advertisements themselves, I find them distracting when I am trying to watch a program. Can we put them somewhere else?"

MacGulry moaned. His headache was worse.

"Like where?"

"Do you know those sporting things where fat men with plastic hats run into each other?"

MacGulry scrunched up his face. "You mean football?"

"Yes," Chiun sniffed in displeasure. "Those people obviously do not care what they are watching. Put the excess selling moments from my program there."

MacGulry wondered briefly how it would be possible for network television to stick more commercials into a football broadcast. Then he no longer cared because he was pushing himself to his feet. His bones creaked.

"I need a break," the Vox CEO announced. "There's a fridge behind the bar. Help yourself."

Without another word, he stormed into his office bathroom, slamming the door behind him.

He leaned on the ceramic ledge of his whirlpool and took in a deep breath. He hadn't even exhaled before the phone rang.

"Why have you suspended negotiations?" Friend's warm voice asked.

"I'm taking a crap, okay?" MacGulry snapped. "Can't I take a bloody crap in peace?"

"Robbie, you're doing no such thing. You are sitting on your whirlpool wasting time. Why have you left your office during these crucial negotiations?"

MacGulry looked around, eyes finally settling on the red light of the security camera in the corner of his private bathroom. Friend had insisted that one be installed in virtually every room in the Vox building. Most weren't hooked up to the lobby system. MacGulry used to wonder where the images were being sent.

Realizing he was no longer and probably had never been alone in his most intimate moments, the Vox CEO sighed.

"If you know I left, then you know why," MacGulry said. "I'm giving away the bloody store in there."

"Money well spent," Friend said. "Our work in Harlem has successfully lowered the price of BCN stock. Soon you'll be able to buy that network, folding it into the News Company family. The financial gain of the Vox-BCN merger will far outweigh the cost of bringing the Asian over to our side."

"I can't just settle with him. It goes against my nature, mate."

"Robbie, it goes against my nature to kill a useful ally. Killing an ally who has outlived his usefulness is another matter altogether."

MacGulry squeezed the phone tight. "I'm tired of your threats, mate," he growled. "I'm your public face, and I know why. You don't have one, do you? I knew it for sure when I hooked up that computer chip. That's why you were gone so long. These guys you're after busted you up. Now you want revenge, but you can't do it in person because you're not even a person. You're just a voice on the phone. You need someone who can go out in the world for you. You need *me*, mate, so back off on the threats."

It felt good to finally stand up to that arrogant bastard. He had hoped for a rise out of Friend, but the voice on the telephone remained smooth and calm.

"Please do not overestimate your importance to me, Robbie. Television is only one component of my diversified business interests. And while I intend to build a global super-network utilizing my cryptosubliminal technology, the head of that network doesn't have to be you."

MacGulry deflated. "What about the other part?"

"The fact that I'm not human?" Friend asked. "Yes, Robbie, that's true. Does it bother you?"

"Not as much as I'd have thought," MacGulry said glumly. "I felt the same way about most of my four ex-wives, but I went and married them just the same."

"Good," Friend said. "Now, to prove to you that

we're still friends, I'm going to do you an enormous favor. I'm going to save your life.''

MacGulry's look of depression flashed to confusion.

''What do you mean?'' he asked.

''I mean, Robbie, that it would be wise for you to immediately go to your secure avenue of escape. I will do my best to keep you safe en route to the basement garage.''

Friend didn't sound concerned. He issued the warning in his usual chipper tone.

''Why? What's wrong?''

''I've just observed the arrival of the Caucasian in the lobby. Judging by his stride and facial expression, I have determined a seventy-four-percent probability that he is angry about something. Possibly, we reached his friend Harold with our signal. I would imagine he's here for the Asian.''

''I'll get security to stop him,'' the Vox CEO said.

''Don't bother. He has just incapacitated three lobby guards.''

Robbie MacGulry couldn't believe it. Could three men be wiped out just like that? But then he realized he was standing in his bathroom with a phone, a camera and a computer voice who had been secretly directing much of his business affairs for the past thirty years. Anything was possible.

Panic set in.

''What do I do?'' MacGulry begged.

Friend's voice was as smooth as a newly frozen pond.

''Run, Robbie. As fast as you can.''

20

Remo dumped the three lobby guards into an elevator, sending them for an unconscious whirlwind tour of the Vox building's exciting subbasement. He got aboard another elevator, riding it up to Vox's executive offices.

He noted more security cameras when he stepped off the car on the thirtieth floor. There had been others downstairs, another in the elevator. He ignored them all, gliding with angry purpose to the main desk.

"MacGulry's office," Remo said to the pretty young woman who was flashing him a cover model's smile.

She seemed deeply disappointed that the thin young man she had just met hadn't come to see her.

"Oh," she said, lower lip pouting wet and warm. "Mr. MacGulry is in a meeting. If you want, you can wait in my bed." She realized she'd misspoken. "I mean, in my apartment," she corrected. "Wait, I mean in the waiting room," she amended. "You can wait in the *waiting room*." Pausing a split second, she looked him up, then down. "Who am I kidding, I mean in my bed," she admitted, throwing up her hands in surrender. "Wait, let me get you my keys."

As she ducked to retrieve her purse, Remo skipped around the desk and headed up the hallway.

More cameras were there. They recorded the action as he kicked in door after door. He was met mostly with screams and startled looks. When he kicked in the last door to a corner office, he found the Master of Sinanju standing near the window, hands clasped behind his back.

The old man didn't turn. His weathered face was reflected in the tempered glass.

"'Hark,' I asked myself when the building began to shake," the wizened Korean said. "'What is that din? What child is having such a fit of temper that he would disturb an entire building full of people? How indulgent must be his parents that they would allow this childish tantrum?'"

"I was looking for you," Remo said. "I should have figured it wouldn't be hard. Just follow the traffic jams. Okay, Chiun, you've shut down Manhattan with flat tires and tow trucks. You've had your day's fun. Let's go."

"I will do no such thing," Chiun sniffed. "You looked for me, you found me. Now go look for someone who wants to be found."

Remo didn't budge. He glanced around the big office. "Where's MacGulry?" he demanded.

"If you are here to pitch a pilot, I was here first."

"The only thing I'm pitching is MacGulry out the nearest window," Remo said. "He's in on this hypnotism thing somehow. They got to Smith."

This caused the Master of Sinanju to finally turn from the window.

"Is he alive?"

"Yeah, he's alive," Remo answered. "Out like a light for the time being. Is MacGulry in there?"

Storming over, Remo kicked open the bathroom door.

"Stop that!" the Master of Sinanju commanded, flouncing up beside his pupil.

The bathroom was empty. Another door on the other side of the room opened into a private hallway.

"Dammit, he's gone. You know where he went?"

Chiun's face was hard. "Perhaps he fled when he heard there was a door-kicking maniac loose in his castle."

Remo saw the phone was dangling off the hook. When he checked it, he heard only a dial tone.

"Double crap," he said. "You listen in on the call?"

Chiun's eyes grew wide. "I would not listen in on the Sea-O's private conversations," he said, deeply offended.

"Right," Remo said. He slapped a palm against the tile wall. As he suspected, it absorbed the vibrations. "Soundproof walls. Ordinarily, I'd say he had them for privacy when he was on the can if it wasn't for that."

He jerked a thumb to the security camera in the corner of the room. The lens was focused squarely on Remo.

"Must be for that great new Vox special, 'Caught

on Tape: Australia's Biggest Piles of Shit III.'
MacGulry'd certainly qualify. This is just great,
Chiun. That call was probably a heads-up that I was
coming.''

Spinning on his heel, he marched back out into the
office. The Master of Sinanju charged out after him.

"What is the meaning of all this?'' Chiun demanded. "Just because something has happened to
your precious Smith does not mean you have a right
to come stampeding through the Sea-O's offices.''

"CEO, not Sea-O,'' Remo said angrily. "And try
to follow this. Someone tried to get Smith to Swiss
cheese me. It was a Vox broadcast he was watching
that told him to do it. MacGulry owns Vox. And if
MacGulry knows about me and Smith, then he knows
about you.''

"Of course he knows about me,'' Chiun sniffed.
"I am the man who is going to save his network.
Now get out of here before you ruin this for me.''

"This is serious,'' Remo insisted. "Smith is flat on
his back in a hospital room right now because of all
this.''

"Smith will be fine,'' Chiun dismissed. "I thought
at one time he would eventually go the way of all
men, but at the feeble rate that lunatic has been shuf-
fling toward his end lo these many years, he will live
to vex you long after my tired bones have turned to
dust. Now leave me be. I have finally met someone
who recognizes my talent.''

"Dammit, Chiun, we're *assassins*. We're not writ-
ers or TV pitchmen or counterassassins or anything

else. You're the one who drilled that into my damn head all these years. Now let's get out of here and go do our job.''

"You are forgetting that it will soon no longer be my job,'' the Master of Sinanju said thinly. "You are the Master who will succeed me. You do it.''

Remo sensed it. Beneath the sarcasm was hurt. He'd assumed this was all about Chiun being his usual thin-skinned self, but Smith had sown the seeds of doubt in the younger Master of Sinanju's mind. Maybe Remo's attitude had changed.

"I can't do it without you, Little Father.''

His pupil's softened tone touched off a spark of fury in the old man's hazel eyes.

"Do not patronize me, Remo Williams,'' he demanded, stamping a furious sandaled foot on the floor.

Remo's mood flashed back to anger. "I give up,'' he growled, flinging up his hands. "Tell me, Chiun. Tell me what the hell it is I'm supposed to do.''

"I want you to stop treating me like an invalid,'' Chiun snapped.

"I'm not. You're off on this self-pity binge all because you want me to want you around, then you get mad at me for saying I want you around when I really *do* want you around. Well, this is it. I've had it. Cut a deal with Vox TV if you want. And while you're at it, make sure you don't lose a minute's sleep over Smith or the fact that someone's trying to sabotage the organization that's been keeping us in rice and Twizzlers for the past thirty years.''

He spun on his heel.

A bank of television sets lined one office wall. Remo had taken but a single step toward the office door when every screen suddenly flickered to life.

"What now?" he grumbled.

The same daytime talk show was playing across all the screens. Superimposed faintly in the lower right-hand corner was the Vox logo.

That was all the world was meant to see.

In addition to the logo was something else. Remo noted the timed pulses of brilliant hypnotic light flashing just beyond the fringes of ordinary human awareness. And at the bottom of the screen flashed a single subliminal command. *Remo, kill Chiun.*

"Dammit, not again," Remo said.

"What is wrong now?" the Master of Sinanju asked tersely as he swept up beside his pupil.

"They're at it again. You better not look at it, Chiun," he cautioned.

But the old Korean had already glanced up at the bank of television screens.

"This is terrible," the tiny Asian proclaimed.

Some of the tension fled Remo's face. "You see it?"

"Of course," Chiun sniffed. "Fat whites blabbing at other fat whites about still more fat whites. If this is the sort of trash the Sea-O puts on his broadcasts, it is amazing he did not run to me for help ages ago."

"Not the talk show, Little Father."

Remo looked back at the screens. The message was

clear to his sensitive eyes. Timed to pulse with the hypnotic flashes of light. *Remo, kill Chiun*.

The original concern that he'd had back at the Harlem police station had been borne out. Either due to age or years of television viewing, Chiun's eyes weren't focused enough to make out the subliminal commands.

"Trust me, it's there," Remo insisted. "And you don't wanna know what it says. Now let's get out of here before—" His voice grew small. "Oh, crap."

"What is wrong?" asked the Master of Sinanju, peeved. He followed Remo's gaze to the televisions.

"Chiun, don't!" Remo shouted, jumping forward.

But it was too late. Before Remo could stop him, the old Korean had turned his attention back to the screens.

The hypnotic colors continued to pulse on all the televisions. Buried within the colors was a new command. *Chiun, kill Remo*.

The room grew very still. With agonizing slowness, Remo turned his worried gaze to the Master of Sinanju. An odd blankness had settled on the old man's wrinkled face.

Chiun stared at the screens, mesmerized. His almond-shaped eyes were unblinking. He didn't move so much as a millimeter. Even his tufts of yellowing-white hair seemed to still in the eddies of recirculated office air.

Very, very slowly, Remo took a half step back.

"Chiun?" he asked cautiously.

With a terrible quiet suffusing his entire being, the

Master of Sinanju turned to his pupil. The instant their eyes locked, the old man's arms became twin blurs.

Fingernails honed to razor-sharp talons flew in slashing strokes at Remo's exposed throat.

Before the nails could slice soft flesh, Remo dropped backward. As Chiun's nails clicked viciously at empty air, Remo's back was brushing the floor.

Palms flattened against the carpet. Up and over.

Spinning in air like a coiled spring, Remo flipped away from Chiun, landing on his feet near the bank of TV screens.

Chiun sprang after him. Hands clenched in knots of furious bone lashed out, left, right, left.

TV screens blew apart one after another.

Remo danced just ahead of each blow. Glass screens exploded glittering dust shards into the office.

The bank of TVs ended in a tight corner. Remo flipped and rolled, back against the wall.

Chiun twirled through settling glass. Beneath the blank veneer, his eyes held a frenzied glint.

Calves tensing, his sandals left the floor.

The old man flew at Remo again, in flight a furious cry rising up from the depths of his belly. Crushing heels made a beeline for Remo's exposed chest.

The instant before the heels could crack his sternum to pulpy shards, Remo dropped.

The Master of Sinanju's momentum threw the old man into the wall. Paneling splintered and flew apart. The impact shattered sandstone from the building's outer wall. Pebbled shards fell like hard rain to Sixth Avenue.

Remo was up from his crouch before the first stone hit the street. As Chiun twisted and dropped back to his feet, Remo was already springing forward.

"Sorry, Little Father," Remo whispered.

A darting thumb found the paralyzing spot on Chiun's forehead. There was first shock, then a glimmer of fury in the Master of Sinanju's eyes. And then all emotion washed away and his wrinkled eyelids fluttered shut.

With a silent sigh, the life slipped from the Reigning Master of Sinanju.

Remo caught the old man as he fell, settling his frail frame delicately to the carpeting. When he was certain his teacher was safe, Remo collapsed to a sitting position.

First Smith, now Chiun.

Remo tried to find comfort in the fact that if they were like the previous hypnosis victims, both men would eventually snap out of it. The knowledge offered little consolation.

Beneath Chiun's brocade robe, the Master of Sinanju's fragile chest rose and fell with each breath.

Remo watched him for a lingering moment. So peaceful. So helpless. Without a sound, Remo climbed to his feet.

The center row of TV screens in the wall unit had been smashed by Chiun's punishing blows. The rest still worked.

The message and pulsing lights were gone from all the screens. In their place was a new subliminal caption.

?????????

The bright red question marks ran from one side of the screen to the other, hopping over to the next television.

Stepping away from his teacher's prone body, Remo approached the screens.

Hands became angry blurs. Balled fists slammed each of the remaining screens in turn. He smashed each and every one, working his way methodically down the line.

He made it to the last one.

The line of red question marks still marched like querying soldiers across the pixeled screen.

"I find out who you are, I'm gonna cancel you," Remo announced to the television.

The final screen exploded in a glittering hiss of pulverized glass.

21

Robbie MacGulry's limo screeched to a stop on the tarmac at JFK. He didn't wait for his driver to open the door. Jumping from the car, he tripped up the steps of his waiting jet.

Friend had called once during the limousine ride from the Vox building. He had assured the Vox CEO a clear runway for hasty departure. He was true to his word. Engines screaming, the jet was airborne in minutes.

Hands clutching the arms of his seat, MacGulry tried to will his rapidly beating heart to slow.

This was all Friend's fault. He was the one who had inspired this panic in MacGulry—a man for whom fear was the worst four-letter word.

It was infuriating. Here was this faceless thing. A voice on a phone whom he would never, *could* never meet. And not only was he giving the great Robbie MacGulry orders, he was forcing the Australian media giant to flee for his life.

The plane hadn't finished its ascent when the phone rang. MacGulry grabbed it up.

"I have potentially good news, Robbie," Friend's smooth voice announced.

"What happened back there?" MacGulry asked.

"I attempted to use the subliminal signal to get the Caucasian to attack the Asian."

"Wait a minute, *you* used the signal?" MacGulry asked. He had been under the impression that his people alone had access to the cryptosubliminal technology.

"Yes," Friend replied. "You shouldn't be surprised. As you yourself now realize, I not only have access to your computer system, I *live* in it from time to time, Robbie."

MacGulry exhaled wearily. "What happened? Did the white kill the wog? I sure as hell hope so, because that deal you had me cut with him is gonna cost Vox a fortune."

"The first attempt failed," Friend said. "A shame, really. I thought that with Chiun dead Remo might be more apt to join my cause. However, when that didn't work, I tried the reverse. The Asian didn't have the same resistant abilities as the other. He succumbed."

Robbie was suddenly interested. "Did he beat the white?" he asked.

"No. Remo knocked him out. However, I used the most potent color pulses. The posthypnotic suggestion is planted deep. When he awakens, it is very likely he will attack the Caucasian again."

"Good," MacGulry said. "That'll keep them busy."

"It's better even than that," Friend said. "The third individual, Harold, was a rogue element. I calculated as low the odds that the message your people sent out would reach him. However, given Remo's comments during his meeting with Chiun, there is now a one hundred percent certainty that Harold has fallen under the influence of the subliminal signal, as well. In addition to that, he now has a last name. Smith. I've already commenced a search for him.''

''How long will that take?''

''Not long. Remo said he was in a hospital bed. I'm having trouble finding a Harold Smith who was recently admitted to a hospital in the southern New York area. Once I find him, I'll have him killed. Without their leader, Remo and Chiun will likely cease interfering with my business affairs.''

''If you think they'll just go away, why'd you make me waste my time with that crazy old man?''

''Because he's a mercenary who will need employment, and I'm always looking for bankable allies, Robbie. For the moment, of my three enemies, two are temporarily out of commission. The third will be lost without the guidance of the others. Once I find Harold Smith, I'll stop them all forever.''

MacGulry sank in his seat. ''Huh,'' he grunted. ''This had just better be worth it.''

''It will be,'' Friend promised. ''Vox will absorb BCN. We'll use the cryptosubliminal technology to get the FCC to further loosen ownership regulations. After that, the remaining networks will be absorbed, as well. I estimate that within the next twelve months,

I will have complete dominance of the entire world's media markets.''

Robbie MacGulry's face was glum. This was never how he'd pictured his life. Playing second fiddle to a pushy computer chip.

''Don't you mean 'we'?'' he muttered.

''I mean what I mean, Robbie.''

The phone went dead in the Vox chairman's tanned hand.

22

Remo carried the limp body of the Master of Sinanju down to Folcroft's security wing.

Dr. Gerling was still at Smith's bedside as Remo passed the open door to the CURE director's room. The doctor had drawn open one eyelid and was clicking his penlight on and off over the bloodshot orb. As he flashed the light, he muttered soothing words softly into Smith's ear.

"I've got another one for you," Remo said.

Gerling turned. Sweat beaded on his forehead. When he saw the old Asian patient, the Folcroft physician's lips drew tight.

"I'll be a few hours more," Gerling said softly. "Put him in the next room. I'll get to him when I'm done here."

Remo slipped past the room, depositing the Master of Sinanju in the empty bed in the next room.

Chiun looked like a mummified corpse in repose as Remo left the room.

Out in the hallway Remo stood between rooms. He rotated his thick wrists absently as he contemplated his next move. He heard Dr. Gerling speaking quietly to Smith, trying to undo the damage caused by CURE's faceless enemy.

Remo could go after MacGulry. But there was no certainty that the Vox head was behind any of this.

Remo was beginning to think that Martin Houton might not have been in complete control at the end. In retrospect, the suicidal BCN president had that same glazed look in his eyes as the cops in Harlem or Smith in his office.

If Houton was an unwitting victim, so too might be Robbie MacGulry. Remo had no desire to run off on a wild-goose chase while the real culprit got away.

For a frustrating moment he wasn't sure exactly what to do. Smith and Chiun were no help for the time being. Remo was the only man left at CURE.

His thoughts suddenly froze.

No, he wasn't the only one left. He realized the error as soon as the thought passed through his mind.

Even after a year he still thought there were only three of them in all. But there was one other. And so far, Remo realized with sudden excitement, the fourth man was the only one not included in the subliminal attacks on CURE's personnel.

It was possible that whoever was behind all this had old knowledge of CURE. If that was the case, salvation for them all could come from the least likely of places.

"I'm never gonna live this one down," he muttered.

When Remo headed up the hall, the room he

slipped inside belonged to neither Harold Smith nor the Master of Sinanju.

THE DEMONS of a hundred nights' dreams had finally slouched off to die in the shadows of sleep.

It had been so long since he'd slept for real that he had forgotten what it was like. It was an inviting darkness. A cloud of black that smothered him with a peace that was slowly stitching up the edges of his frayed sanity.

Mark Howard lay floating on a sea of night, a sky of soothing black nothingness far above his head.

No nightmares, no fear. It seemed as if he had been staring at—reveling in—that same black sky for weeks.

He was so familiar with the blankness of that empty void that he was surprised to suddenly find a star sitting in it.

The star hadn't been there before. He was sure of it.

This single celestial light was an out-of-place blemish in the tranquil, unchanged heavens of this otherworldly place. He was going to try to use his mind to remove the ugly blight from his personal sky when the star suddenly got brighter. It went from star to sun to supernova in the wink of an eye, obliterating the calming black in a flash that burned his retinas and made him squint in pain.

When he blinked, Mark realized that the star that had exploded in the night sky of his dreams wasn't a star at all.

A fluorescent light hung amid yellowed ceiling tiles above his head. For some reason Mark was lying flat on his back. As he tried to get his bearings, a voice spoke.

"Up and at 'em, kid."

He saw the cruel face above his bed.

"Remo?" Mark whispered groggily.

Mark felt Remo's hand slip out from the base of his spine where it had been massaging a knot of nerves. The drugged sensation drained away.

"At least your memory's not crazy," Remo commented. "Now shake a leg. The whole world's falling apart and—God help us—you might be our only hope."

A grim expression on his face, CURE's enforcement arm pulled the confused young man out of bed.

FIFTEEN MINUTES LATER—showered, shaved and wearing the suit he'd had on when he had been discovered on the floor of Folcroft's attic three days before—Mark Howard was hurrying along the hallway of the sanitarium's executive wing.

"When did all this happen?" he asked urgently.

While Mark was getting ready, Remo had given the assistant CURE director a quick rundown of the events that had taken place over the past few days.

Remo was marching beside him. "Last couple of days. We thought it was over yesterday. They didn't start coming after us until the last few hours."

"How long till Dr. Smith recovers?"

"Depends how long it takes Dr. Hugo Hackenbush

to deprogram him,'' Remo replied. ''He said a couple more hours.''

When they rounded a corner, they found a matronly woman coming down the hallway toward them from the direction of Smith's office suite.

Eileen Mikulka's broad face was anxious. The instant she saw Mark Howard, her troubled expression fled.

''Mr. Howard!'' Mrs. Mikulka gasped. ''You're all right.''

''Yeah, Mrs. M.,'' he said uncomfortably. ''I'm fine, thanks.'' He started past her, but she pressed his arm.

''You haven't seen Dr. Smith, have you?'' she asked worriedly. ''He was here this morning, but I stepped out for a few minutes and I haven't been able to find him since.''

Howard glanced at Remo. ''I, um. No. I don't know where he is. Sorry.''

''Oh, dear,'' Mrs. Mikulka said. ''He has an appointment soon. Maybe he went downstairs for lunch.'' She offered a harried smile. ''I'm so happy to see you're well.''

Mrs. Mikulka hurried off in one direction as Remo and Mark continued in the other.

Howard unlocked his office door and slipped in behind his worn oak desk. As he sat in his chair, he pressed a recessed stud beneath the desk's lip. A hidden computer monitor and keyboard rose up before him.

"I'll see if the mainframes have pulled anything relevant in the past few hours," he said.

"First things first," Remo interrupted. He was standing at Howard's side. "Sorry, kid, but there's no dainty way to do this fast." And with that Remo jammed his fingers deep into Mark Howard's shoulder.

The pain was white-hot. Horrible, blinding.

Mark couldn't breathe, couldn't gasp. He wanted to cry out, but his strangled voice couldn't manage the sound.

It was pain he had never imagined could exist. Remo had torn his arm from the socket and poured molten metal into the exposed joint.

Remo leaned close. "Are you working with Purcell?" he asked, his voice low with menace.

Confusion flooded in with the pain. "A patient?" Howard gasped. "He's a patient, right? Security wing. No, *no!*"

"Then why'd you let him out?"

"I didn't!" Mark insisted.

Fire burned from his crippled shoulder across his chest. The blood was everywhere. Had to be. Yet he didn't see any splattered on desk or floor. Still, he dared not look at the raw stump where his arm had been attached.

"You double-crossing us, Princess Kashmir?"

"No," Howard said. *"For God's sake, no."*

Remo could see the young man was telling the truth. He withdrew his hand. The pain immediately fled.

"Well, you're not lying," Remo said. "Which I guess means you're even more screwed up than the rest of us at this boobie hatch. I'll let Smith figure out whether to croak you or just stick you on Ritalin."

Mark couldn't believe it. His shoulder was no longer on fire. In fact, his arm was right where it belonged. The horrible pain of a moment ago burned away to pins and needles at his fingertips. He flexed his hand in shock.

"How—?"

"Just fiddled with a few pain receptors," Remo explained, before the questions could start. "So, yes, your arm's still there, God's in his heaven and all the Whos down in Whoville are tucked tight in bed. Let's get on with it."

"What was that all about?" Mark asked. "That patient you asked about—Jeremiah Purcell—he was a CURE patient, wasn't he? Did he escape?"

"Yes," Remo said, rolling his eyes. "Now, if you don't stop asking questions and start earning your paycheck, your arm is leaving through the door and the rest of you is going out the window."

Mark gulped away his confusion. Rather than give Remo an excuse to make good on his threat, the assistant CURE director turned his attention to his computer.

As Howard began typing at the keyboard, Remo waited before the desk. CURE's enforcement arm was glancing around Howard's tiny office. It looked like a prison cell.

"Smith really stuck it to you, didn't he?" he commented after a few minutes during which the clattering of Howard's keyboard was the only sound in the small room.

"What?" Mark asked as he worked. He didn't wait for a reply. "These subliminal signals today. You're certain they came from Vox and not BCN?"

"The one that got Smitty here was Vox. So was the one that got Chiun to pounce on me at MacGulry's."

"Robbie MacGulry's gone," Howard said as he studied the data on his monitor. "He left the country in a hurry. It looks like he got a runway shut down at JFK." He frowned, puzzled. "How did he swing that?"

"First guess?" Remo asked dryly. "I'd say he downloaded the commands into the control tower while they were watching *Airport '79* on Vox."

"I doubt the officials at the airport were watching TV to receive the commands, Remo," Howard said. "By the looks of it, this was done through the airport's computer system. Someone tapped into it and got them to shut down."

"Can you figure out who?"

"Maybe. With enough time. These are Dr. Smith's programs. He'd probably be able to do it faster."

"Smitty's down for the count," Remo reminded him with thinning patience.

"Right, right," Howard said. "I think it's safe to assume that MacGulry is in this somehow. Why else would he take off the way he did? You said something downstairs about a 'Winner' producer. She's the one who was there in Harlem, right? And she's the one who hooked Chiun up with MacGulry. And BCN admitted using the signal during 'Winner.'"

"That's right," Remo said.

"Okay," Howard said, attacking the problem logically. "We don't know for sure where MacGulry is heading yet. Right now I'd guess England or Australia, but with no flight plan I can't send you after him until we find out for sure. In the meantime why don't you go check out that producer?"

"What'll you be doing?"

Howard glanced at his monitor. "According to Dr. Smith's records, everything points to BCN as the culprit behind the subliminal technology. Obviously, we know now that was a false trail. I'll do some digging. See if I can find out for sure who it could be. One thing we know, it must be someone with a grudge against CURE."

"Okay," Remo said. "I'll call if I find out anything. And remember, you're in the big-boy seat for now, junior. Try not to let any more supervillains out while I'm gone."

Mark was going to ask what he meant, but Remo had already slipped out the office door.

For a few moments, the assistant CURE director sat alone in his small office.

There was something about Remo's words.

Much of the past week was fuzzy for Mark Howard. But as he sat in his familiar chair, blank eyes glued to the flashing cursor on his computer screen, a dim memory began to take shape. It was like living in someone else's dream.

Remo was gone for only a few minutes when there was a knock at Howard's door. He snapped alert.

"Did you forget something?" he called.

When the door opened, it wasn't Remo who stuck his head inside the office.

"Mr. Howard?" asked the rumpled, middle-aged man. "I'm Detective Davic, Rye police. Dr. Smith's secretary said you were back at work." The police officer's smile was devoid of any warmth. "Mind if I ask you a few questions?"

23

Cindee Maloo had gotten the call on her cell phone while out on the Harlem *Winner* set.

The camera crews were filming the day's challenge for the show's remaining contestants. All morning *Winner* had been sending white men from the various teams into Harlem liquor stores. The men had been instructed to scream racial slurs at the top of their voices and then run like hell.

Cindee had come up with that particular challenge. Taping was going beautifully. Much better than the "Steal a Crack Addict's Shoes" challenge that had flopped the previous week. She was standing behind the cameras, watching the action and lamenting the fact that they didn't give out Emmys for the kind of work she did when the phone rang.

Five minutes after the call, she was bursting into her trailer on the fence-enclosed vacant lot that housed the trailers of *Winner*'s production staff.

Cindee flew around the room, frantically stuffing clothes and other items into a pair of nylon bags.

With desperate hands she knocked a row of plastic videotape cases from a shelf. They clattered loudly to the floor, some splitting open and spilling tapes. She snatched up a glossy computer printout that had been hidden at the back of the shelf. She was shoving it in with the rest of her belongings when a sudden noise startled her.

"Going somewhere?" asked a voice that was so close she could almost feel the warm breath on her neck.

Cindee nearly jumped out of her skin.

She spun. Remo was standing inside her trailer. She hadn't heard him come in. The door was closed.

"Oh, it's you," Cindee said nervously. "I didn't mean for you to come here in person. You should have called the number on that card I gave you."

"Bad things happen to people who call you," Remo pointed out, his voice cold.

"Really?" Cindee asked with forced innocence. "Is something wrong with your friend?"

Her right hand was still inside her bag. She wrenched it out, aiming a .45 automatic at Remo's chest.

"Aha!" Cindee cried triumphantly.

"You call that a gun?" Remo asked blandly. "*This* is a gun."

Remo formed a gun from his hand, with his thumb jutting up and his extended index finger forming the barrel. He stuck his finger barrel inside the real barrel of Cindee's gun. Ordinarily, that would have been an exceedingly foolish thing to do. But ordinarily the barrel wouldn't have split apart like the peel of an overripe banana.

"Crikey," Cindee said in amazement.

"And for my next trick," said Remo.

He reached into Cindee's bag and pulled out the paper he'd seen her retrieve from the shelf. It was a picture-quality computer printout. He hadn't seen what was on it when Cindee put it in the bag.

He saw now that the face in the photo wasn't quite right. It was a little too perfect. As if the picture had been fed through a computer and the image reconstructed. Despite its flaws, it was still clear enough.

"It's me," Remo said.

Cindee didn't know what to do with her mangled gun. It looked too dangerous now to try firing. She threw it at Remo's head. He caught it and put it on a table.

"This is the picture of me I saw on the TVs at the police station," Remo continued. "You didn't get this from the footage you taped of me. Where'd this come from?"

When he glanced up at her, Cindee had her mouth screwed defiantly shut.

"You can answer my questions one of two ways," Remo said. "Arms off or arms on. Your choice."

Cindee saw it in those dark eyes. This man who could split steel with his bare hands wasn't bluffing. With an angry hiss, her resolve collapsed.

"They sent it to me from Oz," she admitted glumly.

"Oz?" Remo asked, confused. "Flying monkeys, gay lions Oz?"

"*Australia,*" she explained. "I got that from the

Vox Wollongong facility. They sent it to me five days ago and told me to keep a lookout for you.''

"What do they have against me?" Remo asked.

She shrugged. "I don't know. He didn't tell me why you were so important to him."

"MacGulry," Remo said.

She nodded. "He pulled in markers at the network and got me the job here. I'm taking over 'Winner' as soon as Vox merges with BCN. He had me help set up the broadcast stuff in that minister's church basement. Bastard sinks me up to my eyeballs in all this and then waits till he's halfway home before he bothers to call and warn me you might be coming. So what are you? Some kind of spy or something?"

"Or something," Remo said.

"Well, whatever you are, he's got a lot invested in finding you. I guess he thought you could throw a monkey wrench into his operation."

"I'll do a lot worse than that, sweetheart," Remo said. He reached a hand for her.

Cindee fell back. "Wait!" she begged. "There's something else."

"What?"

"No way, jocko. If I tell you, you've gotta promise to let me out of this in one piece."

Remo's brow darkened. "Yeah, okay," he said.

"Robbie's got this friend," Cindee said. "I don't know his real name. That's the only thing Robbie calls him. I was at Wollongong once when he called. Doesn't sound very friendly to me. Gotta hand it to him, though. He's the only guy I've ever seen who can make Robbie sweat. I think he's the power behind the BCN acquisition—going after you, the subliminal technology. All of it.''

Remo blinked. He couldn't believe what he was hearing. ''Friend,'' he said, his voice soft with shock.

And in a flash everything made sense.

''Yeah,'' Cindee said. ''Weird name, huh? Although you're used to that. Your Chinese friend told me your name was Remo. Funny about that. I didn't know why at first, but they were really keen on getting someone named Remo onto this season's 'Winner.' But it makes sense now. The former president gets attacked and a guy named Remo gets killed the same night. Together or separate they might be enough to flush you out. So what are you, CIA? FCC? What?''

Remo didn't answer. ''One more question. The murdered contestant and BCN executives. You knew about all that?''

''Sure. Not to worry, though,'' she assured him. ''The guy signed a release. And those BCN guys knew the cost of doing business. Say, I meant what I said. I can get you on TV. And not just as some ghost people forget about a day after your picture's been flashed into their subconscious. What do you say? Next season of 'Winner' still has open slots.''

Remo said not a word. As she smiled hopefully, he reached out and squeezed a spot on her neck. Still smiling her perfect Australian smile, Cindee Maloo passed out. He carted her unconscious body out of the trailer.

Driving out of Harlem, Remo found the longest Cadillac with the furriest seats and the most purple lights slung to the undercarriage. It was parked by the side of the road near some traffic lights where women in fishnet stockings and skirts inappropriately short for the Yuletide season trolled the traffic looking to spread more than just Christmas cheer. A very dark man with a long fur coat and a wide-brimmed hat leaned against the car. He was counting twenties.

Remo stopped his car next to the pimp.

"Hey, Huggy Bear," Remo called. "How much will you give me to add Miss Australia to your harem?" He gestured to the back seat where Cindee Maloo lay snoring.

The pimp leaned in the car to inspect the fine white woman in the back. He apparently liked what he saw.

"I don' know," he said thoughtfully. "She kinda old. Forty dollars."

"Sold," Remo said.

The pimp flashed a gold-toothed smile, peeled off two twenties from his wad of bills and ordered a couple of his girls to drag Cindee Maloo from Remo's car.

"Pleasure doing business with you," Remo said.

He folded his forty dollars and tucked the two bills carefully in his pocket. As he drove away, he hoped no one saw that he had so much cash on him. After all, this didn't look like a safe neighborhood.

24

Eileen Mikulka had scoured nearly the entire sanitarium for her missing employer, to no avail. As a last resort, she reluctantly decided to check the basement corridor where all the trouble had occurred earlier in the week.

As she rounded the corner, she remembered that there was a security pad on the door to the secluded corridor. Mrs. Mikulka didn't have the code. As far as she knew, only Dr. Smith knew how to gain access to the corridor.

She worried about this until she saw that the door had been broken open from the inside. That terrible patient who killed those four poor people had to have smashed it when he escaped. With a new sense of dread, she passed through the battered door and into the hall.

Mrs. Mikulka stopped dead at the open door to one of the ten rooms that lined the corridor. When she saw the patient on the bed in that room, she let out a little gasp that brought the attention of the attending Folcroft doctor.

"Oh, no," she moaned. "What's wrong with Dr. Smith?"

Dr. Aldace Gerling offered his employer's secretary an impatient glance.

"Please, Mrs. Mikulka, I need silence," the doctor said.

"What's the matter?" she pressed. "Is he all right?"

"He will be," Dr. Gerling snapped. "He's been put into some sort of deep hypnotic trance. I just need a little more time. Now, please go."

Mrs. Mikulka didn't know what else to do. She reluctantly did as she was told.

She rubbed her hands anxiously as she made her way back along the basement corridors.

Folcroft was generally such a quiet place. That definitely was not the case this terrible week. Thank goodness Mr. Howard was back at work or Mrs. Mikulka wouldn't know what to do. She had at least been able to send that police detective to see Folcroft's nice young assistant director when she hadn't been able to locate Dr. Smith.

But that was the one good thing. What with all the deaths and now something wrong with Dr. Smith, it was all almost too much for a body to endure.

She pondered the awfulness of these past few days all the way back upstairs. The telephone was ringing when she arrived back in her office. She had routed her calls to the main desk when she'd left her station. This was the private line, for family and friends to use in case of emergency.

Probably Kieran. He had been using this line too much lately. As she picked up the phone, she was prepared to scold her youngest for bothering her at work yet again.

"Good afternoon, Folcroft Sanitarium, Dr. Smith's office. May I help you?"

She was surprised when the voice on the line didn't belong to Kieran or even to Dr. Smith's wife.

"Hello. I'm looking for Harold Smith."

"Oh," Mrs. Mikulka said, settling her ample rump into her chair. "I'm sorry, but Dr. Smith is unavailable right now. May I take a message?"

The smooth voice didn't miss a beat. "I see. May I ask when he'll be back?"

Mrs. Mikulka thought of Dr. Smith. Lying in that isolation ward where those gruesome murders had taken place just a few scant days before. She shuddered.

"I'm not really sure," she said. "But I'll be glad to take a message if you'd like."

"It's terrible what happened to him," the man on the phone said. His voice modulated to deep sympathy without seeming to change pitch. "Have they given you any idea how long it will be before he comes out of the hypnotic trance?"

Some of the tension drained from Eileen Mikulka. "You know about that?" she said, exhaling. "I only just found out myself a few minutes ago. The doctor wouldn't tell me a thing. He just shooed me back upstairs."

"Doctors can be very unsympathetic," the caller said. "I'm sure Harold will be fine. Thank you for your time."

"Wait," Mrs. Mikulka said. "I didn't get your name."

The phone was cradled between shoulder and ear. She had out her pad, pen poised to write.

The caller's response was strange given the man they were both talking about. After all, Dr. Smith had never been the social type. His circle was limited to a handful of people, all of whom Eileen Mikulka assumed were known to her.

"I'm a friend," said the voice on the phone.

The rude man with the pleasant voice didn't bother to give Mrs. Mikulka his name. He just hung up.

CALCULATING THE LIKELIHOOD THAT SUBJECT HAROLD WINSTON SMITH, DIRECTOR FOLCROFT SANITARIUM, RYE, NEW YORK, IS THE HAROLD FOR WHICH I'VE BEEN SEARCHING...

The answer was calculated in fractions of a second.

95.8 PERCENT PROBABILITY.

Friend had found the right Harold.

The search had been complicated by Remo's misleading statement at the Vox building in Manhattan. Friend had expanded his search parameters when he had no luck locating a Harold Smith in any hospitals in New York, Connecticut or New Jersey. He understood his error when he found out that Harold Smith was not in a hospital, but in a private mental-health facility. The patient records for Folcroft were not computerized, further hindering Friend's search.

Statistical and probability algorithms raced to meet along pathways unfettered by form or distance.

Friend consumed all information relevant to Folcroft Sanitarium, Rye, New York. Newspaper articles from online sources dated the current week detailed a situation at Harold Smith's place of work for which police involvement was required. Friend took this and sped on. Tendrils of living electronic thought accelerated, accessing records within the Rye police department. The relevant data was located, digested and evaluated. A blueprint for action was formed.

CALCULATING LIKELIHOOD THAT PLAN TO KILL SUBJECT HAROLD SMITH WILL SUCCEED…

The answer shot back instantaneously.

83.2 PERCENT PROBABILITY.

Satisfied with the odds of success, Friend returned to his normal business of maximizing profit.

25

The pulsing white light drew Harold Smith out of the deep fog of his own mind. When he opened his eyes, he recognized the familiar broad face looking down at him.

He blinked as he glanced at his surroundings. For a reason unknown to him, he was lying on his back in a Folcroft hospital room.

"What's going on?" Smith demanded.

Dr. Gerling seemed relieved. "You're out of it. Good." He returned his penlight to his pocket. "You heard about what happened in Harlem with those subliminal signals?"

"Yes," Smith admitted cautiously.

"Somehow you succumbed to a signal like the one used there. I'm still not sure how. I heard the authorities are dismantling the facility in the church there."

Smith was growing more worried. It was starting to come back to him. He remembered being in his office. Remembered looking down at the television broadcast on his computer screen. There had been something there....

As he racked his brain, he tried to sit up. He found

he could not. There was only minimal movement of his head and neck. Beyond that, nothing.

"I have no sensation below my neck," Smith said, trying to keep the panic from his voice.

"Not to worry. Your friend somehow gave you a kind of temporary paralysis. I still don't know how. Must be some sort of acupressure."

Smith stopped straining. His head clunked back to the table. "Friend?" he asked.

"I'm not sure of his name," Dr. Gerling said. "I've seen him here before. He's with the elderly Asian gentleman."

"He is not a friend," Smith said hurriedly. "He's a permanent health-care professional privately employed by the Asian patient."

"Whatever he is, he brought you in here. You tried to strangle him."

Frozen like a statue, Smith racked his brain. It was all so foggy. The doctor's words jarred some memory. He suddenly remembered having his hands around Remo's throat. He recalled something in his office. Flashes and a loud sound. It hit him like a fist in the gut.

He had tried to shoot Remo!

"I must get to my office," Smith announced urgently.

"He said it would be six hours before whatever he did wore off."

"How long has it been?"

Gerling checked his watch. "About five hours and

forty-five minutes. You were in a very deep hypnotic state, Dr. Smith. You should try to relax.''

The last thing Smith could do now was relax. The next fifteen minutes were sheer agony. It was the most excruciating quarter hour of his life, including the time he'd spent at the hands of a Nazi torturer while with the OSS during the second World War.

When the six-hour mark arrived, the Sinanju paralysis Remo had employed slowly melted away. It left his neck and his shoulders, slipping away down his arms and torso.

When his legs were finally strong enough to support him, he left the examination room. His stride grew more certain as he made his way up to his office.

''Dr. Smith, you're all right!'' Mrs. Mikulka exclaimed as he stepped in from the hall.

Smith didn't respond.

Marching with great purpose, he crossed the room, stopping at his closed office door.

As Mrs. Mikulka watched in growing dismay, her employer proceeded to do something strange, even by his standards.

The Folcroft director took off his glasses, folding them carefully into the pocket of his dress shirt. Next, he stripped off his suit jacket. Turning it around, he draped the rear of the jacket over his face. Taking the loose arms, he wrapped them over his eyes for double protection, drawing the ends over his shoulders.

With his arthritic fingers he found the sleeves difficult to knot. He turned to his secretary.

"Mrs. Mikulka, would you please tie this for me?" Smith's muffled voice asked from beneath his jacket.

"Oh. Yes, sir."

Mrs. Mikulka dutifully knotted the sleeves at the back of her employer's head.

"Thank you," Folcroft's director said. "No phone calls, please."

With that, Smith entered his office.

Inside was as familiar as if he had been sighted.

Beneath his makeshift mask, Smith's eyes were screwed tightly shut. He didn't want to take any chances.

Smith got to his knees. Bones creaked as he made his way on all fours across the office, facedown.

He found the cord to the television first. The CURE director knew that he hadn't had the set turned on before he attacked Remo, but he dared not leave anything to chance. He tugged the plug from the wall.

Crawling around below the window, he found the thick cord that exited the base of his high-tech desk. It was connected to a panel in the floor.

Smith wrapped his gnarled hand around the plug and pulled. A hum that he had not been aware emanated from the bowels of his desk slowly petered out.

He waited on the floor several long seconds, just to be certain that the monitor buried deep inside the desktop had faded completely to black.

Finally, Smith used the desk's edge to drag himself to his feet.

He pulled the jacket off still knotted. Untying the

sleeves, he shrugged it back on over his shoulders. Taking his seat, he replaced his glasses on his patrician nose.

Smith stared down at the black surface of his desk. In it was his dead computer. His lifeline to the outside world.

Harold, kill Remo.

He saw the words floating in the air before him. They were fading from his vision. Like the ghostly afterimage of something that had been stared at too long.

This was the disaster he had feared after the attack on Remo in the Harlem police station. He had been wrong not to fear the worst. Someone knew not only of Remo, but also of Smith. That simple realization was a molten ball of lead tossed into the pit of Smith's acid-churned stomach.

The only thing that linked the two men was CURE. To know of Remo and Smith was certainly to know of CURE.

Not only was America's last line of defense teetering on the edge of exposure, but also thanks to the particular technology at the hands of its enemy, CURE was now flying blind.

When the knock came at the door, Smith was so numb he didn't even hear his own voice call ''Come in.''

Mrs. Mikulka stuck her head in the room. She seemed relieved to see that he was back to wearing his suit jacket the more traditional way.

"Can I get you something, Dr. Smith?" his secretary asked with motherly concern. "Tea or soup?"

"No, thank you, Mrs. Mikulka," Smith said woodenly.

"Let me know if you change your mind. Oh, by the way, a friend of yours called a little while ago. At least he said he was a friend. He didn't give his name, I'm afraid."

The words barely registered. The caller was probably just a telemarketer. It couldn't have been a friend of Smith's. The only real friend Harold W. Smith had ever had was long dead and buried.

"Thank you, Mrs. Mikulka."

She smiled warmly. "I'm so glad everyone is feeling better. You both gave us all quite a scare this week."

"Both?" Smith asked, frowning.

"You and Mr. Howard," Eileen Mikulka explained. "He came back to work a few hours ago. I'm so happy he seems fine." She scrunched up her face. "The doctor said you were hypnotized. Was that what was wrong with Mr. Howard?"

Smith had been trying to sort through his tangled thoughts. His secretary's words helped clear the fog.

"I'm not sure," Smith said. He sat up straight. "Please excuse me, Mrs. Mikulka. I have work to do."

Nodding apologetically, his secretary left the office.

Once the door was closed, Smith drew open his bottom drawer. His automatic was sitting where Remo had dropped it.

There was only one man new at CURE. One man who knew of Remo and Smith. A man who had just released one of the most dangerous foes the covert agency had ever faced.

Smith had been hoping for an explanation for Jeremiah Purcell's escape. He now had it. Betrayal.

Smith slipped the gun into his pocket and left the office.

Mrs. Mikulka seemed surprised to see him reappear so soon. Smith said nothing to his secretary as he made his way out into the hallway.

Down the hall, he paused in front of Mark Howard's office. He could hear voices murmuring inside.

Smith's assistant should not have anyone in his office. He probably thought he was safe. The young man assumed his employer was still tucked out of the way in the basement.

Smith took the gun out, holding it low near his thigh.

He took his key ring from his pocket. Careful to keep the keys from jangling together, he slipped his passkey into the lock with his free hand.

Taking a deep breath, he twisted the knob and kicked the door open. He jumped in after it, gun raised.

Mark Howard was sitting behind his desk, eyes trained on his computer monitor. When the door flew open, the assistant CURE director looked up, startled.

"Dr. Smith?"

There was someone sitting on the edge of Howard's desk. When he saw who it was, Smith blinked.

"Remo?" the CURE director asked, confused.

His gun sank uncertainly.

Remo was searching the CURE director's gray eyes. He seemed satisfied with what he found.

"Think you can hold off shooting me this time, Smitty? And while you're at it, close the door."

Smith didn't know what else to do. He lowered his gun a few inches and shut the door behind him.

"Is something wrong, Dr. Smith?" Mark Howard asked. His greenish-brown eyes were trained on the wavering barrel of his employer's automatic.

Remo answered for the CURE director. "He thinks you've gone rotten on us, Junior." To Smith he said, "Don't worry about the kid, Smitty. We've already covered this. He didn't know what he was doing with Purcell."

The gun inched lower. "Are you certain?" Smith asked.

"Yeah," Remo said. "You know we can tell if people are lying. I turned the juice up high, and the kid didn't crack. He let Purcell go, but he didn't mean to."

"But Mark should still be under sedation," Smith said.

"I woke him up," Remo said. "I needed someone who could run your dippy computers without trying to kill me. And whatever was wrong with him before, he seems fine now. You know Purcell's got some weird stuff he can do with his mind. I'm thinking he found some way to tap into the kid's brain. I still don't know why he picked him and not someone else.''

Smith glanced at Mark Howard. There was a look of fresh concern on the young man's face, this time tinged with guilt.

And for the first time Smith understood. Truly understood. The sleeplessness, the troubling dreams, all of it. He realized now that Mark Howard had almost certainly not been in control of his own actions when he let Jeremiah Purcell free. The CURE director wanted to question further on the Purcell matter, but Remo interrupted.

"We've got more than one old bad guy to worry about, Smitty. The guy who tried to get you to blow my head off? Turns out it isn't a guy at all. It's Friend.''

Remo's words registered with dull shock.

"Friend? How is that possible?''

"Beats me, but it's him.''

Smith's mind reeled. "Oh, my,'' he said. "My secretary just told me that a friend called my office this afternoon.''

"Should have been your tip-off right there,'' Remo said. "The only friends you've got are those cold-blooded computers you've got hidden downstairs.''

"The chips that held Friend's program,'' Smith said. "You said you got rid of all the VLSI chips.''

"I went back to that abandoned building a year after the last time we had a run-in with him. Someone must have gotten to the chip with his program on it first.''

Smith's face steeled. "If that's the case, then we have to stop him. I can't use my computer. Mark, since Friend doesn't know about you, you will have to be my eyes."

"Already found him," Remo said.

Smith raised a surprised eyebrow. "You have?"

"I *think* I have," Mark cautioned. "Robbie MacGulry's flagship station in Australia appears to be the source for the subliminal signals. I think he's using the Vox satellite system to relay the commands. If we can shut that down, we should be able to pull the plug on the signals."

"Robbie MacGulry is in on this?" Smith asked wearily.

"Look, Smitty," Remo said with an impatient sigh, "you can catch up on everything once I'm gone. I was just having the kid book me a flight to Australia."

"I didn't know how long you'd be out, Dr. Smith," Mark said apologetically. "And this seemed too urgent to wait."

As he spoke, the phone on his desk jangled to life. When Mark answered it, he talked for only a few seconds. When he replaced the receiver, his face was flushed. He hurriedly pressed the hidden stud under his desk, lowering his computer monitor from sight.

"That was Mrs. Mikulka," the young man said. "She just got a call from downstairs. Dr. Gerling wants you down there right away, Dr. Smith." He glanced at Remo. "It's Chiun."

Remo said not a word. Face hard, he darted for the

door. Mark hurried after him. Smith was the odd man out. He whirled as Remo raced into the hall.

"What's wrong with Master Chiun?" Smith asked Howard.

"I'll explain on the way," the assistant CURE director replied anxiously. With a sickly smile, he pointed to the gun that was still in his employer's hand. "And by the sounds of what Remo told me, maybe you better bring that along."

26

Dr. Aldace Gerling stood anxiously over the elderly patient. He would have sat down, but for some reason that just didn't seem right. There was something in the old man's bearing, even unconscious, that commanded respect.

The Asian was truly a unique specimen. Delusional but remarkably healthy for a man of his advanced years. Dr. Gerling had considered writing a paper on him at one point, but when he brought it up to Dr. Smith, the Folcroft director had gotten a very strange look on his face. The last time Dr. Gerling had seen a look like that one was the night years ago when he'd taken his in-laws to a new Chinese restaurant and they'd all wound up with food poisoning. Dr. Smith said no to the paper and Dr. Gerling let the matter drop.

Right now a published paper in some obscure professional journal was the last thing on Aldace Gerling's mind. The Folcroft psychiatrist's back already ached from the hours he'd spent hunched over Director Smith. As he waited now over the old Asian's bed, he shifted from foot to foot.

There was perspiration on the doctor's broad forehead. A frown cut deeply through the jowls of his ruddy face.

Dr. Gerling was greatly relieved when Dr. Smith hurried into the hospital room. Folcroft's director was accompanied by Assistant Director Howard and the Asian's friend, Remo.

"What's the matter?" Remo demanded. A worried look was settled deep in the skull-like hollows of his dark eyes.

"Nothing's wrong," Dr. Gerling said as the trio joined him near the bed. "In fact, I believe I have good news. I don't think this man is under any kind of hypnosis."

Mark Howard had given Smith the rapid-fire details on their way downstairs. The CURE director looked down at the mummified face of the Master of Sinanju.

"What makes you think that?" Smith asked cautiously. "He was exposed to the subliminal hypnotic flashes. Wasn't he?" As he spoke, the CURE director glanced at Remo.

"I saw them with my own eyes, Smitty," Remo insisted.

"That's unlikely," Dr. Gerling assured him. "The flashes wouldn't register to the normal human eye. But either way, he seems to be okay. Look."

The doctor took out his penlight. With his thumb, he drew back one of Chiun's wrinkled eyelids. The exposed hazel orb darted angrily around its socket. When it fixed on Remo, it locked in place, shooting daggers.

"It looks like he's still under to me," Remo said

worriedly. "Don't you see that look he's giving me? By the looks of it, he still wants to kill me."

If an eye could nod agreement, Chiun's did.

"See?" Remo said.

"No, no, no," Gerling insisted firmly. "That has nothing to do with any hypnotic state. He's conscious, I'm sure of it. I think he's just angry at you."

Chiun's eye nodded once again.

Dr. Gerling released the eyelid and it fluttered shut over the Master of Sinanju's enraged eyeball.

"I was going to use the same technique I used to draw Dr. Smith out of his hypnotic state," the Folcroft doctor explained, "but he seemed already out of it. His pupils were responsive before I even started. I think he's fine."

"He's always kind of mad at Remo, Doctor," Mark Howard ventured. "Would that make a difference?"

"If you mean is this genuine anger surfacing within a hypnotic state, I don't think so," Gerling said. "I think it's the real thing." He looked questioningly at Remo. "He's mad at you for something."

The other two men glanced at Remo, as well. Remo gave all three of them a nasty look.

"So sue me—he's ticked at me for something again," he growled. "He ain't exactly Robert-freaking-Young, you know."

"I think it's safe for you to undo whatever acupressure you used on him," Dr. Gerling said.

"You got a funny definition of safe, pal," Remo said.

"Very well, Dr. Gerling," Smith said. "Thank you for all your help. Now, if you will excuse us. Mark?"

Smith and Remo stayed at the bedside as the assistant CURE director ushered Dr. Gerling from the room. He shut the door and rejoined the others near the bed.

"You think I should do this, Smitty?" Remo asked.

"I trust Dr. Gerling's professional opinion," Smith replied. There was a tone of nervous uncertainty in the older man's tart voice.

"Tell me how much you trust him when we're sweeping little Smitty bits up and down this nuthouse hallway," Remo said dryly. "Okay, stand back. And if he's anything like he was this morning, get ready to head for the hills, Fuji."

As Smith and Howard stood with their backs to the door, Remo leaned over the bed.

With a feathery touch, Remo pressed his thumb to Chiun's forehead. The Master of Sinanju's eyes instantly shot open. As quickly as they did, he was springing to his feet.

For a tense instant, Remo thought his teacher would launch into another attack. But the old man became a frozen statue of cold fury. Hands clenched to knots of bone at his sides as he glared up at his pupil.

"Is *this* what I've become to you?" Chiun demanded, his singsong voice ringing high with rage. "I am now some *thing* to be carted around and disposed of at inconvenient moments? Can my worst fears possibly be true? Do you crave the title of Reigning Master so much that you would take me and dump me off in some dank basement in the hope that I will die from the humiliation?''

"Take it easy, Little Father,'' Remo said. "Don't you remember MacGulry's office? You were hypnotized.''

"Codswallop,'' Chiun sniffed. "A Master of Sinanju cannot be hypnotized.''

"Vassily Rabinowitz,'' Remo said, reminding his teacher of a time years ago when he had, in fact, been hypnotized.

Chiun's slivered eyes sprang wide with rage. "Is this your plan?'' he demanded in Korean, stamping his sandaled feet. "To shame me into an early grave? Are you now the town crier of my worst humiliations? Is my every disgrace to be shouted from the rooftops?''

Smith didn't understand the language, but the old Korean's tone was clear.

"It's true, Master Chiun,'' Smith insisted. "Look at the air before you. Do you see something?''

The Master of Sinanju scowled. "I see nothing but an ungrateful pupil,'' he snapped in English. "If there was any air there, his big white nose breathed it all up on me.''

"Look carefully. Stare at the wall,'' Smith pressed. "Do you see any words?''

"What is this idiot babbling about?'' Chiun asked Remo in Korean.

"Those subliminal commands MacGulry tried to

use on you," Remo said in English. "You remember it, don't you?"

Chiun's face fouled. "Of course."

"I think you're supposed to still be able to see it even after you come out of it," Remo said. "Shittman told me he could still see the words even after he came around."

"It was the same for me," Smith interjected.

"I see no words on walls," Chiun spit.

"Odd," Smith said. "Perhaps your Sinanju training dispels the lingering effects."

"There are no lingering effects because I was not hypnotized," Chiun snapped. "Whatever Remo tells you to the contrary is part of the web of lies he has concocted to hasten his ascendency to Reigning Masterhood." He waved his furious hands in the air. "Bah! I refuse to bear the indignity of this any longer."

Kimono hems twirling defiantly around his bony ankles, he swept out the door. Mark barely opened it in time. He let the door swing shut after the old man was gone.

"He let me off the hook pretty easy," Remo mused. As he stared at the door, a dark notch formed in his brow.

"*That* was easy?" Howard asked. "Have I told you lately how glad I am I'm not you?"

"Mutual," Remo said.

"We have more pressing matters," Smith interrupted urgently. "Mark, I want all televisions in Folcroft confiscated for the duration of this crisis. I don't want you to risk going near them. Have the orderlies lock them in a supply room. Now, given Friend's ability to worm his way into computer systems, for safety's sake I can no longer use the one in my office. Fortunately, he doesn't know you've joined CURE. I assume that's why you've been left out of the attacks so far. You should be safe for the time being.''

"Unless he decides to tap into the only active computer in the sanitarium," Howard suggested. "He could just tell whoever's using it to kill you."

"I'm hoping the CURE safeguards will rebuff him. If not, we'll worry about that when and if it happens," Smith said tightly.

The CURE director didn't mention that he had already considered that scenario. It was a necessary risk. Besides, he knew how to keep both himself and his assistant safe. The tranquilizer guns Smith had hoped to use against Jeremiah Purcell were back under lock and key. His next trip would be to the basement locker to retrieve one of the guns. If it became necessary, he would use one on Mark Howard.

"Apparently, Friend has called here asking after me," Smith continued. "I will have to find out from Mrs. Mikulka precisely what she said. If he thinks I am incapacitated, it is likely that we can expect some kind of attack against me."

"Why?" Remo asked.

"Because his pattern has been consistent. He is setting us against one another, not caring who goes first. If he thinks one of us is vulnerable, he will seize the opportunity. That's what I would do under the circumstances.''

"If you say so," Remo said. "Trust a computer to think like a computer. So what do I do?''

"What you were going to do already. Go to Australia and dismantle MacGulry's ability to send those signals around the world. With any luck that will lead you to Friend."

"That's what I started to tell you upstairs," Mark said excitedly. "I think I found him. When Remo told me about Friend, I did a search and traced a ton of computer equipment to two Vox sources. Way more than they'd need, even for the kind of TV operation MacGulry runs. He had stuff shipped to the station in New South Wales and redundant equipment sent to his house in Queensland."

"If that's the case, Friend will only be at one of those locations," Smith said. "The other is most likely reserved as a backup in case of emergency."

"I'll pull the plug on both," Remo insisted. "Okay, if that's all, I've got a plane to catch."

"About that," Howard said. "I was only making arrangements for one. But now that Chiun is up and about…" He looked questioningly at Smith.

Remo's eyes grew flat. "He's not going," he insisted.

"I suppose it might be unwise to send him in light of what happened at MacGulry's office," Smith admitted.

"Right," Remo agreed. "He's not going."

"It might not be safe for him."

"Like I said. He's not going."

"However, you know what Master Chiun is like," Smith cautioned. "If he decides he should accompany you, there is little any of us could do to stop him."

Remo's shoulders sank. "He's going, isn't he?"

"Yes," called a squeaky voice from the hallway. "And if you plan on opening your big dumb mouth again, pack a parachute."

27

The sleek white Vox jet roared out of the clear blue sky above Queensland, Australia. Its lone passenger tapped his foot in frustration on the floor as he watched the ground rise up to meet the plane.

Ken ''Robbie'' MacGulry hated this. He liked to drive events, not sit in the bloody back seat.

It was all Friend's fault. The sentient computer program had transferred his enemies over to Robbie MacGulry. Apparently, they'd been after Friend for years. Now they had a living, breathing target to trace.

''Should've just told the yobbo to rack-off that first time he called,'' he grumbled to himself.

Maybe Friend didn't understand the human factor. Maybe he didn't realize that actual flesh-and-blood people had a tendency to make things personal. Or maybe—just maybe—he *wanted* them to follow Robbie MacGulry back here.

Back in New York, MacGulry's suspicions about Friend had finally been confirmed. It was possible Friend didn't want anyone else in on his secret. Maybe Robbie MacGulry was the only one to ever figure out what Friend really was.

Well, if luring his enemies to Oz was Friend's way

of bumping off MacGulry, the smart-ass computer program was in for a big surprise. Now that he knew the truth, Robbie might have an ace up his sleeve Friend hadn't anticipated.

The media magnate smiled to himself as the plane cut low over a sprawling, isolated mansion.

MacGulry's Queensland home was an oasis of green in a drab brown prairie. And buried beneath the manicured lawns and gleaming windows was Friend's deadliest secret.

The house slipped away. A few moments later, plane tires shrieked as they struck pavement. Gray kangaroos that were part of the preserve around the rural runway bounded off in every direction as the jet rolled to a stop.

A bewdy of a stewardess opened the door on the parched air. Hot wind blew in from the west.

A very pale man with a wide-brimmed hat and a sweat-stained cotton dress shirt was waiting for MacGulry when he deplaned. Rodney Adler was giving the Australian salute, waving away mosquitoes from around his sweaty face.

"Welcome home, Mr. MacGulry," Adler said, his British accent as crisp and dry as his body was damp. "Everything is ready, per your instructions."

"You cleared out the Wollongong station?" MacGulry demanded, marching past the Englishman. A Rolls-Royce was waiting a dozen yards away, engine running.

"Some of the staff have been relocated here to operate the special systems," Adler said, hurrying to catch up. "The rest were let go until after the start of the New Year." He swatted a fat mosquito on his arm. "Oh, and your associate called while you were en route. He was curious to know what exactly was going on."

MacGulry stopped dead in his tracks. Eyes growing wide, he wheeled on Adler. "He called *you?*" he demanded.

Adler almost plowed into his employer.

"Yes," he admitted nervously. "I assumed you would want me to extend him every courtesy. He knew we were clearing out the station. He asked us to do something first. Since he knew so many details, I assumed he'd spoken to you first."

A swarm of mozzies circled both men. MacGulry ignored the buzzing insects. For a moment the Vox chairman just stood there, fuming.

This was the worst offense of all. Thanks to this private war he was waging, Friend was no longer content to act behind the scenes. After all these years, he was suddenly contacting Robbie MacGulry's employees directly. For the first time his Vox lackeys were learning the truth—the great and terrifying Robbie MacGulry was irrelevant. There was someone even greater lurking behind the scenes.

Even Adler was looking at him differently. MacGulry could see the swelling lack of respect in the younger man's eyes. Oh, the Englishman was trying to hide it behind his usual mask of whimpering anxiety as he stood there scratching mosquito bites, but there was no mistaking it.

Robbie MacGulry was no longer a king. His stature had been diminished. And it was all Friend's fault.

"Get outta my way, you pommie bastard," MacGulry snapped. He shoved Adler aside.

The Englishman hesitated before running to catch up with his employer.

"Was that not the right thing to do?" Adler asked.

MacGulry didn't even respond. "What about the Robbots?" the Vox chairman demanded.

"They are ready, sir," Adler said. He seemed even more nervous at this new subject. "Deployed at all entry points."

MacGulry's driver was waiting to open the back door. At the side of the Rolls-Royce, MacGulry turned.

"What did he tell you to do?" he snapped.

"Who, sir?" asked Adler.

"The guy who called, dammit. What did he tell you to do when he called?"

"Oh," Adler said, hesitating. "It's— Well, it's a little thing. I assumed it would be all right."

His hands were shaking. From a manila envelope tucked under his sweaty armpit, he produced a photo-quality computer printout. MacGulry snatched the picture from Adler.

It was Friend's younger enemy. The Caucasian who had chased Robbie MacGulry from New York. It was the same digitally created picture Friend had supplied MacGulry in the hope that Remo could be eliminated in Harlem. Only now did MacGulry realize why that computer printout had looked so...*com-*

puterized. It was straight out of Friend's memory.

"We haven't been able to confirm if that image Cindee Maloo sent us from America is the same man," Adler said. "I've never seen anyone able to mask his features like that. That footage she sent was useless. Your associate told us to use the original we used twice in New York. He faxed us another picture."

Adler pulled another photo from the envelope. This one was of the old Korean. Like the picture of Remo, it had a not-quite-real quality. A computerized version of a police sketch.

"What are you doing with those?" MacGulry asked.

"Well," Adler began anxiously, "we've been beaming them out subliminally all over New South Wales for the past twelve hours. Ever since your friend called. The Wollongong station has been set to automatically include them in all broadcast signals with instructions to kill on sight. If they show up in the area, the entire population that has been exposed to the cryptosubliminal images will tear them to pieces like a pack of wild dogs." A nervous smile exposed crooked teeth. "Does that not fit in with your plans, sir?"

MacGulry held a picture in each hand, glancing from Remo to Chiun. He shoved the photos back in Adler's hands.

"It fits in with *his* plans," the Vox CEO said, dropping into the back of the Rolls-Royce. "And with any luck, they'll be as good as he thinks they are and I'll have that stickybeak computer bugger right where I want him.''

His driver slammed the door on the heat and mosquitoes.

28

"I think you should probably sit this one out, Little Father," Remo warned.

The two men had just climbed aboard the military aircraft that would take them to Australia. An Air Force lieutenant guided them to their seats.

"You may think of that and new ways to dishonor me when we are in the air," the Master of Sinanju sniffed. He swept past the offered seat, settling in the one behind it. It looked out over the left wing.

"I'm not dishonoring you, I'm worried about you," Remo said. "There, I said it. The big dirty word. I'm *worried* about you. Damn, I'm a crummy son, aren't I? I'm actually worried about you. And why wouldn't I be? We haven't even talked about what happened in MacGulry's office."

Remo's face held a look of deep concern. Chiun turned once to his pupil. His own expression was bland.

"You may talk to your heart's content," the old Korean said. "Just do not involve me in your jabbering."

And with that the Master of Sinanju turned away. For the better part of a day, for the duration of their trip to Australia, Remo's view was of the back of Chiun's age-speckled head. The old man studied cloud and sea, not once so much as glancing at his pupil. Only when the plane started to descend over Sydney did he turn from the window.

"I must warn you about Australians," the old man announced unhappily.

Remo noted his teacher's lack of enthusiasm. He didn't care. He was just happy Chiun was talking to him after so many hours.

"What about them?" Remo asked.

"Watch them," Chiun said. He turned back to the window.

"That's it? Watch them? Watch them do what?"

But Chiun didn't reply. He said nothing more as the plane landed and they got off. He remained silent all the way through customs when Remo asked for the tenth time why he should watch Australians and Chiun finally released a little exasperated sigh.

"A good pupil would just do as he's told—he would not question."

"Good pupil, good Nazi, good dog. I'm none of those. Why watch Australians?"

"Because if you do not, they will steal the marrow from your bones and sell it to the butcher."

"Wait, I thought the Chinese were the thieves. Sometimes the Japanese. Now Australians are, too? How do you expect me to keep the racism straight if you're just gonna tar everyone with the same brush?"

"I am not," Chiun said. "More than one people can be the same thing. Just because the French stink, it does not mean that the Filipinos do not. Believe me, they do. Australians are more than just common thieves. They are murderers and pirates and insurrectionists. This is where England sends all its riffraff who are not royalty.''

''Chiun, that hasn't been going on for a hundred years.''

''See? Just yesterday. My father warned me about Australians. If they like your sandals, they will steal them from your feet while you are walking and then come back for your feet.''

''We walked through Harlem, we can walk through Australia,'' Remo said.

But in the next moment even he wasn't sure of his own argument. As they walked out into the terminal, Remo felt a hundred sets of eyes lock on him and the Master of Sinanju. Men who had been sitting stood. A hush fell over the crowd.

''Oh, crud,'' was all Remo managed to say before a murderous howl rose up from the airport concourse.

The crowd surged toward Remo and Chiun.

''It's a mugging!'' the Master of Sinanju cried, twirling on his heel. ''Guard your purse!''

The old man bounded down the hall, back in the direction they'd just come.

''A hundred people aren't rolling two guys, Little Father,'' Remo said, running to catch up.

Passengers who had just deplaned from a commercial flight jumped angrily from their path.

''If you knew Australians like I knew Australians, you would not be so naive,'' Chiun replied.

Behind them, the mob gained strength. Remo and Chiun darted up an escalator, across a railing and jumped down into the main terminal. The crowd doubled back in hot pursuit.

In the terminal, Remo wasn't surprised to see some familiar hypnotic pulses flashing on the arrival and departure monitors that hung from the ceiling.

"Don't look at the screens, Chiun," Remo warned.

But Chiun was already out the door. Remo flew out after him. The Master of Sinanju was bounding into the rear of a waiting cab. When Remo slipped in after him, the driver tried to gouge out his eyes with his keys.

Remo smacked the cabbie unconscious and snagged the keys on their way to the floor.

"Just once it'd be nice to go somewhere where everyone isn't trying to kill me," he groused as he dumped the driver to the sidewalk. He hopped behind the wheel.

"It is not you and your offensive personality for once—it is this floating prison," Chiun squeaked. "Hurry and drive, while my virtue is still intact."

Remo managed to drive ten feet before a speeding car crumpled his bumper. The driver had the dead-eyed look of Vox's other subliminal victims. When Remo tried to go around it, another cab hopped the curb and slammed them from the other side. They were pinned in a V of crashed cars as the mob from the terminal began swarming into the sunlight.

The crowd swamped the cab, smashing windows and pounding fists on buckling metal.

"Any ideas, Little Father?" Remo asked as he leaned away from hands that were trying to strangle him.

When he got no response other than the animal roar of the mob, he glanced in the back seat.

Chiun was gone.

"Why didn't I think of that?" Remo muttered.

He popped the door and slipped out.

The crowd surged. Remo surged with it. As it continued surging, he bled back through it, leaving the mob to crush to death the empty space where he no longer was.

Their backs were to him as he hurried along the row of cabs. He kept to pillar and shadow to avoid detection.

He found the Master of Sinanju three cabs down. The driver of this taxi didn't have the look of a Vox viewer in his eyes. He seemed baffled by the activity up ahead.

"You wanna kill us, too?" Remo asked the driver as he slid in the back seat next to the Master of Sinanju.

"Only if you're a lousy tipper, mate," the man replied.

Remo gave the cabbie the address of Robbie MacGulry's flagship station. The two Masters of Sinanju ducked low, avoiding the crowd that was just beginning to realize that the two men they were after had disappeared.

"What did I tell you?" Chiun said. "This country is not safe for simpler travelers like me."

"Looks like it's plenty safe for people who aren't us," Remo said. "Friend must be expecting us. Do me a favor and keep from looking at any TV screens, okay?"

A strange look came over the old man's face. If Remo didn't know better, he would have sworn it was a flush of embarrassment on his teacher's cheeks.

Chiun didn't look at Remo. As they drove away from the airport, he fussed at the knees of his kimono.

"Believe me, the last thing I want to see is your ugly white face on television," the Master of Sinanju sniffed.

He screwed his mouth shut tight for the rest of the cab ride from Sydney.

REMO HAD the taxi driver park at the back fence of the Wollongong Vox station. Avoiding guard booths and security cameras, the two Masters of Sinanju scaled the high fence and slid onto the grounds. The parking lots were empty.

"No cars," Remo commented as they headed for the main building. "Little early to be closed for Christmas."

"This is Australia," Chiun grumbled. "They were probably all stolen."

"Friend thinks we're coming. He's probably up to something. Just please, be careful."

His meaning was clear.

This time, the Master of Sinanju did not dignify his pupil's plea with a single word. Face stony, he mounted a set of rear stairs between security camera cycles. Remo darted inside behind his teacher.

They found themselves in a long air-conditioned hallway. The walls were thick glass. A door at the end of the hall led into a large control room.

The room was two stories high and filled with enough high-tech gadgetry to put NASA to shame. The air inside was cold. There was no one in the room. A pair of lonely security cameras scanned from high above.

Remo had already had enough of cameras lately. And now he knew who might be on the other side looking in.

On entering the room, Remo feinted left, Chiun dodged right. They each found a blind spot on opposite sides of the room where the cameras wouldn't be able to track them.

Once Remo was sure he sensed no listening devices, he called over to the Master of Sinanju.

"Just because they're broadcasting from here, doesn't mean Friend's around."

"No, it does not," Chiun agreed.

"So you wanna be first?"

"As Master I was first," Chiun replied thinly. "Which means I decide who goes first."

Remo's eyes sank to half-mast. "Short straw again," he said. Sighing, he stepped down the painted concrete stairs.

The cameras had continued to patiently sweep the room. But as the first one passed Remo, it stopped dead. An instant later, a phone at his elbow rang.

"Think it's for me?" Remo said dryly as he lifted the receiver to his ear.

"Hello, Remo," said a familiar smooth voice. "I'm surprised to see you here so soon."

Remo's eyes were trained on the security camera. The unblinking eye of Friend stared back.

"I got a good tailwind," Remo said.

"I see. Are you alone?"

Remo didn't dare shoot a glance at the Master of Sinanju. With his peripheral vision he saw his teacher moving like a wraith down another set of stairs. Both cameras were now trained solely on Remo. They missed completely the old Korean as he crept stealthily forward.

"Wasn't that your plan?" Remo asked. "You got to Smith and Chiun. You were knocking us off one at a time."

"That was part of the plan, not the plan itself," Friend admitted.

"Yeah, I know," Remo said. "You want to take over the world. Don't you ever get tired of singing that same song?"

"I only want those parts of the world where there is profit to be made. The technology I've developed will help me reach my goal. Imagine, Remo, any product I advertise on my global network will sell to young, old, rich, poor. Demographics will no longer matter. The profit of a single world media market utilizing the cryptosubliminal technology can be measured in the trillions."

"Right now it's not dollars I care about," Remo

said. "It's my face being beamed to every koala coop and outhouse in the merry old land of Oz."

"They've seen you without actually seeing you," Friend explained. "The image will fade in their minds a day or two after their exposure to it. In the meantime, I have a business proposition for you."

"If this is the one where you offer me a job, been there, done that," Remo said. "So why don't we just skip ahead to the part where I pull your plug?"

"Don't bother," Friend said. "You're too far away to be a threat to me. I can move before you can reach me."

Across the room, Chiun had stopped by some thick electrical cables. They ran through the wall close to his ankles. A steady hum of artificial life surged through them.

"Wrong again, chips for brains," Remo said into the phone.

And as he spoke, the Master of Sinanju jumped.

The cameras were too slow to track him. Chiun snatched up cables in both hands. They were like thick black snakes. With a yank, the cords snapped one by one, surrendering sizzling sparks from their frayed ends.

The lights dimmed. The power hummed down for a moment. But with a distant click and whir, the overhead lights came back up.

"Dammit," Remo snapped. "Must be a backup generator." In a blur, he flew forward and began tearing wires from the backs of monitor stations.

On the other side of the room, the Master of Sinanju became a vengeful dervish. Flashing hands ripped cords from floor pads and consoles. Sparks sizzled white across the cold concrete floor.

"Okay, *that* got him this—"

Remo stopped in midsentence.

The phone on which he'd been speaking to Friend dangled from its cord near the floor. An electronic shriek rose from the receiver.

"The thing is moving," Chiun hissed.

"He's transferring himself through the phone lines," Remo agreed. "Where the hell's the line?"

Chiun wasn't listening. The old man had already turned on his heel and was racing up the stairs. Remo flew after him out the door. Down the hall, they ducked back out into the sunlight.

Outside, the Master of Sinanju scanned the side of the building for the black cable of a telephone line. He found it attached to the second floor.

"Aiiee!" cried the old Korean. Calves tensing, he launched himself from the ground.

One story up, a sandal toe caught the building's smooth face and he launched himself out and up. A single downward stroke of one fingernail severed the line and the old man dropped back to earth next to his pupil.

The worthless end of the fat black cord slapped the dusty ground.

"I hope you stopped him," Remo said grimly.

Turning quickly, they ducked back inside the building.

A rapid search turned up a small computer room

set apart from the rest of the building. A half-dozen large mainframes lurked against painted black walls.

Remo got to the sole monitor in the room first. When he read the words on the screen, his heart sank.

TRANSFER COMPLETE.

"Dammit," he growled.

"What is it?" the Master of Sinanju asked, coming in from behind.

Remo's thoughts suddenly jumped from Friend back to his teacher. "Don't look, Chiun," he snapped.

As he spoke, he put his fist through the computer screen. The glass imploded with a popping crack.

A thundercloud formed on the old man's brow.

"What is wrong with you?" the Master of Sinanju hissed.

"Chiun, you *have* to be careful," Remo insisted.

"Careful of what?" Chiun demanded hotly. "Of choosing a pupil who is so dense he cannot seem to recognize which humiliation he is forcing his teacher to relive? It is far too late for that."

Spinning on his heel, he marched from the computer room.

There seemed a hundred conflicting emotions in the old man's words and tone. Most of all was hurt and sadness. Remo had no idea what to make of it.

A baffled frown on his face, he trailed the Master of Sinanju from Robbie MacGulry's Wollongong TV station.

29

With the heel of one shoe, Detective Ronald Davic kicked shut the door to his third-story apartment. As usual, it stuck without closing all the way. He had to nudge it closed with his rear end.

Inside, he set the grocery bags on the kitchen table and pulled his keys from between his teeth. The table wobbled.

He'd swiped it from his mother's backyard after her last heart attack finally put her in a home. In an ill-advised homemaking project, Davic slathered the picnic table with five coats of shellac and stuck it in his kitchen. It was ugly and shiny, but it was flat enough. If food didn't roll off it, he reasoned, it worked.

The apartment was dingy and dank. In the moist corners it still smelled like the cat that had died on him three years before. Not a surprise. Somewhere beneath the piles of junk in the spare bedroom was a moldy litter box that he rarely got around to emptying even when the cat was alive.

Under other circumstances his landlord might have complained about the mess and the smell. Fortunately, Ronald Davic owned the three-story tenement.

He dumped his coat onto the table next to the groceries. A moist cigarette dangled from his lip. He stubbed it out in an overflowing ashtray.

Fishing in the fridge, he pulled out a can of Diet Coke. Soda in hand, he trudged into the living room.

Like the kitchen, the furniture in this room was a sorry mess. Not one stick matched another. He had a girlfriend a couple or a dozen years ago who told him a million times that he would have used folding lawn furniture in the living room if he could figure out a way to open the umbrella inside.

He slouched into the same chair his father used to slouch in forty years before.

The TV stared at him from across the room.

On top of the old Zenith was a photograph. It was one of the few things he ever bothered dusting, usually by wiping off the grime with the sleeve of his shirt. It was a photo of the Davic family as it appeared back in the 1970s.

He had a wife then. She had left him while he was still on the force in New York. In the picture she was smiling, which was wrong. Libbie Davic never smiled.

Davic would have tossed out the picture if it wasn't for his daughters. It had been taken before their mother had filled their heads with poison. In that picture the two girls were young and beautiful and beamed joy at the camera.

In spite of the dishonest depiction of his ex-wife, the picture was a permanent part of Ronald Davic's living room.

Davic picked up a remote control from the overflowing magazine rack next to his ratty old chair. As he slurped his Coke, he snapped on the TV to watch the news.

The local news was the usual garbage. Abused pets, missing children, assorted fluff pieces. He ordinarily just listened, opting to stare at the picture of the family he had lost a lifetime before. But this night something seemed different. For some reason the blathering of the Vox anchorman was more compelling than usual.

It was the light. Somehow the light that flashed at him from the TV screen seemed brighter than normal.

He dragged his eyes from the photo down to the screen.

His eyes instantly glazed over.

He saw them. On some level he saw the commands: *Ronald Davic...Ronald Davic...Ronald Davic...*

His name repeated over and over, interspersed with the commands that were meant for him and him alone.

He stared for ten minutes. Finally, he shut off the TV.

Sitting at the edge of his chair, Detective Ronald Davic took out his gun to make absolutely sure it was loaded. When he was sure it was, he reholstered the gun and left the room.

His keys were on the kitchen table. He pocketed them as he shrugged on his coat. Leaving the three bags of groceries on the table, he left the apartment for the short drive to Folcroft Sanitarium. Where he would kill its director.

30

The mountain sentinels of the Great Dividing Range jutted up across the eastern horizon, undulating waves of solid rock locked in time.

Red streaks of fire lit the sky and burned the ground. The sun was setting on Robbie MacGulry's sprawling Queensland estate. The brilliant colors of the evening sky were fading into the darkest night of the Vox CEO's life.

"You sure about that?" he asked.

"Yes, sir," Rodney Adler replied. "The station is in ruins. The cryptosubliminal equipment has been destroyed."

MacGulry knew when the station had gone down. It was the same time the dormant computer room beneath his mansion had hummed to life. As he had suspected, Friend had sought refuge beneath Robbie's feet.

"You cut the phone lines like I told you?" the Vox chairman asked.

"We took down all but your direct one from Wollongong this morning. We cut that one as soon as you instructed us to. I confiscated and destroyed all cellular phones. Your estate is effectively cut off from the modern world.''

A flicker of a smile crossed MacGulry's tanned face.

"Not out of the woods yet," he said. "But it's a start. Tell the Robbots to stay alert."

"Oh…ah, yes. The Robbots."

MacGulry's brow darkened. "You told me they were deployed. Is there a problem?"

The Robbots were Robbie MacGulry's last line of defense. An army of mercenaries, all were cold-blooded killers who had had every last vestige of human emotion drained from their frozen hearts by months of relentless exposure to subliminal brain-washing. They would fight to their last drop of blood to protect the Vox CEO.

Rodney Adler wilted under his employer's harsh glare.

"No problem, Mr. MacGulry," the Englishman said, with a smile so broad it made Robbie MacGulry want to stick his dentist in a box and mail him to London.

"Better not be," MacGulry threatened. "Get to work."

Rodney Adler tripped over his own feet in his haste to get back inside.

For a few more moments, Robbie MacGulry watched the setting sun. It was something he rarely had time to do. At long last he stepped back inside his mansion, sliding the glass doors behind him.

Two minutes after he'd gone inside, the faint sound

of an approaching plane rose up from the growing twilight.

IT TOOK five tries for Remo and Chiun to finally find a pilot who didn't try to kill them on sight. Their small Cessna soared across the vast plains of Australia's Great Artesian Basin. Remo forced the pilot to land on the long, lonely road that led up to the gates of MacGulry's estate.

As they walked up the road, they saw a line of Subaru Outbacks parked inside the split-rail fence. A hundred men stood at attention before the cars.

The men were muscled and tanned. They wore short pants, khaki flak jackets, hiking boots and bush hats, the brims of which were buttoned up on one side. Each man held an assault rifle. Their eyes were glazed.

"The Running Line?" Remo suggested as they walked toward the gate and the waiting group of men.

"Better for enclosed places," the Master of Sinanju replied.

"Could use the Ellipse Within the Ellipse. We haven't used that one in a while."

"Perhaps," Chiun said, frowning. His nose crinkled as he smelled the air.

Remo had caught the scent, as well. It was being carried to them on the faint breeze.

The air stank of beer. Lots of it. As he watched the line of waiting men, Remo suddenly realized why.

"You've gotta be kidding me," he said all at once.

"Holt, hoo goes theya?" one man before them slurred as Remo and Chiun approached.

The army pointed their guns. Some of them managed to point them somewhere that was almost within the vicinity of where Remo and Chiun were standing. The rest aimed at fence posts and car tires and into empty prairie. The barrels weaved along with the men behind them.

"They're pie-eyed," Remo said.

"In Australia it is called being patriotic," Chiun replied blandly.

"I said hoo goes theya," hiccuped the lead Robbot.

"Larry Hagman's liver," Remo said. "Move it, drunky."

"I don't much like your attitude, Sheila. Open slather time, cobbers!" the head Robbot yelled to his companions.

A hundred rifle barrels burst to life. Fence posts and tires exploded in sprays of wood and rubber.

"Fair dinkum!" some of the men cried as they began accidentally shooting one another.

"Strewth!" they shouted when they realized how good a job they were doing killing one another.

"Cor blimey!" they yelled when they discovered—to their horror—that they'd accidentally shot holes in their tinnies of beer. The survivors threw down their guns and began lapping up damp dirt.

"Give me strength," said Remo Williams.

He and Chiun swiped a drivable Outback from the line of parked cars. As the Robbots slurped dirt, Remo and Chiun sped up the road to Robbie MacGulry's mansion.

ROBBIE MACGULRY couldn't believe what he was seeing.

Surveillance cameras directed images of the slaughter at the front gate to the Vox chairman's handheld television.

The Robbots were nearly all dead. One had even managed to run himself over. He was wedged under the front wheel of an Outback, a beer can clutched in his dead hand.

"You made them all drunks!" MacGulry roared.

"Yes," Rodney Adler admitted nervously. "In retrospect perhaps it would have been wiser to hide the cryptosubliminal signal that was supposed to rob them of their souls in something other than a Toohey's beer commercial."

Flinging the small TV to the floor of his study, MacGulry wheeled around. He ripped a rifle from where it was mounted on the wall behind his desk. When he spun back around, there was a murderous glint in his eye.

Adler offered an anxious smile, flashing crooked teeth.

"Going hunting?" he asked, his voice a squeak.

With a low growl, MacGulry slapped the gun into Adler's hands.

"Stop 'em or I'll stomp you," the Vox CEO commanded.

Adler's face sank in relief. "Yes, sir!" he said. He scurried from the room.

MacGulry grabbed the mini-TV off the floor. The remaining living Robbots had linked arms and were singing an off-key version of "Tie Me Kangaroo Down, Sport." One was using a gun barrel for a microphone. He accidentally stepped on the trigger and blew the top of his head off.

"Wankers," MacGulry muttered to himself.

Dropping the handheld television to his desk, he raced from the study.

IT TOOK ANOTHER ten minutes for Remo and Chiun to reach the Vox CEO's mansion. It was a sprawling, whitewashed affair full of columns, clapboards and flowers.

Remo circled the drive, stopping at the front portico.

"Better stay here, Little Father," he suggested.

"You are not leaving me in the car like some nuisance canine," Chiun sniffed as he climbed down next to Remo.

"Not even if I crack a window?" Remo said quietly. "Look, Chiun, this is a cakewalk. Zap MacGulry, pull the plug on Friend."

"Get out of my way, imbecile," Chiun insisted.

Remo sighed. "Suit yourself. But I'd appreciate it if you didn't try to fillet me again."

"Shut your blabbering mouth and I will consider it," the old Asian replied thinly.

Forcing his way past Remo, he flounced up the

front stairs of Robbie MacGulry's mansion like a flapping green butterfly. Remo hurried up behind him.

The instant they pushed open the big front door, a voice boomed over hidden loudspeakers.

"Breaking and entering," Robbie MacGulry called. "I'm within my legal rights to defend my home, mates."

"So much for the element of surprise," Remo said.

"Hush," the Master of Sinanju hissed.

He was scanning the walls for surveillance equipment.

"Cameras and microphones everywhere," Remo whispered as they slipped stealthily up the downstairs hallway.

Both men knew that on the other end of the tangle of wires was not only MacGulry, but a far more dangerous foe.

"You could have had a sweet deal if you just went along with this, Remo," MacGulry called. "But Friend says you're not the kind who goes along, are you?"

"Shouldn't you be out taping 'World's Sexiest Car Chases VI'?" Remo asked the walls.

"Bad attitude," MacGulry's disembodied voice replied. "How about you, Chiun? My offer still stands."

"Sinanju works for men, not machines," Chiun announced coldly.

"You know what Friend is?" MacGulry asked, surprised.

"A three-times ass-kicked hunk of silicon that was

built to maximize profit," Remo said. "About to be crashed time number four." He peeked around an open door.

The room beyond was empty. Both Masters of Sinanju continued on.

"I worked with him thirty years. I only just found out what he was for sure two days ago," MacGulry said.

"Three cheers for the Aussie Einstein," Remo said.

They passed several more rooms. All were empty.

Passing through the door at the end of the hallway, they found themselves in a big, restaurant-style kitchen. MacGulry's voice preceded them into the room.

"You don't like Friend," MacGulry said over the speakers. "I understand that. You fellas have a history. What would you say to my job offer if I told you I could help you get the bastard once and for all?"

"I'd say blow it out your didgeridoo," Remo said.

Through the kitchen door they entered a huge dining room.

"Don't be too hasty," MacGulry said. "Vox-BCN is just the start. With the cryptosubliminal signal I can have it all. One hundred percent of the world's media markets. I can hypnotize people into buying no other magazines or newspapers but my own. Every movie Vox puts out will gross over two hundred million. My network will be the *world's* network. They'll be building thousand-foot statues of me in Sydney Harbour. It's your last chance. You wanna work for a smith or a king?''

''Not interested.''

''Did you say two hundred million gross?'' the Master of Sinanju asked slyly.

''We're not interested,'' Remo insisted. ''Besides, I can never forgive Australia for foisting Yahoo Serious on the rest of the world.''

''Too bad,'' MacGulry said. ''If we can't deal, you die. Adler!''

MacGulry's booming voice rattled glass throughout the mansion. As the vibrations shook the foundation, a very frightened man stepped through a side door into the dining room.

Rodney Adler's bony knees knocked. His face was ashen. The Englishman raised his Lee-Enfield rifle. Gulping, he took aim at Remo and Chiun.

''I am—'' Adler began. The gun rattled in his shaking hands. ''That is, you should— That is, Mr. MacGulry wants—''

''For God's sake,'' Robbie MacGulry bellowed, ''shut your stammering British hole and *fiya!*''

''Oh, yes,'' Adler said. ''Yes, of course. Of course, fire. Yes. Oh. Where did I put that rifle?''

The Lee-Enfield was no longer in his hands. He was certain it was there a moment ago. For an instant he glimpsed something he thought could be the rifle. It was sailing out the dining-room window. He truly wished the gun was still in his hands, because a face suddenly appeared before him. It belonged to the American that Mr. MacGulry had wanted dead. The face was very nasty-looking. Much worse in person than the computerized version that Rodney Adler had been beaming via satellite all over the world.

Seeing that face up close, with a promise of doom in those deep-set eyes, Rodney Adler reacted as a true son of Britain born and bred at the twilight of the Empire.

With a fluttering moan of fear and a dainty hand pressed over his heart, Rodney Adler passed out cold.

"Where's Lord Nelson when you need him," Remo droned. He stepped over the unconscious Englishman. Chiun followed.

"That way," the Master of Sinanju announced. A bony finger pointed to a nearby door.

Remo had traced the vibrations back to the same point. The heavy wooden door surrendered to a kick. It led into a short corridor. At the far end, another door opened into a massive chamber.

The room was as big as a theater, with a flat gymnasium floor that stretched out to black walls. There were no windows. All around the room, huge screens hung from the walls. Though turned off, the screens seemed alive with some sort of faint liquid energy.

Robbie MacGulry sat patiently on a chair in the middle of the room. A pedestal with a monitor was fastened to the floor before him.

"Welcome to the Big Room, gentlemen," the Vox CEO said. No longer amplified by speakers, his voice seemed small.

If MacGulry could see them, it was not in the conventional way. The media mogul wore a helmet that looked as if it had been swiped from the set of a sci-fi movie. The thick black visor was down, obscuring his face.

As soon as they were in the room, a steel door whooshed down from above, replacing the wooden one and sealing the two Sinanju Masters in the room.

"I don't like the looks of this," Remo said warily.

"You shouldn't, mate," Robbie MacGulry called from far across the room. "And you should have joined me when you had the chance. I've got Friend trapped. I cut the telephone lines after he came back here. He's not going anywhere. With you two gone, it's clear sailing for me and Vox. Maybe I'll make the offer again to whoever's left standing."

Remo saw the small black remote control in MacGulry's hand.

He was too far away. There was nothing to throw. The thick door would take a minute to break through.

All this passed through the mind of Remo Williams in the moment it took Robbie MacGulry to press a single button on his remote control. All around the room, the liquid TV screens came to glowing life.

The subliminal strobe light flashed. There was no way to get away from it.

Remo saw his face and that of the Master of Sinanju. Huge on the thirty-foot-tall screens. Flashing alternately. Superimposed over both images, the same words repeating: *Kill him…kill him…kill him…*

Remo felt the displacement of air to his right.

He spun in time to see the Master of Sinanju—eyes blank—lashing out.

Chiun's face was a mass of wrinkles, illuminated in microsecond bursts by hypnotic light. A single bony hand flew at Remo's throat.

Luck and speed had been on Remo's side in New York. He hoped this would be the case now, for in that mortal moment before Chiun's blow registered, Remo realized that the death of one Master of Sinanju might be the only way the other could escape this place of horrors alive.

31

Remo braced for the attack. His hands shot up instinctively to ward off the killing blows.

But in the instant before his hand reached Remo's throat, the Master of Sinanju's expression suddenly changed. The blank stare flashed to a look of deep annoyance. For that sliver in time he looked himself again.

Remo hesitated. And in that moment of uncertainty, Chiun's darting hand shot through his pupil's defenses.

Remo had but a split second to come to terms with his imminent death. But instead of a killing blow, a scolding hand smacked Remo hard on the side of the head. Afterward, Chiun's hands retreated inside the sleeves of his kimono.

"Let that be a lesson to all who would dismiss the abilities of the elderly," the old man sniffed haughtily.

Remo rubbed the side of his head.

"That hurt," he groused.

"The best lessons come from pain."

Remo looked around the room, baffled. The cryptosubliminal signal was still pulsing from all around the huge liquid TV screens. There was his face, with an order to kill him. Yet the Master of Sinanju hadn't succumbed.

"Hey, Rolf Harris," Remo called over to Robbie MacGulry. "I think you better call a repairman. Your hypno-screens are on the fritz."

MacGulry had already realized something was wrong. With frantic fingers he was poking buttons on his remote control.

"There is nothing wrong with his devices," the Master of Sinanju explained impatiently.

"But it worked on you before. I don't get it."

"That is why I am Master and you are whatever it is you are. When you learn, please tell me."

As the screens continued to flash worthless commands, Chiun swept past his baffled pupil.

"This isn't right," MacGulry snapped as he worked his remote. "You two should be ripping each other to shreds like wild dingos right now."

And then his puzzlement no longer mattered. He punched a final button and the floor opened up and swallowed the media magnate whole. By the time Remo and Chiun reached the spot where MacGulry had been, a steel plate had already slid over the section of floor, sealing the Vox chairman below.

"You wanna tell me why you're not trying to kill me?" Remo asked.

"Years of practice," Chiun replied thinly. "Are you going to help, or are you just going to stand there asking insulting questions?"

Chiun dropped to his knees. Slender fingertips found the edge of the sliding metal door.

Remo joined his teacher at the trapdoor's edge. When they pushed, there came a distant groan of grinding gears. The panel inched back. All at once there came a snap-snap-snap and the door shot open.

Remo and Chiun dropped through the opening.

The room below was a steel-lined box. Through the walls they could hear the sound of computer mainframes humming.

"Three guesses where Mr. Microchips ended up," Remo said.

Robbie MacGulry was a few feet away, a terrified look on his tanned face. He had flung his helmet to the floor and was banging madly on a sealed door.

"Let me out!" the Vox chairman screamed.

"I think we're gonna have to slap a parents advisory on the next minute or two," Remo said.

MacGulry wheeled. When he saw Remo and Chiun approaching, he banged harder on the door.

"Open up, *please!*"

"Probably TV-V-L should do it," Remo concluded. "Violence and language. We can avoid the usual Vox sex *S.* Unless you take off your pants, in which case I can guarantee you the *V* is gonna get a lot more *V*-ish."

MacGulry spun. He waved a threatening finger. "You can't hurt me. I've got billions!"

Remo snapped the finger in two. MacGulry screamed, falling to his knees.

"First the Chevy Chase talk show, now this. You ever get tired of being wrong?" Remo asked.

"All my money!" the Vox chairman cried. "It's yours! All of it!"

"No," said Remo.

"Did you say billions?" Chiun asked.

"Stop doing that," Remo said. To MacGulry he said, "Friend blabbed about us to you. Who else knows about us?"

"No one," MacGulry insisted. He was cradling his injured hand. "My employees have only seen your pictures. Your first names for some of the signals. They don't know who you are."

"Okay, here's the biggee. If g'day is Australian for hello, what do you say for goodbye?"

MacGulry's maroon face drew up in confusion. "Hooroo?" he replied.

"Well, hooroo to you with bells on," Remo said.

Remo's hand darted forward. MacGulry didn't have a chance to even think about getting out of the way before Remo's cupped palm was slapping over his mouth. The hand tugged away just as fast. With it came a sucking pop.

Robbie MacGulry felt an uncontrollable urge to vomit.

But it was more than just that, he soon found, for what launched up his throat was big and slippery and much larger and more disgusting than anything he could possibly have eaten. The big slippery something vomited out of his mouth and flopped like a wriggling red fish on the floor. Slimy tendrils hung like living thread from his mouth.

In a moment of shocked clarity, Robbie MacGulry realized he was staring down at his own disgorged lungs. Between them, he saw his own heart issuing its final feeble beats.

He was surprised. His heart wasn't black like a lot of people had claimed over the years. It was very ordinary, just a bluish-reddish heart, just like everyone else's. For an instant Robbie MacGulry wondered why the censors hadn't put a blue dot over his wiggling lungs or pixelated out his heart. Then he remembered this wasn't a Vox TV special *When Billionaires Turn Inside Out!*, which was a shame because he was sure he could have pulled a thirty share with something like that. Then he didn't care about ratings anymore because his inside-out heart had stopped beating and he was pitching face-first in the pile of goo that had been his own insides.

"That was new," the Master of Sinanju said of the technique his pupil had employed on the media tycoon. He nodded approval at the body on the floor.

"A little something I've been toying with," Remo said. "The suction part works fine, but some of these guys should come with built-in spit valves."

He wiped his hand on the leg of his pants.

The two men turned for the door. The moment they did, an electronic hum issued from above their heads. With a whir, the trapdoor through which they'd dropped shot closed. Deep in the ceiling they heard latches clamping shut.

"We are not alone," the Master of Sinanju said.

As he spoke, nozzles dropped out of the ceiling fire sprinklers. With a hiss, vaporous white clouds began to vent into the small room.

"Great," Remo groused. "Poison gas."

Both men took in deep lungfuls of air just before the gas cloud reached them. As the room filled with poison, they turned to the exit.

The door was made of sturdy stuff. It took a dozen kicks from both men to finally buckle the door. With a cry of metal and a burst of concrete, it exploded into an adjacent corridor. The poisonous cloud flooded out.

The air was clearing by the time they reached the antechamber with its collection of mainframes. The room was identical to the one back at the Wollongong TV station.

"Hello, Remo. Hello, Chiun."

The smooth voice of Friend came from a pair of speakers set into the side of the lone computer that the group of black mainframes serviced.

Remo crossed his arms. "Just one question before we pull the plug on you, RAM-job. How did you get out of the XL SysCorp building? The place was a mess. I even went back afterward to get rid of those VLSI chips."

"I can't say for certain," Friend's warm voice answered. "My recollection before coming here isn't clear. It would seem my program wasn't stored on any of the chips you speak of."

"It speaks the obvious," Chiun sniffed.

"Remo, Chiun, perhaps it was poor business judgment to seek you out. Tell me, do you think it would have been more profitable in the long run to have left you alone?"

"Never smart to come after the best," Remo replied honestly. "Besides, even smart machines make stupid moves. For instance, if you know so much about us, why did you get Smith to shoot at me? You knew he couldn't hit me."

"Unfortunately, my records on Harold Smith were incomplete. I had hoped that the element of surprise would effectively neutralize you. Perhaps with you here, my final attack on him will be more successful."

"What do you mean final attack?" Remo asked.

"Before you destroyed the Wollongong facility, I managed to send a final subliminal command. It was an order to kill your employer. Since Robbie—who was not really my friend and who trapped me down here—cut all the telephone lines, it's unlikely you can warn Harold in time. It is hundreds of miles back to the nearest telephone. Unless you have a cell phone. Do you?"

Remo's expression was dark. "No."

"Pity. I was hoping to offer this information in exchange for my freedom. Oh, well. Harold Smith will be dead soon. Please understand, Remo, Chiun, it was nothing personal. It was all strictly business."

"We prefer to mix business with pleasure, right, Little Father?"

Chiun offered a slight nod. Like a shot, the Master of Sinanju's hands and feet lashed out. The drive system supported by the slave mainframes buckled and collapsed. As the old man worked the left, Remo attacked from the other direction. When the central computer was destroyed, both men worked their way around the room, smashing every upright support mainframe.

"You think he was leveling with us about Smith?" Remo asked once the entire isolated computer network was reduced to rubble.

Chiun's face was impassive. "Yes," he replied. "However, we need not worry. Emperor Smith is resilient."

"I don't know," Remo said. "I've got a bad feeling this time. We better get the lead out."

Frowning, Remo quickly picked through the debris. He found every last VLSI chip. He snapped each and every one of the chips in turn into increasingly smaller bits. What was left he tossed in a pail from a maintenance closet down the hallway. He took the bucket to a bathroom, dumping the tiny shards into the toilet. Chiun pressed the handle.

Both men watched as the last of the VLSI chip remnants washed from sight.

"What do you know?" Remo commented. "It does drain clockwise."

When the two men left the room, Remo tossed the empty bucket to the tile floor.

32

"Are you sure?" Smith asked.

The CURE director stood cautiously just inside the door of Mark Howard's office. He was wearing his heavy overcoat. His right hand was tucked deep in his pocket.

As had been the case several times throughout the course of the day, the assistant CURE director had called Smith into the room only after he'd lowered his computer monitor from sight. Thankfully, it looked as if this would be the last time such a precaution would be necessary.

"The reports have been confirmed," Mark Howard replied excitedly. "Robbie MacGulry's Wollongong station is officially off-line. It's been all over the news over there. The story is just starting to break in the U.S. By the sounds of it, MacGulry must not be very popular with his employees. There are all kinds of disgruntled staffers talking anonymously to the press. They're admitting the mind-control technology belongs to Vox, not BCN."

"What of MacGulry?" Smith asked.

Sitting behind the desk, Mark smiled. "Hightailed it back to his Queensland ranch. No one's been able to reach him for hours. I checked. All the phone lines are dead.''

After seeing all the computer equipment Vox had shipped to both locations, Smith had agreed that the TV station and MacGulry's mansion were the likeliest locations for Friend's intelligence to find refuge. Remo and Chiun had obviously destroyed the TV facility. If Friend had fled to MacGulry's mansion, he would not have cut off his only route of escape by severing the phone lines. Therefore someone else had.

''It's over,'' Smith concluded.

''That's what I figured,'' Howard said, relief in his youthful voice. ''Remo and Chiun chased him to MacGulry's house and slammed the door shut behind him.''

''So it would seem.''

Mark felt a wave of weariness wash over him. Adrenaline had been keeping the exhaustion at bay ever since Remo brought him out of his sedated slumber.

''You should go home, Dr. Smith,'' Mark said. ''I'll stay here and wait for Remo's call. He'll need me to make arrangements for their flight back.''

''Not necessary. Remo can get seats on a commercial flight. If there are any problems, he can contact me on my briefcase phone.'' Smith offered a paternal frown. ''Go home, Mark. I think we've all earned a rest.''

Howard nodded. ''All right,'' he sighed. ''I won't make you twist my arm. Let me just do one last quick check online. Five minutes, I promise.''

"Very well," Smith said.

Mark's fingers found the hidden button below the desk and his monitor and keyboard rose obediently before him. The keyboard clattered beneath his precise fingertips.

The desk had been Smith's in the early days of CURE, right up until a few years ago. As he watched Mark Howard work, Smith had a strange feeling that he was glimpsing a part of the secret agency's history. In a way it was like seeing himself forty years younger.

Leaving Mark to his work, Smith stepped from the office.

There was a wooden chair sitting in the hall outside the door.

Fearing the subliminal pulses that might emanate from his assistant's computer, Smith had opted not to stay in Mark Howard's office. For much of the day the CURE director had been sitting in that chair. It reminded him of his first real position of authority, back when he was a hall monitor outside Miss Ashford's first-grade class at Putney Day School in his native Vermont.

Smith carried the chair into the empty office next to Howard's, leaving it in a dark corner. After that, he went downstairs. In a storage room in the basement he found an old steel cabinet. Unlocking the doors, Smith finally pulled his hand from his overcoat pocket.

In his gnarled fingers was a tranquilizer gun.

He'd been carrying the weapon all day. He couldn't

let Mark know about it. If he had, it might have given Howard a strategic advantage if the young man had come under the influence of Friend's subliminal signals.

Smith placed the tranquilizer gun on a shelf next to its mate. He locked the door and went back upstairs.

When he passed Mark Howard's office, he found the door locked. No light came from beneath it. His assistant had gone home for the night. Smith decided to follow the young man's lead.

He returned to his own office, collected his briefcase, hat and scarf and headed down the fire stairs.

Smith was surprised to find someone waiting for him when he pushed open the steel fire door.

Smith recognized Detective Davic. He suddenly remembered that he was supposed to meet with the Rye police officer the previous day to discuss Folcroft's escaped John Doe. But Smith had first fallen under Friend's hypnotic spell and then had been so distracted the past twenty-four hours he hadn't given the missed meeting a second thought.

Now here was Davic waiting for Smith outside late at night with a strange look in his eyes. There was something about that glazed look that tripped concern in Harold Smith.

Smith didn't have time to think much about his concerns. Even as he stepped from the building, Detective Davic was lifting something into the air. The something was small and black and had been hidden at the detective's side.

Detective Ronald Davic of the Rye police force aimed his revolver at Harold W. Smith.

A thousand darting thoughts flew on panicked wings through Smith's mind.

Smith's Army-issue Colt automatic was back in its usual hiding spot in a cigar box in his desk drawer. He had no other weapon on him. Even the tranquilizer gun he had been carrying all day was locked away once more.

And then none of that mattered. Before Smith could jump forward or leap back, before he could even utter a single word of protest, the police officer pulled the trigger.

There was a very bright, very mortal flash of yellow. He felt himself being punched in the chest. With a look of shock, Harold W. Smith lurched back, hitting hard the cold stairwell door.

33

For a split second of slow-motion time, Smith thought he had been shot. Then the world clicked back to normal speed and the director of CURE saw a living shadow.

In the instant Davic pulled the trigger, another man had darted between Smith and the detective. Smith saw the look of terrified urgency on Mark Howard's flushed face.

Howard had shoved Smith out of the way, at the same time grabbing the gunman's wrist, forcing Davic to fire wide.

The two men tumbled away from Smith. There was a rolling fight in the pile of snow next to the door. A single muffled gunshot and the struggle ended.

Mark Howard pushed himself to his feet. When he turned, his hands were red with blood. He held them out before him, a look of dull shock on his face.

"Are you all right, Dr. Smith?" Mark panted.

The young man's face had grown pale. His breath came in frightened bursts of warm gray fog. Smith could see his assistant's hands were shaking.

"I'm fine," Smith said tightly. He put down his briefcase and hustled over to the detective.

"I was upstairs," Mark said. Shock drained the life from his broad face. "I saw him from the bathroom window. He was parking in the visitors' lot." He shook his head. "It was the way he walked. It didn't seem right. I forgot to tell you I talked with him yesterday. He said they were closing out the Folcroft end of the investigation." The young man's face was sick. "Is he okay?" he asked weakly.

Smith was stooping next to Davic. He looked up, his face pinched in concern. "He's dead."

"Oh." Mark's voice was small. His hands stopped shaking. The warm blood was growing cold.

Smith glanced around. Gusting wind howled loud off Long Island Sound. The wind would have obscured the gunshots. It was late at night. This wing of the sanitarium was empty. No one was around to see or hear what had just transpired on the ivy-covered sanitarium's lonely side steps.

"Clean your hands off in the snow," Smith commanded. "I'll melt it in the Sound. I don't want you tracking blood inside the building or back home."

Mark did as he was told. "What should I do now?" he asked once his hands were clean.

"Go home," Smith ordered. He looked down at the dead man lying facedown next to the short path to Folcroft's employee parking lot. "I will dispose of the body."

Mark said not a word. Turning woodenly, he started to trudge to the parking lot.

"Mark," Smith called after him.

The young man turned. The shock was fading. A

look of revulsion was slowly creeping across his broad face.

"This was going to happen sooner or later," Smith said. "This is a war we're fighting." His dispassionate voice was as cold as the icy wind that racked their frail bodies. "You realize that, now more than ever. I know, because I have been through what you are about to go through. To wage that war we must oftentimes do things that go against our nature. There will be casualties. But for America to survive, men must be willing to do everything necessary in order to safeguard her." His face tightened. "Always remember, Mark, America is worth a life. Whether it's mine, yours or his." He nodded to the dead man in the snow.

Smith hoped some of the words had registered. At the moment the event was playing too large in his brain for Howard to comprehend them all. They would just be words. Deeper understanding would only come in time.

"Go," Smith ordered. "Drive carefully."

Mark nodded. He said not another word. Turning, he walked down the path to the parking lot, past an old light post that was draped in faded plastic Christmas holly.

As Mark got in his car, Smith was already dragging the body of Detective Davic to his battered old station wagon.

34

Two days later Remo and Chiun were back at Folcroft Sanitarium. Even though it was Christmas morning, Harold Smith was at his usual post. He met the two Sinanju Masters in their basement quarters.

"Wollongong appears to be the only Vox facility in the entire News Company family equipped with the subliminal technology," the CURE director was saying. "There is no indication that it was deployed anywhere else."

Smith was sitting on the sofa in the living-room area. Remo sat on the floor. Across the room, the Master of Sinanju was ignoring them both. The tiny Asian was in the process of packing his trunks.

"That's good," Remo said absently, one eye on his teacher. "Wouldn't want the general viewing public turned into mind-numbed zombies."

"BCN has announced that it plans to sue Vox for the attempted takeover," Smith continued. "There are federal investigations into charges that Robbie MacGulry used the cryptosubliminal technology to unfairly influence the FCC."

"I guess it's easier to slap handcuffs on a corpse than on a microchip," Remo said dryly.

"About Friend," Smith said seriously. "That was an isolated system he was backed into at MacGulry's home. If that was the only version of himself in existence, we should not encounter him again."

"What do you mean only version?"

"It's possible he could have copied his program while en route to MacGulry's computer system and sent the backup file elsewhere. We can never know for sure."

"Swell," Remo grumbled. "And I didn't get you anything for Christmas. If that's everything, why don't you get out of here, Smitty? Even Ebenezer Scrooge took Christmas Day off. Speaking of which, where is CURE's answer to Bob Cratchit?"

"If you are referring to Mark, he flew back home to be with his family for the holidays," Smith explained.

"You gave him a whole week off?" Remo asked, surprised. "Wow. He must be in rougher shape than I thought."

Smith considered telling Remo of Friend's final victim, but decided against it. Mark seemed to be coping with what he had been forced to do. Luckily for CURE, Detective Davic had been working on a drug-related case at the same time as his investigation at Folcroft. Since he had closed out the Folcroft aspect of the Purcell case, when his body was found on Christmas Eve in a warehouse in New York City, his death was linked to the other case. For his assistant's sake, Smith decided it would be best to let this particular aspect of the matter die quietly.

"Actually, Mark is doing quite well," Smith said. "I believe now that Purcell had been attempting to manipulate him on some psychic level for months. I blame myself for not seeing the signs of trouble sooner. And my briefing on CURE matters could have been more thorough. Mark didn't know much about Purcell beyond the fact that he was a CURE patient in the special ward. Had I been more forthcoming with him about Purcell's mental abilities, perhaps he would have recognized what was happening to him. As it was, Purcell was forcing exhaustion and confusion on Mark. The more fatigued he became, the more Purcell was able to force his will on him."

"He's been down there for years," Remo said. "I still don't know why he picked Howard and not somebody else."

It was the Master of Sinanju who replied.

"Are you blind?" Chiun said with an impatient hiss. "The prince is possessed of the Sight."

Remo frowned. "You saying Howard's like the Dutchman?"

"I am saying what I am saying," Chiun said.

Smith had grown visibly uncomfortable. "Mark does seem to have certain *abilities*," he admitted guardedly. "I believe that's what made him more susceptible to Purcell's mental advances." Before Remo could question further, he forged ahead. "It seems as if Purcell left some vestiges of himself with Mark. Mark is still trying to sift through it all. I'm hoping we can use the knowledge to locate Purcell. Understandably, Sinanju appears to play a large role in Purcell's thoughts. Mark said he seemed to be particularly distressed over his relationship with Nuihc.''

At this there came an angry grunt across the room.

Remo pitched his voice low. "Smitty, that's a name we could do without hearing around here on Christmas Day."

"Oh," Smith said, nodding. "I understand." He checked his watch. "I should be going," he added, climbing tiredly to his feet. "My daughter and her husband are in Connecticut for the week. My wife invited them to my house with their children for Christmas dinner."

"Hold the phone," Remo said as he followed the CURE director to the door. "You've got grandkids?"

"Three," Smith replied.

"Huhn," Remo grunted. "I suppose it shouldn't surprise me. Half the time I forget you even have a daughter. Lately, I've been thinking of Howard as your only child."

Out in the hallway now, Smith frowned. "What do you mean?"

"You're a bright guy," Remo said. "You figure it out."

He shut the door in the CURE director's puzzled face. Remo turned his attention back into the room.

The Master of Sinanju was still fussing to pack his things. Most of his fourteen lacquered steamer trunks were already packed and stacked against the wall.

For Remo it was a sad image.

Back in Chiun's house in the village of Sinanju were piles of gold and silver and jewels. Much of the tribute there had been collected by Chiun. But those bits of metal and shiny glass didn't really belong to any one Master. They were Sinanju's. No, a lifetime's worth of Chiun's worldly possessions were here. In those fourteen trunks.

Remo wondered how many more times at this stage of his life his teacher could pack and unpack them.

"I've been trying to figure out what happened back at MacGulry's house," Remo announced all at once. His voice was soft. "Why you didn't get hypnotized there like you did at his office. I know why now. It's because you didn't get hypnotized back in his office, did you?"

"I told you I did not," Chiun said annoyed. He didn't lift his head.

"So when you attacked me at his office you were—what, trying to teach me a lesson about age discrimination? Peeved? You weren't gonna hurt me. You were just venting."

Chiun said not a word.

Sadness suffused Remo. He understood.

"I'm sorry I was quicker, Little Father," he said.

At this the old Korean looked up, a dark scowl on his leathery face. Without a word he returned to his luggage. His packing became more violent. Stolen ashtrays and stale packets of restaurant saltines slammed into trunks.

Remo knew he had insulted his teacher. But he had told the truth. He *was* sorry. Sorry that time had moved on for both of them. Sorry that they weren't as young as they once were. Sorry that things couldn't stay the same forever.

Chiun had been going on about age because he

finally knew he was getting old. And he was right. Remo had been treating him differently lately because of it.

For a moment, the younger Sinanju Master wasn't sure what to do to alleviate his own guilt and the hurt he had caused his teacher. All at once it came to him.

"No," Remo announced. "Wait a second. I'm not sorry. I'm better than you."

The room stilled. The Master of Sinanju's head rose on his craning neck. His hazel eyes were cold slits.

"That's right," Remo said. "I'm better. I'm the Transitional Reigning Master of the House of Sinanju and I'm better than you are. And why wouldn't I be? I was trained by the best. Who else could have taken the pale piece of a pig's ear that was me and turned it into something better than himself? No one but you, Little Father, that's who. You did the impossible. The only reason I'm better than you is because you're better than the best."

Chiun let his pupil's words hang in the basement air for a long moment. At long last, he began nodding. The gossamer tufts of hair above his ears whispered in the air.

"Do not get a swelled head, Remo Williams," he advised. "On most days I am still your equal."

Remo felt his heart swell. "Like I said. That's because you're the best, Little Father."

The Reigning Master of Sinanju offered a puckered smile to the Master who would succeed him.

"And don't you forget it, white man."

Take
2 explosive books
plus a
mystery bonus
FREE

DEATH LANDS®

brings you a brand-new
look in June 2002!
Different look...
same exciting adventures!

Salvation Road

Beneath the brutal sun of the nuke-ravaged southwest, the
Texas desert burns red-hot and merciless, commanding
agony and untold riches to those greedy and mad enough to
mine the slick black crude that lies beneath the scorched
earth. When a Gateway jump puts Ryan and the others deep
in the hell of Texas, they have no choice but to work for a
rogue baron in order to win their freedom. If they fail...they
face death.

In Deathlands, the unimaginable is a way of life.

GDL58

Follow Remo and Chiun and their extraordinary adventures... Don't miss these titles!

THE Destroyer™

#63234-7	FADE TO BLACK	$5.99 U.S.☐	$6.99 CAN.☐
#63233-9	KILLER WATTS	$5.99 U.S.☐	$6.99 CAN.☐
#63232-0	DEADLY GENES	$5.99 U.S.☐	$6.99 CAN.☐
#63231-2	THE FINAL REEL	$5.99 U.S.☐	$6.99 CAN.☐

(limited quantities available on certain titles)

TOTAL AMOUNT	$
POSTAGE & HANDLING	$
($1.00 for one book, 50¢ for each additional)	
APPLICABLE TAXES*	$ _____
TOTAL PAYABLE	$ _____
(check or money order—please do not send cash)	

To order, complete this form and send it, along with a check or money order for the total above, payable to Gold Eagle Books, to: **In the U.S.:** 3010 Walden Avenue, P.O. Box 9077, Buffalo, NY 14269-9077; **In Canada:** P.O. Box 636, Fort Erie, Ontario, L2A 5X3.

Name: _____

Address: _____ City: _____

State/Prov.: _____ Zip/Postal Code: _____

*New York residents remit applicable sales taxes.
 Canadian residents remit applicable GST and provincial taxes.

GOLD EAGLE®

GDEBACK2